To Jo. It took some time, but we got there, so thank you.

To those who said I could, and especially those who said I could not.

To Alison, thanks for the sweeping and dusting, then and than.

To my family and friends who acted as a sounding board for so many years, they were always patient and constructive.

To my fellow writers who encouraged me, explaining I should hurry my ass up as they wanted to read the damn thing.

—Phil Hore

The order of
THE DRAGON

AN AMUN GALEAS AND SEBASTIAN VULK ADVENTURE

BOOK ONE OF THE
BLOODLINE TRILOGY

PHIL HORE

RAVEN'S HEAD
PRESS

NEVER SAY NEVERMORE

NEVER SAY NEVERMORE

First Edition • January 2016 • Raven's Head Press • Copyright © 2016 Phil Hore • All rights reserved.

Editor: Michael R. Hudson
Cover Art: Arantza Martinez

PUBLISHERS NOTE

Raven's Head Press
Ravensheadpress.com
ISBN-13: 978-0692620441 • ISBN-10: 0692620443

The order of
THE DRAGON

PHIL HORE

PROLOGUE

My name is Amun Galeas and it is hard for me to fathom that I now live in an age of instant communication. But then again, I've said similar things about many an age for as long as I can remember and I assure you I have lived too many lifetimes that I should even bother counting anymore. I am going to relate a true story to you. One that I, and my associates of the time, lived through. I have all of this, along with countless other stories, written down in a volume of diaries but I so detest that word as it seems to me necessary to be preceded with "dear" and although I do use that word in my writing it is almost invariably linked to the fairer sex. Rather I keep—journals—but I am afraid that you wouldn't be nearly as entertained in the reading of them since I use a lot of, I think the term today would be shorthand, as well as a lot of rudimentary drawings of characters and places encountered in each, shall we say—adventure. It is best that I relate them to you directly and I hope to be sharing many, many more of these with you should I be around to do so and, of course, if you are interested in hearing them. I call this adventure The Order of the Dragon and the year it took place was 1888.

CHAPTER ONE

At the time I had thought it a dream, some spooky apparition of a sick mind.

The distance of time has offered me some clarity on the subject, and I now understand the dream was indeed no dream at all but rather a vision of things to come. Of course with such things, once the meaning was clear it inevitably arrived too late.

To tell the tale with as little embellishment as possible—a long time failing of mine I am afraid—it will be necessary to start at the beginning. Not the beginning of my own tale mind you as that is long and tedious and I fear it would have you in the land of Morpheus by the end of the telling, I'm actually speaking of the genesis of this tragic tale.

I had been awake for some hours, though where I was, and in fact who I was, escaped me at the time. All I knew was that I lay in a large bed in an enormous room. Majestic windows full of light made up one side of the room, while the opposite wall was filled with fine paintings and tapestries. From the style I could tell that most were of some eastern origin, though I recognized none of them.

A single large mirror hung on the wall nearest the foot of the bed. In it I caught a glimpse of someone wearing a linen nightshirt and with a head tightly wound with a gauze bandage. With a start I realised that it was my own image that was quizzically returning my gaze. The large red stain bleeding through the front of the bandage made it look more like some mystical turban that you would find topping a street charlatan with all the magical prowess of a turnip.

Next to the bed lay a large earthenware jug that I hoped contained water, yet when I moved to pour myself a glass I discovered both my arms were tied to the posts of the bed, a fact that had escaped me until this time. Upon inspection I discovered my legs were afflicted by a similar fate. All this just added to the growing list of anxieties I found myself starting to suffer.

Since I was going nowhere, I busied myself inspecting the rest of the room. Having been clearly blessed with astounding observational skills I noticed the door at the far end of the room had opened at some point and the figure of a well-dressed gentleman was now standing at the far corner of my bed.

"I see you're finally awake."

My new companion was a tall, powerfully built man with a large, handsome moustache. He looked to be long in years, yet he carried himself with the grace and energy of a much younger man. An ink black top hat sat perched on a crown of silver hair, adding to the image of his age. He pointed to my bound arms. "I'm afraid we had to place you in restraints for your own safety as we feared you might hurt yourself. You had several violent fits while you slept."

"I suppose a thank you is in order then?"

"Not at all, we were only too happy to help." The man smiled as he sat down on a small chair next to the bed.

"With all the generosity you have already bestowed upon me, I feel guilty to ask a boon of you?"

"Name it." He asked, his grey eyes falling hard on mine.

"I was wondering if I could trouble you for my name and current location. I seem to be having trouble remembering either at the moment."

Several emotions ran across my benefactor's face. First he seemed wary, then bemused. "Oh my boy, what a predicament you find yourself in. Unfortunately I can offer you no relief from your first question, as I am afraid I have no idea who you are. As for the second, you find yourself in my care and in my house at Islington."

"London?" I said, grasping onto the tiny piece of information like a life raft. "But how is it that I am here then?"

"I apologise, but that is a question you will have to find out for yourself. I made what inquires I could and have found out nothing. There has been no mention of anyone matching your description as missing. The only knowledge I have to offer is that my oldest daughter discovered your prone body before our gates. Fearing you dead she had you brought inside. On inspection she found you to be very much alive and, except for the nasty blow to your head, in, what appears to be, exceptionally good health." He gave me a smile and a wink as he tapped his own head in the general area of my wound.

"Bringing you inside, she also noticed the finery of your clothing and deduced that you must be a man of substance. On further inspection we could find no documentation, nor any money, thus we came to the conclusion you'd come afoul of one of the unruly characters that seem to populate the streets today. We put you to bed, where you have stayed for the last two days. I must tell you we were growing concerned and had given you until this morning to show signs of improvement before we called for a doctor."

A look of confusion and pain must have come across my face as the room began to tilt and spin. I felt myself falling back towards the bed as a wave of nausea washed over me.

"Forgive me my friend. I should have realised how weak you are. Layback, sleep and when you awake I shall tell you the rest of your tale while you take some nourishment. But for now, rest and worry about nothing."

I later recalled that as my eyes closed the man gave me the most quizzical look.

When I woke again my room was bathed in warm, honey hued sunlight. At the foot of my bed lay a pile of neatly folded clothes, and beyond that a small table with a single chair placed firmly in a pool of light streaming through one large window.

On the table lay a tray covered with pastries and bread rolls. A bowl held fruit and a large crystal jug contained what I once again hoped to be water. Seeing all this food brought me to the realisation that I was damnably hungry.

With care I extracted myself from the bed and was well pleased to find I was no longer bound to anything. I stumbled on weak legs towards the food laden table, and once seated gorged myself on the banquet as though I had not eaten for days. If my generous host was to be believed, apparently this was an accurate statement.

As I ate my body seemed to respond. What had started as hunger quickly grew to an animal type lust to feed. It was not until I had eaten every morsel on the table and drunk all the water that I felt sated.

"That is what I like to see, a man with a healthy appetite! To me that above all else tells me that you, my friend, are on the mend!"

I slowly turned in my chair and gave my benefactor a nod as I wiped any remaining crumbs from my face.

"I know, I know, you have many questions, but please dress and then I will give you a tour of my home. I think the exercise will do you some good and I will answer your queries as we go." At that he bowed, backed out of the room, and closed the double doors as he went.

"I must say it is a relief to be taking in some fresh air again."

We both were taking a slow, steady stroll down an exquisitely manicured lawn. At the far end was a brick wall that encompassed not only the garden but also a series of buildings at the far edges. There was even a large glass greenhouse.

"I do not mean to cast dispersions on your house, nor your hospitality, it's more that I am relieved to be up and moving about."

"As are we to see you up and about my lad," agreed my host as he gave me a friendly pat on the back, "but now if you feel reinvigorated, I would have you make acquaintances with the rest of my family."

"Indeed sir," I said with enthusiasm. "Lead the way so that I may have the pleasure and give my thanks to them."

Walking about the house my benefactor had introduced himself as Dominique Stamford, and his magnificent home was called Stamford House. His family had once been one of the landed gentry that England used to be teeming with, but somewhere in the past some great uncle had invested much of the family fortune in the South Seas Company. When that particular financial bubble burst it not only took down many of those in the government who had supported the shaky scheme, it also ruined a number of England's older, established families.

After all the debts were repaid and more than a few family members had been sent to the New World to escape the clamouring hands of their vengeful family members, Stamford House, and only Stamford House, remained in the family's coffers.

To restore their fortune the men of the family had entered the one business open to English gentlemen with little experience in anything other than being gentlemen, the military. Most never returned from their service in the distant corners of the empire, meaning the once numerous Stamford clan was whittled down to General Wilberforce Stamford, his only surviving son, Colonel Dominique Stamford, and the colonel's two daughters.

As the Colonel guided me through a garden full of the most wondrous flowers and trees, he explained his father, the General, spent much of his time in the large greenhouse, and the old man had requested a meeting with me after I was done with the grand tour.

I have to admit as lovely as the garden was; it seemed little more than a facade. It felt like the flowers and sculpted hedges were trying too hard to look like the grounds of an affluent household, and somehow were failing. There was something amiss here. Between the trees and shrubs I could see men I assumed were the gardeners, hard at work completing the upkeep such a field of beauty required.

"Through here my good fellow." Gestured my host towards a pair of large glass doors facing the lawn. We passed through these and entered a room so large I estimated it ran the entire length of the house. The room was well appointed with fine furniture, an abundance of art, and the curtains were drawn across the large windows, darkening the interior.

"This is the Great Dining Hall," Stamford noted as we walked in, "and this is Beatrice, my wife."

I stepped forward and clasped the hand of the young, blonde woman before us, bringing it up to my lips. "My lady, I wish to thank you for allowing my recuperation in your lovely home." In the flickering light of the numerous lit gas lamps Beatrice Stamford proved to be a most handsome woman; her linen and lace dress hugging a body full of curves and hidden promises.

"My, how gallant." She smiled warmly. "A trait most uncommon these days."

"Sadly the times we live in I am afraid. The hustle and bustle of this modern metropolis seems to have weeded out most of the niceties we once had time for."

"Well put," agreed the Colonel, "we are indeed living in a time that seems to be losing its grip with its past in order to run towards a supposed wondrous future." His sarcastic tone hung there for all to hear.

"Change is not a bad thing, in moderation." I said, happy to be talking about something other than the state of my head.

"I fear my husband mourns for a time gone by when life seemed simpler." Beatrice admitted, looking with sympathy at her husband standing by her side.

Next the Colonel presented a young woman who must have been near the same age as Mrs Stamford. "This is my youngest daughter, Lucinda."

"Pleased to meet you." The girl smiled, taking my offered hand. Her skin was the colour of fine porcelain and her dark, watery eyes were deep pools that any man with blood running though his veins would happily dive into. "I apologise that my sister Robyn is not here at the moment, but I am sure she would be pleased to see you up and about."

"Thank you. I hope to catch up with her at some stage and pass on my appreciation personally for finding me and recusing me from my stricken state."

"I am sure Robyn will show up eventually to accept your thanks, but for now we have no time for such idle chat." The Colonel took a seat and was followed to the table by the two ladies. The table was large enough to operate as a raft if London should ever flood. "We have an injured guest with a most urgent problem."

"Is that so?" Asked Beatrice, turning her intense gaze towards me. "And what, pray tell, would that be?"

"Our guest has no memory of who he is, much less how it was he arrived here."

"Really, how extraordinary?" Beatrice giggled with delight.

"Beatrice..." Lucinda gasped, before bestowing a sympathetic look on me that could have melted granite, "...that must be terribly...confusing."

"Well, it certainly has not been the most pleasant feeling, but I must say my present company is doing much to alleviate any anxiety I had been suffering." Barely had I got the words out when a loud crash pierced the pleasantness of the table.

Through one of the side doors to the dining hall, about half a football field away, clattered the remnants of what must have been afternoon tea. Through the chaos of broken crockery and shattered finger sandwiches and cream cakes stalked a young woman I assumed to be Robyn. Wearing a blue dress that highlighted her sky blue eyes, the Colonel's eldest daughter seemed to be at least the same age as her mother, though far less...graceful.

"Father, you really have to do something about these servants."

Behind the girl a maid and butler darted about the doorway,

snatching up food and porcelain shards before they could be trampled into the rug or scratch the room's gleaming hardwood floor. I noticed the butler gave Colonel Stanford an odd look of exasperation, suggesting the entire affair had been Robyn's fault. The look Stamford gave back was one of sympathy, as though he knew it was, but what could he do.

Lucinda was out of her chair in a flash and giving her big sister a warm hug. "Look who is finally up," she said through an embrace that was not enthusiastically returned.

Unprompted, I stood, walked over to the sisters and took the older daughter's hand. "I believe it is to you that I owe my rescue and subsequent good fortune."

Robyn returned my warmth with a long, cold look, before curtly dropping my hand and walking past me. "It was nothing. Charles did most of the work."

Dumbfounded at the lack of civility, I tried to mask my shock by asking the others, "Charles?"

"Grandfather's batman." Lucinda explained, taking up my recently discarded hand and leading me back to the table. As we sat a new service of tea and cakes arrived and everyone helped themselves. I sat down to a steaming cup of black tea and a bun, whose twin I had seen roll through the door, across the floor and under a sofa just a few minutes earlier.

"It would seem I owe this Charles a thank you as well."

"Thank the help?" Robyn gasped, refusing a pastry and sipping from a cup of naked black tea. "You will next say we should thank the tree for the apple or the cow for the milk on the table."

"Civility is never a coin misspent Robyn." Mrs Stamford smiled, though her eyes suggested she was far from pleased.

"And when I need advice from you Beatrice, I'll be sure to ask for it." The hard way Robyn bit out her mother's name made the growing tension between the two women practically palpable.

"Not at the table ladies, not today," ordered the Colonel from under his twitching moustache. "We have a guest."

Clearly unconcerned about what I saw or felt, much less what her family thought of her, Robyn picked up her cup and drained it. She then stood and stalked out of the room without another word. What servant's encountered her during this awkward retreat made sure to give the girl a wide birth.

"I apologise for my daughter's behaviour," Mrs Stamford said with a gracious smile, "She's been going through a rather tough time."

"Her fiancé ran off with her best friend." Lucinda leaned in and whispered in a voice everyone at the table could clearly hear.

"That's enough of that," the Colonel said to the girl, though with none of the anger he had just laid upon the two older Stamford women. Already it was obvious the angelic Lucinda was the apple of her father's eye.

"Well it's true," she smiled coyly as she bit into a pastry.

A large, balding uniformed man entered the room and asked for my attendance. With a last sip of tea I stood, thanked the Stamford family again and followed close behind to visit with General Stamford.

CHAPTER TWO

My guide proved to be Charles, the General's batman.

"I believe a thank you is in order." I suggested as we walked towards the distant greenhouse.

"Me sir?"

"I was informed it was you who carried me inside when my unconscious body was found near the house gates."

"Oh, that sir. Well yes, it was me, so you are most welcome."

Outside, someone had taken all the morning's wondrous sunshine and put it in a box. Dark grey clouds had replaced the blue sky, and they could not have been more threatening if they had been carrying a pistol.

Inside the greenhouse the heat was beyond stifling. Having walked only four steps, I found myself taking my coat off, undoing some of my shirt buttons and gasping deeply for air like a fish flopping about on the floor of a rowboat. The sickly sweet stench of manure, rotting vegetation, and flowering orchids was intense and it reminded me of another garden long ago.

Deep inside the gloomy room sat what had once been the imposing figure of a man. Though I had never met General Wilberforce Stamford, I recalled seeing images of the man in newspapers during his prime. The man that sat before me could not even be called a shadow of his former self as a shadow carries substantially more weight.

The General sat in a wheel chair, his legs buried under a heavy wool blanket. "Take off whatever you need to, I understand how hot it is in here."

I sat on the chair before the man, lowering myself to what was clearly a more comfortable viewing angle for the old man. "A pleasure meeting you General Stamford."

"You know me?" he asked. "I was under the impression you'd lost your memory."

"I have, at least I seem to have lost most of it. Snippets, however, filter through. I remember seeing you in a paper some years ago."

"Back when being a hero of the crown meant something. Yes, those days are well behind me now."

"If I may ask, exactly what happened?"

"Damned if I know, damned if anyone knows. I've had dozens of doctors and quacks of every persuasion poke and prod me. The general consensus has me catching something in a foreign jungle or swamp that is yet to be seen or described by science. The only thing they all agree on is there is nothing that can be done, so all I do now is sit, day by day, waiting and wasting away."

"That is no way for a man to live."

"It's no way for anyone to die either young man. All I do is spend my days in here receiving warmth like one of these damnable orchids, sucking in all that nourishes me from the wet, warm atmosphere. I do believe I am even starting to smell like one of these damn plants." He was too, but I was too polite to point this out. "So here I sit, waiting to die, existing in an environment similar to the one that likely put me here in the first place. Funny how life can turn out sometimes."

"Funny is not the word I would use," I admitted.

The General gave me a long, thoughtful look. "No, I suppose not."

While we had been talking a servant had entered silently and placed a large glass of ice water next to my seat. I picked up the glass, making sure not to let its perspiring surface from the greenhouse's humidity slip through my equally perspiring hands. Having drained half the glass in one long swallow, I ran its cool surface across my brow before returning the vessel to the table. It only took a moment but most of the ice had already melted.

"Would you like something stronger? I can no longer imbibe myself, but you are more than welcome to partake."

"No, no thank you, strong alcohol may not be advisable at the moment," I said as I tapped my bandaged head.

"Of course, of course."

"So, if I am not being too rude, why did you have me called before you?"

"The house seldom has visitors these days, and I far less. The chance to talk to someone new is one of the few luxuries afforded me in life."

"Surely your family…"

"…my family wants nothing to do with me," the old man spat, "if it was not for the fact that Stamford House is mine I doubt they would even remain in the same city as me. Luckily the family's modest fortunes these days are tied up with the estate, and as such, with me. Even if they refuse to speak to me, at least I know they are close and safe."

"Safe?"

"It's a dangerous world, a fact you surely must have personal and intimate knowledge of." One skeletal hand, wrapped in a dark spider web of veins, opened up and a single finger tapped the side of the old man's almost hairless head in roughly the same place my wound was situated. "But you are correct to enquire, that is not the only reason I have asked you here today."

I sat back and took up the glass of water. After another long swallow I replaced it back on the table, allowing the General time to get his thoughts in order. "You must be very careful in this house. Things do not end well for men who visit us here."

"Is this a none-to-subtle warning for me to keep my hands off your granddaughters? I assure you no such thought…"

The old man waved off what I was saying like a bothersome fly. "No, no, nothing like that. I am sure you are an upstanding and honourable fellow. There is no implication here. I am being very literal. Watch yourself during the time you remain here and make sure you leave at the first opportunity. Too many young men have been ensnared within the trap of my family, and very few have ever escaped our clutches."

I recalled the old General had seen a lot of action during his long military service for Queen and country, and many a young man wearing his uniform had followed him into battle and never returned. Somehow I knew this was not the sort of loss he was talking about.

Before we could recommence our talk a clock at the far end of the room struck three. Immediately a door behind the General's chair swung open and another servant entered. Without saying a word he took hold of the old man's chair and wheeled him about and out of the room. The General did not look pleased about this, nor did he do anything to stop it.

Apparently dismissed, I picked up my jacket and walked out the door I had come in through, happy to leave that sweltering hell behind.

CHAPTER THREE

The afternoon air was soothingly cool after the stifling greenhouse and I decided to take a walk through the garden. No sooner did I put a foot on the path though that I found Robyn Stamford walking beside me.

"Stay away from my grandfather."

"And good evening to you Miss Stamford," I replied warmly.

"What did the old man want from you?"

"To show me his paper daisies. I must say he certainly has a fine crop coming in this season. Did you know they were a favourite of Napoleon? He even grew them on the island of St Helena while a prisoner there."

"You think you're being clever. There is nothing sadder in this world than a man who thinks he is being clever."

"I bow to your expertise on the failings and foibles of men."

We continued walking down the garden path in silence. I smiled away the time and even stopped to watch as a butterfly on gossamer wings of orange and white fluttered and flitted from one flower bud to another. Next to me the delightful Robyn Stamford harrumphed, unsure how to proceed and far too stubborn to let me have the last word. What a sight we must have made as we then continued strolling down the path.

I stopped again and inspected one of the more picturesque blooms the garden presented, and could feel Robyn had reached the end of whatever good grace she had been holding onto. In frustration the girl grabbed my elbow and forced me to turn and face her. She then snarled in a most un-lady like way, "Stay away from my grandfather, stay away from my family, and stay away from me."

I held back a reply and allowed the girl to storm off. Though she was clearly angry with me over I knew not what, I had learned a long time ago you get nowhere antagonizing young women. They have a nasty habit of turning vindictive and can make your life a living hell, so best to avoid that particular pitfall whenever you can.

I spent a few minutes watching a team of four gardeners planting a semi-mature tree of a variety I was not familiar with. The men struggled to lower the specimen into the deep hole they had dug, and once safely nestled inside three of them began shoveling dirt over the exposed roots. I did not see where the fourth man had gone, but assumed he was retrieving some unseen supervisor to inspect their work thus far.

Perhaps it was my wounded head or having not recovered from the heat of the greenhouse, perhaps I was still pondering the conversation with the lovely, if not somewhat disturbed, Miss Stamford. Whatever the case I never gave the timing of the gardener going missing with my own arrival a second thought. It was a mistake I could easily have regretted.

Leaving the tree and its sweating trio of workmen, I decided to take the long way back up to the house through a grove of mature trees, far older than the one being planted. Amongst this grove were statues of men I did not recognise, some of who were protecting women who looked the sort I too would like to have known a little better. If that required protection from some unknown danger, well I could do that. There were also small outbuildings along the way, carefully hidden from the main garden and the house. Some of them I assumed were used for potting and others perhaps for storage of tools. It was as I passed between two such buildings that the missing gardener stepped out from behind a shrub and hit me very hard over the head with his shovel.

CHAPTER FOUR

My head hurt.

Actually my head had already been hurting before my run in with the flat end of the shovel. It had been hurting ever since I woke up in bed, what was now starting to feel like days ago. What I meant to say was my head no longer simply hurt, it was now a source of complete and utter misery. It felt as though the shovel had split my skull in two and was still sitting there, like some handyman's Excalibur, waiting to be drawn out by the true king of England.

Before my vision swam the face of my attacker. For some strange reason he looked concerned.

"Are you kidding around Amun? Did I hit you too hard?"

Though a reply formed, it somehow got lost on the way out.

"Come on, I did not hit you that hard."

"Frzzberker blitwort," I said.

"Hmm, maybe I did hit you to hard."

Though most of my motor functions seemed to have deserted me, the sharp pain from my head kept my mind focused enough to keep an eye on what my attacker was up to. He first got up and looked about, perhaps to make sure his ambush had remained unseen and there was no one rushing to my rescue. Next he returned to my side and removed a small tobacco tin from his top pocket. This he opened and from within removed a butterfly very similar to the one I had seen earlier during my walk with Robyn Stamford.

The gardener took the insect and, forcing open my mouth with his left hand, and placed it on my tongue, before forcing my mouth closed. He then clamped one incredibly powerful fist over my mouth and nose and almost politely said, "Swallow."

As hard as I tried to squirm from under his embrace, the man effortlessly held me in place. "Swallow!" he said again with more force.

Already I could feel the fragile creature's body dissolving in my mouth as my body tried to dislodge the irritant by drowning it in saliva. I could feel the harder parts rubbing against the roof of my mouth, and then starting to migrate down my throat as the butterfly disintegrated.

"Swallow…it…" the man said again, perhaps sensing my ability to resist disappearing along with what air was in my lungs. "For god's sake Amun, just swallow the damn thing."

Finally my chest heaved and spasmed as blissful unconsciousness approached. Just before I blacked out I felt my throat automatically swallow, and once my attacker was sure I had not somehow faked everything, he released me.

With a gasp, fresh cool air flooded my lungs and my amnesia melted away like, well, like a butterfly on your tongue.

CHAPTER FIVE

Though I rarely intervene on the activities of men, somehow enough people know about my past to ensure I occasionally still receive visitors in distress, hoping I have some knowledge or advice that could help them survive their time of need. Most are just lazy people with lazy issues and those I happily send away. Occasionally something or someone appears with a tale to tell that catches my attention. In these instances I am happy to help as the world can be a dull place at times, so a new challenge or even just something to pass the time is a jewel to be treasured.

If you are of the opinion the butterfly was some magic potion that gave me back my memory, well you are correct. I hate insects, I hate every kind of insect, but very specifically I hate butterflies. Certainly they look very pretty, and that is their evil genius. Underneath the gaudy colours and great luminous wings lies a filthy creature of coarse hair and black, spider-like bodies. Have you ever looked closely at one of their heads? I mean really closely? Those enormous alien eyes, the giant proboscis that makes them look more like a drinker of souls in some thirteenth century religious manuscript about the tortures of hell rather than something little girls like to paint on their bedroom walls. Butterflies are the painted strumpets of the animal kingdom and I do not trust them one little bit!

The horror and disgust of having the incarnation of evil in my mouth helped trigger the destruction of the intellectual block I had placed in my mind days ago. After so many years I had become a creature of habit and lazy days. I have always tried to avoid work, confrontation, or stimulation where I could, but to remain living in the standard I do—and that requires money. This, of course, means when I do work I do so to get paid so I can go right back to my comfortable chair and my books. Knowledge, like any skill, requires upkeep, and I need time to remain the genius I believe myself to be.

The fellow that stood over me was Sebastian Vulk, and we had known each other for a long time. Certainly he did not like everything I did, and I was none too happy about his success with the ladies (a problem) and his inability to gamble (not so much a problem as an ongoing tragedy that threatened to doom us both). Not only did Vulk bring his own unique gifts to our…acquaintance… he was also of such a great age that he too was also often up for an adventure to alleviate the boredom that came from being wealthy and idle. His association with me ensured he got plenty of that. He was what you would perhaps call a friend. I wouldn't though, as I had very little time for the man, but you may well consider us as such.

"Feeling better?" Vulk asked, hauling me to my feet with little effort, than patting my backside down as though I was a clumsy child. "I know this is a little earlier than you asked, but things seemed to be progressing too fast for you to be lying about in bed."

Taking my first unassisted steps, Vulk guided me down one of the rear paths to a section of the garden that seemed unused. As we walked he filled me in.

"I joined the ground staff like you suggested, and what a miserable lot they have turned out to be. Most of them are discharged soldiers who had served with the General, though recently a number of the older men have retired and been replaced by men who had served with the Colonel. Most are as mean as the day is long, and none of them know the first thing about gardening, which is probably the only reason I got the job."

As we neared one large brick wall that I assumed ran the perimeter of the estate, Vulk pointed out a large pile of rubbish and what looked like a discarded barn door. "What I want to show you is under there, and as far as I can tell no one I have encountered has had anything to do with it."

Unsure what 'it' was, I approached the slab of wood carefully and tilted the access gate up by one corner. Underneath was a shallow pit, and about two feet down was the body of a man; well I assumed it was a man, and circumstances would later prove me correct.

Vulk saw my surprise. "It would seem you were right on the money about this place old boy."

CHAPTER SIX

"Do you think we should dig him out?" I asked Vulk, kneeling by the hole and peering in.

"And by 'we' do you happen to mean you want me to dig him out?" None to subtly Vulk tried to hide the spade he had been carrying behind his back.

"Guess that means he's staying in there. Would have been nice to know how he died." I said, trying a little emotional blackmail.

"That's easy enough, he's been exsanguinated."

I look from the corpse to Vulk, and then back at the corpse. "How can you tell?"

Vulk gave his nose a little tap. "No blood, and I do not mean on the body, I mean there is no blood anywhere near that body or in it. You are looking at something that is little more than a dry husk."

Reaching down, I completed a quick search of the man's pockets that I could reach. This revealed nothing, so exasperated; I grabbed one sleeve and yanked hard, pulling the arm free of the earth. Sitting on one finger was a ring I recognized from a description I had been given days earlier.

Finding the ring and retrieving the ring, however, turned out to be two different problems. After a number of tugs it was clear the ring was there to stay.

"Out of the way," Vulk called out as he raised his shovel and brought it down with a loud 'CHUD'. "There you go," he said, pulling the ring from the now dismembered digit and tossing it to me. There are no words for how open my mouth was during the dismemberment.

As I mentioned, the ring fit a description I had been given to me by Mr Thomas De Gois, father of a missing boy by the name of Jerome De Gois. The lad had also been the fiancé of Miss Robyn Stamford, and the family knew how much the boy loved the girl and had become suspicious when he disappeared and the Stamford's claimed he had run away with someone else. Normally I would never have bothered with such an investigation, but the Stamford family had caught my interest after I did a little research on their history, and the boy's father also offered me a lot of money, and I mean a truly obscene amount of money to find their son.

Before arriving at the house I had investigated the boy's disappearance and almost immediately great holes had appeared in the Stamford story. There had most certainly been train and ship tickets as they had claimed, purchased in the name of Jerome De Gois and Miss Julie David, the girl he had supposedly run away with. Yet enquiries at the hotel where the pair had allegedly stayed before their departure revealed no description of the lovers. No one at the station, nor the port where the ship had sailed from could remember anyone resembling them, and a letter sent to the shipping line's office at their port of destination in New York revealed no one had actually occupied their cabin during the crossing. Certainly none of this was proof of any wrong doing as the couple may well have laid down a false trail themselves, ensuring anyone following them, such as a vengeful Stamford posse, would waste time chasing phantom passengers, allowing them to merrily sneak away in the opposite direction. I mean De Gois, after all, was running from a bride whose father had at one stage an entire army ready to die for him. Surely out of the ranks he could find a few lads willing to do him a nasty favour to find and eliminate the man who'd just broken his daughter's heart.

Of course I was no longer pursuing that line of reasoning because this had been too obvious, and history has taught me nothing is ever that easy. The body lying at my feet was proof my suspicions had been correct.

"Are there anymore?" I asked Vulk, who was busy keeping an eye on the rest of the garden to make sure we were not disturbed.

"Anymore . . . bodies, you mean?"

"The girl to be exact. I expect Miss David will be lying about here somewhere as well."

The light seemed to dawn behind Vulk's honey-brown eyes. "His girlfriend. I should have thought of that myself. I haven't found anything, but to be fair I stopped looking once I found him."

"Right, well I have to get back to the main house. Keep up the good work," I said, nodding my head at the body, "and when you get the chance, have a look for the girl."

"I'll do better than that, I'll do a thorough search of the grounds, plus any place a body could be stuffed into. I usually find whenever there's one body, there's going to be more. Like weeds, corpses are."

"A gardener to the end," I said, slapping Vulk on the shoulder and wandering back up the path to the distant house.

CHAPTER SEVEN

Upon returning to my room I found a suit had been laid out on the bed. Remembering someone had mentioned dinner was promptly at six thirty, and the time on the large clock sitting between the two windows of my bedroom read six twelve, I changed and headed back downstairs.

That night I ate with the entire Stamford family, minus the heat loving, reptilian-like General. The tension between mother and eldest daughter was still so palpable it could have been used as gravy for the fine roast mutton that was the centre of the evening's repast.

With my memory back I now had to keep up the pretence of my injury and bumble-mindedness. Robyn Stamford ate only a few morsels, gave me a filthy look, then left. I assumed she was heading out on the town as I had uncovered in my investigations the wild comings and goings of the elder Stamford girl. She was known as a flossy who could be found as often as not in a cheap gin shop as in an upper market wine bar.

"And how was your afternoon?" I asked Lucinda, trying to end the dinner's silence between the main course and a dessert of fruit and cheese.

"I spent the day reading about horses. I'm hoping to learn veterinary skills when school starts up again after summer."

"Do not be getting your hopes up on that, you know what happened last time." Colonel Dominique said bluntly, leaving no room for argument and giving me another little thread to pull at. What had happened last time?

Beatrice's look between the two suggested there was always wiggle room for a daughter against the stubbornness of her father. "And how was your walk?" she then asked me, changing the subject. I recognized a fishhook when I saw one and figured the lady of the house was thoroughly uninterested in my walk and extremely interested in my view on her garden.

"Sadly I was overcome by another spell and I do believe I fell and hit my head again," I explained, pointing to my re-bandaged head where a second, smaller bloodstain was now visible. When I had returned from seeing the body of De Gois I met once more my original saviour, the dapper batman Charles, who took me inside, cleaned my new wound and re-bandaged my head.

"Oh dear," Mrs Stamford said, noticing the new stain for the first time. "It seems you will be staying with us a little while longer."

"We insist." Colonel Stamford agreed, mopping up some of the juices on his plate with a corner of bread. This was an uncultured thing to do and said more about his time in the field than how his parents had brought him up. Mrs Stamford noticed me watching her husband and his bread and gave him a stern look. Clearly this was something the two had disagreed about before, and an issue the Colonel was uninterested in going into again.

"I am in your debt; and thank you for the clothes by the way."

Beatrice smiled at this. "I hope you don't mind but it's one of my husband's old suits. It may not be the most fashionable, but I promise you it is clean."

"Styles come and go but the classics remain forever. It fits as though it had been cut for me."

"I think you look very handsome," Lucinda said as she popped a sliver of apple into her mouth. "I believe you would not be out of place at any ball or coffee house."

"I think I look like a swami about to play my flute and make a rope dance into the air like a cobra." I said to the girl, wiggling my fingers in front of me mystically. "Maybe one day you will accompany me into town and I can take you to lunch and we can see just how many heads we turn together?"

The two Stamford ladies giggled, and Lucinda said she would love to one day get out of the house and accompany me to lunch. The Colonel gave me a look that suggested maybe those blows to the head had knocked loose something other than my memory.

An argument, some discourtesy, and a moment of foolishness in front of my hosts…all in all a successful dinner I felt.

With the ladies retiring to do whatever it is ladies do after a meal, the Colonel and I found ourselves in the billiards room holding cues and smoking cigars and all but ignoring the three balls remaining on the table.

Along the wall were family mementoes from a life hard lived. Weapons and flags were in abundance, showing the career path of the Stamford men through the last dozen decades of military action in the name of the monarchy.

"Any of these yours?" I asked.

"The flag at the end I took from a Russian hill in the Crimea, but the rest are from my forebears. That wall over there is all my father's."

The indicated wall was a wealth of militant souveniring. Flags of nations I did not recognise, weapons I had probably used myself back in the early days. A portrait of the General sat in the middle of this collection, looking more the man I remembered from the old newspaper articles on his exploits.

"The Crimea, that was a few years back was it not?" I asked, recalling I was supposed to have very little memory at this time.

"It feels like a lifetime ago."

"The Thin Red Line?" I asked this as though remembering something from deep within the recess of my mind.

"That was the 93rd Highland Regiment at Balaclava, I was there much later. I began the war standing by the side of Robert Colquhoun, he was the British consul in Bucharest who tried to organize a Polish uprising against the Russians when they annexed the region."

"It did not end well I take it?"

"Mass arrests, the Romanian Revolution crushed under the weight of 35,000 Russians, the people crying to us for help; then screaming at us when we could not provide it. I ended up crawling through the city sewers to escape." Taking a long, calming puff from his cigar, the Colonel let the smoke drift slowly out of his mouth, making him look like some despondent demon. "No, it did not end well at all."

Changing tactics I put my own cigar down and took a shot on the billiard table. The cue ball clicked against the red loudly and began to rebound across the table. As we both watched the ball roll towards a corner pocket a woman's scream pierced the night.

Both of us were out the door and running to the front hall. Here we found a maid burrowing her face into the shoulder of another of the older ex-soldiers who had followed the General into retirement.

On the ground lay someone I had not met yet. Approaching

carefully, I rolled the body over to discover a man's face staring back at me. His throat had been torn out, yet like poor De Gois in his garden, there was no blood.

"Who is he?" I asked the Colonel who stood grimly over both of us.

"Fortey, a footman, any idea how he died?"

"Well I am no expert but that gaping wound in the throat would be my guess."

Outside I could hear the Peep-Peep-Peeping of police whistles growing closer and closer. Men with lit lamps were traversing the grounds outside; looking for an intruder I personally did not think was out there. Whoever did this was just as likely to be inside. In fact considering the grizzly crop Vulk had already discovered sprouting in the grounds, it was more than likely the murderer was standing within a few feet.

First one, than half a dozen bobbies pushed through the house's front door and, while most began cordoning off the area, a particularly large corporal shepherding a handlebar moustached sergeant started inspecting the body. After a preliminary search they looked up and I caught the eye of the sergeant and gave him a subtle gesture not to give me away.

Sergeant Edgar Willkie seemed to catch on and moved his attention back to the body.

With that little issue out of the way I moved through the room, catching snippets of conversations from those gathered about. There were maybe twenty people who had been inside the house searching, and I had seen maybe fifteen more outside with lit torches. Most of those looked like the gardeners, and nowhere had I seen Vulk. Knowing the old dog, he was either held up in some young chambermaid's room, or hot on the heels of the murderer. Honestly, my money was on the first.

Its first official investigator, a large man with muttonchops and a lopsided bowler hat visited an hour after the body had been found inside the Stamford's entry hall. Inspector Frederick Abberline of Scotland Yard entered out of the night, followed by Sergeant Willkie, who I hoped already had a word in the Inspector's ear. The way Abberline studied the body and ignored the gathered crowd, including myself, assured me he had.

With care not to draw attention to myself I moved to the front door and stepped out into the cool night air. I had not noticed how hot it had become inside with so many bodies pressed together. Hanging back from the crowd, I spotted Vulk and he looked concerned.

I made my way to his side and we soon had our heads together, looking just like the other tiny huddles of conspiracy conversationalists about the house.

"Find anything?"

"Like what?" Vulk asked, confused.

"What do you mean 'like what'? Have you found anything to point out who the murderer may have been?"

"Sorry Amun, I just got here and I'm not sure what's been going on." His sheepish grin told me I had been right the first time and he had been with a girl.

'Well, while you have been off dallying diligently with some debutant, someone has snuck inside and killed one of the General's men."

"Which one?"

"A footman called Fortey"

"Damn, he was a good egg."

"I had hoped you were out here, hot on the scent of the killer."

"Well I guess I am now," Vulk said, turning to go.

"That may not be the wisest move right now. Abberline and Willkie are here and they know about me, but not you. It might be better if you just remain in the background until I get a chance to talk to one of them."

"You're the boss, boss." Vulk agreed with a salute, before melting away into the night.

The police were thorough and professional now that Abberline was on hand. They cordoned of the body and then moved the gathered crowd into a large room at the far end of the house. From there they began interviewing everyone, one at a time, in a side room. Willkie made sure I was in the first half of those interviewed.

After an hour a Bobbie came and escorted me down the long hall to a room just before the front entry hall, where the body now lay under a sheet. I recognized this as an old investigation trick, letting those about to be interviewed see the body. If innocent, the person should be upset or dumbfounded by the murder, so this little glimpse should only heighten this. If guilty, the interviewee may be smug, pleased, vindicated, calm, or perhaps recalcitrant at what they had done. Either way, a peek at the corpse could be beneficial to an interviewer.

The Bobbie knocked once, and when no one answered he opened the door and let me inside. Once I was through he closed the door again and likely took post outside to make sure we were not disturbed.

The small room turned out to be an office of some sort, likely attached to one end of the billiards room by its position in the house. Behind a large desk, that I assumed was the Colonel's, sat Inspector Abberline and Sergeant Willkie; two men that, if not friends, were at least friendly acquaintances.

"Take a seat Amun," Willkie said, indicating the solitary chair on my side of the table.

Instead, I stalked the room as though inspecting every nook and cranny.

"Tell us what you know?"

"And good day to you friend Amun. My, that is a nasty looking bump on your forehead. Can we do anything for you, a glass of water perhaps?" I am not sure my sarcastic tone was sarcastic enough for the Inspector. Not even looking, I could tell Sergeant Willkie was grinning as broadly as Abberline was scowling. This was the continuation of a dance the three of us had heel-and-toed many times in the past.

"I don't have time for the niceties, now sit down and tell us what you know." Abberline was clearly in no mood. "It's already late and we have more than a dozen interviews to complete yet."

"Fair enough." I walked back to the table, sat, and ploughed through the answers to the questions they were about to ask. "No, I have no clue what the hell is going on here…yes, if I did know something I would most likely tell you…no, I am not hiding anything, at least I am not hiding anything relevant."

Willkie's grin could not get any wider without both edges meeting again at the back of his head. Abberline just kept up his glare as though he knew I had a sarcasm quota, one that would soon run out.

Holding up my hands, I submitted to the withering glare of the inspector. "I was hired by Thomas De Gois to investigate the disappearance of his son Jerome, who also happened to be the fiancé of the Stamford's eldest daughter, Robyn. My initial investigation showed it was going to be near impossible for me to get inside Stamford House, as the staff was either retired soldiers personally known to General Stamford or servants who'd been with the family for years. In fact the only position I could find going in the house for months was for a gardener."

"You're working here as a gardener? I don't believe it." Willkie laughed. The man could be annoying.

"No. Vulk is working here as a gardener. I had to obtain my entry through far more nefarious and subtle means." I tapped my head as evidence of my plan.

"I was meaning to ask you about your turban, sahib?"

Ignoring the Sergeant, I carried on with my tale. "We arranged to have myself mugged by the household's front gates. The plan was I would be found and taken inside, where I would have no recollection of who I was. This would hopefully give access to the house. I could then take my time during my 'recuperation' and search for any evidence of young De Gois."

"Under false pretences!" Abberline noted something down in that infernal notebook of his.

"Not at all. I planned it so I really did have amnesia. I have some experience with this sort of thing and if you know the right method you can uncover quickly if someone is faking the affliction. When I was brought in I really did have amnesia."

"And who was your assailant?"

I gave the inspector one of my own hard stares. As much as I liked the policeman he was still a policeman and would always try and serve the law. If he felt my crimes warranted it, he would come down hard. "I do not remember."

"Not fully recovered then?" Willkie beamed.

"Exactly."

"All right. So what have you uncovered so far?" Abberline asked.

"Nothing, I have had barely a day and was only just starting my investigation when 'Fortey' out there met his end. I did get to meet the General though, now there is a very sick man. Oh, and watch out for the eldest Stamford girl, that kitten most certainly has claws."

"You think she killed her fiancé?"

"I think my work here has only just begun. I think if you leave my cover intact, at least for now, then you will have a man on the inside of this mausoleum. If you do not give Vulk away you will also have a handy operative on the outside as well—that's what I think."

"Our time is up." Willkie got up and indicated I should follow him to the door. "Any longer in here and it will be suspicious why you're getting special treatment."

That the good Sergeant never checked this action with the inspector told me they both had already discussed the virtues of keeping me undercover and had agreed to continue my charade before I entered the room. They had not known about Vulk though, and before leaving the room I pushed for their promise to leave him in place as well.

All in all the next few days promised to be fun.

CHAPTER EIGHT

The household was in shock.

It was not that Mr Fortey was particularly loved but that he had died in such a horrible way, and in the presence of almost the entire household. Literally all of us must have been only a few feet away, yet no one had heard or seen anything.

If it could happen to a strapping veteran like the footman, it could have happened to any of us.

After a busy and rather painful day I headed for my room, climbed into bed and slept like a log. Certainly I had a chair propped against the underside of my door handle and shoelaces tied around the latches to the large bay windows, but none of that would matter to a man who had taken two solid hits to the cranium within as many days.

I woke the next morning to someone politely but insistently knocking on my door. From the comfort of the softest pillow it had been my fortune to make an acquaintance with in some time, I cracked an eye and spotted the Louis XVI chair still wedged under the door handle to keep it closed.

Mumbling about the unfairness of life, I stumbled out of bed and, with bed socks flopping about my feet like some waterless fish, I managed to remove the chair and open the door.

"Oh my!" the maid gasped.

Realising that turning sideways would only heighten the poor girl's observation of one of the great natural wonders of the world, I instead chose to half close the doors and hide my morning achievement.

"Yes my dear?" I asked nonchalantly.

"Its nearing midday sir and the Colonel thought it best we make sure you hadn't... ummm..."

"...perished in my sleep?"

Amazingly the girl curtsied rather than admit that was exactly what they were all thinking. "Let me dress and you can tell the kind Colonel I will be down directly."

Downstairs the kitchen was abuzz with activity as the cooks

prepared meals for the family, the staff, and the dozen or so police officers stationed at the house since the night before, ordered to stay too keep everyone safe. Of course what they had not told anyone was that they were also there to find any other hidden bodies and to cordon the area off to give the investigating team its best chance of finding the all-important clue that would see someone dangling at the end of a rope.

I joined the line in one of the side rooms off the main dining hall where an army of kitchen hands were keeping the piles of food on the table stocked for everyone to help themselves from. The buffet was first rate, and after a plate of cold lamb, part of a roast chicken and one of the juiciest tomatoes I'd eaten in years, I was off outside to take a rejuvenating walk. Of course this was just a ruse, I was really looking for Vulk, who I found at the end of a rope.

Certainly it was more like twine as he was marking out a stretch of ground where a new flowerbed was to be planted. Dusty and dirty, the man looked happier than I had seen him in ages. "It's the work. I'd forgotten just how invigorating it was to set yourself a task and accomplish it. The joy of seeing a project through to the end, it's almost like being a kid again."

"You remember being a child?" I asked, taking up a position under the shade of a tree.

"Well, it wasn't that long ago."

I gave him a raised eyebrow.

"Ok, it was a long time ago, but certain things stay with you throughout your life. Adult years can stretch on and on, but your time as a child, well that was finite and special."

Looking about to make sure we were alone, I asked. "Find out anything?"

"Besides a lost love of botany?" Vulk said, heeling his spade into the dirt and lifting out a clump of dirt. This he turned over and mysteriously replaced into the exact same hole.

"What you're doing isn't botany, it is…manicuring."

Snuffing at my last comment, Vulk put his head down and dug up another shovel of dirt. "I filled the hole with our friend at the bottom. The bobbies were making a real search last night and I reckon they would have found him the way we'd left him."

"It is amazing how enthusiastic they get when a crime occurs within the gentry."

"Got that right, I cannot imagine them spending any of the effort they did here on the death of a whore."

"Did you find anything else?" I asked, trying to keep him on track.

"There was no sign of anyone moving about the house by nefarious means. The only movement to and from the main building was along the path."

This was important and only confirmed what I had suspected. If the killer had been an outsider, fear of discovery would have kept them in the shadows during their approach to the house. "Anything else?"

"No blood."

"You mean no blood anywhere on the grounds?"

"I mean no blood anywhere. There are no droplets of blood outside, no hint of blood in any of the household garbage that is even remotely human. I didn't even notice any blood within the foyer."

"So our Mr Fortey died the same way as De Gois?"

"Seems so," Vulk agreed, returning to shoveling clods of dirt and rolling them over.

I had to ask. "What are you doing?"

"Turning the soil. This makes the ground softer, allows birds to eat any damaging insects that may be present in the earth and gives the seedlings their best chance of germinating."

My unblinking look made him shrug his shoulders. "I read a book about it all before I came here," and with that explanation I accepted a small oiled cloth bundle from Vulk and left him to his work.

The afternoon passed without incident. I took tea with the ladies of the house as the Colonel was off doing manly, colonel sorts of things at his gentleman's club. He had announced he would not be back until much later.

As the day's light began to bleed out across the horizon, workmen started lighting torches and lanterns along the main approach to the house and throughout the grounds. These lights sent shadows dancing across trees and hedges, and caused more than one person to jump, believing they had seen someone sneaking about.

Inside, the house was also a bustle of activity as the staff made sure most corridors were never empty for too long. No one would be breaking into Stamford House tonight.

I was pleased to see that with the Colonel away General Stamford had joined the dinner table. Lucinda chatted amiably about everything and anything she'd encountered that day; to her the murder of a man she had known her entire life, but likely never had asked a civil question to, was little more than news of the day. To the youngest of the Stamford clan we could have been talking about pirates or bee keeping.

The General spoke little and ate like a bird, then having consumed almost no food and only sipping at the most excellent wine from his own cellar, Charles the batman appeared out of nowhere and wheeled the old man back to his hothouse and flowers.

With no military or male presence around anymore I finally discovered what the ladies do after dinner. They had their own little room of hobbies and trinkets and they kindly invited me to join them there for a glass of port. Within minutes Robyn Stamford also excused herself and was gone. No one seemed that concerned, so I decided not to be either.

Mrs Stamford was a charming and handsome woman and as worldly wise as a mushroom. If the conversation was not about London society, the latest Parisian fashions or fine Italian shoes, she proved uninterested. Lucinda on the other hand was full of life and questions, some of them were poignant, some even insightful, but her unfocused nature meant she too was soon on to other subjects and no true conversation could be had.

I decided, despite their quirks, that I liked the family.

Excusing myself to find a longed for cigar, I had only just made it to the front door when a brusque dandy dressed in all the finery and fashion of the day pushed past me rather rudely. I made sure as I caught my balance that my right foot became entangled with his and he took a rather frightful stumble, only just catching himself before hitting the floor.

"Frightfully sorry, I really must begin to look where I am going."

"Oaf," the dandy said.

"And you are?" I asked.

"Unlikely to answer the questions of someone such as yourself," he answered and stormed off towards the billiards room. I watched as he discovered the room darkened. He then made his way over to where the ladies were still seated. I was unconcerned with any possibility of him being the killer as, with everyone so on edge, and I was sure no one could approach this house without being investigated thoroughly. In fact now that I think about it, the questions that would have been put to him by the police cordon at the front gate were likely the source of his current testiness.

Always one to happily stick my nose in where it could become the most sticky, I decided to follow the Stamford's latest guest and see what he was up to. Clearly he was no killer, but I was pretty sure whatever he was about was going to be something of interest. I entered the ladies parlour just as the dandy cried out.

"But his club will not allow me in and I desperately need to see Uncle Dominique."

"A problem ladies?" I asked, ever the gallant dragon ready to tilt at the dangerous knight. I made a deliberate play of putting my unlit cigar between my teeth, thus freeing up both hands just in case they were needed for some direct pacifying.

Mrs Stamford was the first to answer. "We are fine thank you. This is our nephew, Willie."

"William, my name is William," Willie snapped back.

"Willie, it is a pleasure to meet you again." Walking briskly across the room I offered the young man my hand.

"It's William, and who are you?"

"Well Willie," I grinned around the cigar. "That's a fine question and one that deserves an answer. If only I had one for you."

When a great cloud of frustration roamed across Willie the Dandy's face, it was Lucinda who leapt to his aid.

"This gentleman is our guest. He was robbed out in the street and beaten. Not only did they take all his money, they also stole his memory with a jolly good whack to the head." The way the girl recounted my woes it was clear she was repeating the story the way she had heard someone else say it.

"You have amnesia?" Willie asked.

"I do."

"I do not believe in amnesia. I think it is just a ruse you are playing to help steal from my Uncle."

"Just your Uncle? You do not think I would be interested in stealing from your Aunt here, or perhaps your Grandfather?"

"Grandfather has nothing left to steal, and Beatrice here is no aunt of mine."

And with that Willie the Dandy stomped out of the room.

"Well he is a delight." I grinned at the ladies. "You should invite him around more often."

Though Willie was painfully obnoxious he did have me wondering what he meant. The General owned nothing and Mrs Stamford was not his aunt, clearly more investigation into the depths of the family was required.

CHAPTER NINE

William Langford was the disinherited nephew of the Stanford clan. The bastard son of a younger brother, the family had kept the boy at arms-length by being shipped off to the best schools, which had infused the young lad with the pretentions that he was owed even more. He wanted his cut of the family fortune and refused to hear there was no longer any fortune to cut. The family mausoleum was the only true piece of property left that he could have any claim on, and as traditionally the family home went to the oldest son, and only officially recognised offspring were permitted to be buried in the family plot, even this was tenuous. The truth of this situation seemed to have no hold on the young man though.

You may ask yourself how I could know such information about young Willie. Let us just say servants talk, especially after something unusual happens within the household they work in. A servant's life is one of monotony. Every day they rise before their masters and begin their daily chores. They snatch breaks and meals throughout the day, at times when experience has taught them they are likely not to be called upon. Certain positions in the household also mean they are often the last ones to bed at night as well. It would be easy to become isolated from the rest of the world in a position where your entire universe was defined by the high wall at the end of the garden. Within the confines of such a life any gossip becomes gold, something to be bartered and brandished around the laundry room or larder.

If you ever want to know anything about a household the best place to gain your information is the kitchen table or laundry—as long they are unaware you are listening of course. It is my long experience people are always happy to talk, but less likely to answer questions, especially to someone they deem an outsider.

The appearance of Willie the Dandy was a hot topic amongst the household's women that day. Partly this was because he was a dashing young man, who I am certain many a scullery maid dreamt would notice them and pull them out of their dreary world. This Cinderella fantasy often led to a girl losing her virtue to such a predatory beast behind the linen cupboard, only to find herself forgotten and discarded once the fun and excitement had worn off. In one of those weird twists of fate, it was likely Willie's mother had once found herself in such a circumstance, though the resulting life of her son became far more favourable than the one that awaited most bastards.

My quest for information eventually led to me sitting around a cup of tea talking to Charles in one of the house's numerous side rooms. Fortey had been a close friend, and the footman's death had hit the batman hard.

"We survived Zulus together, we did. He even took a bullet for me at Balaclava, so for him to die in such a way, it's horrid." I was tempted to smell the batman's tea to see if it had been fortified with anything stronger than sugar.

"Did he have any family?" I asked, prompting the old soldier to carry on. I felt like a heel manipulating the man who had offered nothing but kindness to me, but sometimes you just have to do things you do not want to do.

"Nah, none of us in the General's service have family. I think that's partly why he brought us here when he retired. Having served together for so many years, in so many of the world's sewers, I think we had become more of a family to him than his own."

"I was wondering why so many of you had retired with him. It is my experience that soldiers usually head home to long abandoned wives and children once their war was fought."

"Believe me, the thought of a warm bed and a stable home was enough enticement for most of us. When you've spent most of your life counting years of service by the number of boots you've worn out humping from one country you had never heard of before arriving in a fiefdom you soon wished you'd never seen, lugging your kit and weapons with ya', the thought of having a nice warm bed to crawl into every night sounded like heaven."

"And has it been?"

"Oddly no. I mean I have enjoyed my time here, well, until recently that is." Looking off into the distance, I figured the man was thinking of his lost friend. "The General's family makes Stamford House a different type of battlefield. We have to side step Miss Robyn, stay well away from Miss Lucinda, and as for Mrs Stamford…"

"She's a tyrant?"

"She's the devil incarnate. Pretty young wife of an older gent, you can imagine what she's like with the strapping young lads we have working the grounds around here."

"She takes them to her bed?"

"She does not." Charles said flatly, as though such a thing was simple unthinkable. He then pondered what he had said for a beat before adding: "She does all but... her twisted little mind is like a spider's. She likes to smile and flutter those eyes of hers, capturing whoever is her prey that week with her charm and wit. It's all promises and sneaky, shared looks, an accidental brushing of an arm on a shoulder, maybe even the ghost of a kiss in a darkened corridor. Once the poor fool is well and truly hooked, she walks away and never talks to him again as the thrill of the hunt is over. If he gets insistent, it is out the front gate with him and banishment. Happened to one of our gardeners just a few weeks ago."

"Did she ever take an interest in Miss Robyn's fiancé?"

This was clearly one question too many by the searing look the batman gave me. Sensing this was all the information I was going to get, and not looking to cause friction, I made my excuses and headed for my room. Truth was my head was throbbing and I needed a good rest. Sadly I was not going to get it.

My head was inches from the pillow when another scream had me up, grabbing my coat and heading back out the door. I followed the herd and found myself back in the room I had only just vacated.

This time there was a lot of blood. There was blood all over the floor and blood splashed down one wall. There was a line of bloody droplets marching across the rug like good little soldiers, and they ambled out the door into the main hallway. This was the door that I had also used just a few minutes ago when I guarantee you there had be no blood droplets anywhere in sight.

What the room did not contain, however, was a body. Instead there was one of the bobbies who had been stationed outside the house, while the maid who had obviously found the scene was bundled up in the arms of Vulk, sobbing deeply into his broad shoulders. At least I now knew which girl had fallen for the big bad wolf's attentions.

Vulk gave me a look, which I assumed meant 'find me later', so I turned my attention to the room. Peaking over the heads of those before me I noticed, for some reason, everyone seemed to be focused on the large knife with the bloody blade lying next to the chair I had recently been sitting on.

"Well, that is going to be rather inconvenient!" I admitted to no one in particular.

CHAPTER TEN

I was once more seated in front of Willkie to account for my whereabouts throughout the day. It would seem someone had reported my conversation with Charles the batman just before he was killed, if indeed Charles the batman had been killed. We were in the same room as earlier, seated at the same desk and on the same chairs, though this time a large whisky sat in a tumbler before me. The good Sergeant had placed it there, perhaps thinking such a libation would be needed after the last few days' adventures.

When the inspector finally returned and everything was sorted, he began interviewing the staff once more in a separate room. I assumed Abberline was looking for any information about what had occurred, before asking what I knew and my own movements. Yet instead he talked to the Stamford family and a Bobbie appeared and asked that I return to my room and wait to be summoned.

I headed upstairs a little confused, stepped into my room and was surprised to discover some unseen assailant attempting to stave my head in with an old mace. I even recognised the weapon as one that had been decorating the billiards room.

Having spent a lifetime ducking such blows I managed to slip under the clumsy strike, with the mace only glancing the side of my head. This was enough to send me cartwheeling to the floor though, giving my assailant the chance to move in for a coup-de-grace. Instead he found his shin meeting the heel of my shoe when I lashed out blindly. This simple act was enough to buy me the time needed to roll back to my feet and leap out the bedroom door. I managed to stumble about ten steps down the corridor outside, before meeting up with the Bobbie who had told me I was not needed for an interview.

The noise of the fight, the blood streaming down my face from a slight gash on my head, along with the look on my face seemed enough warning to alarm the policeman, who blew his whistle and ran into my room to apprehend my attacker. I swear that damn whistle hurt my head far more than the mace had.

Leaning against the far wall as more policemen chasing the whistle thundered up the stairs and into my room, I considered following them, but the way the horizon had begun to tilt suggested I should continue with my effort to keep the wall from tumbling down.

The first policeman soon reappeared in the corridor, hefting the mace with a smug look of accomplishment on his face. The villain had vanished into thin air, which was both a little unsettling and unsurprising. So far the household had suffered two deaths and most likely a third, and during the most recent murders the killer seemed to have vanished into thin air.

Another murder, another attack, another whisky, and another interview with Willkie and Abberline. I ignored both the drink and my growing need to fill the empty void between us with quips and japes; instead I sat silently and waited for the inspector to commence his inquisition. Not for the first time the policeman surprised me.

"Working on the theory you had nothing to do with the batman's death, is there anyone you can think of that would want to kill him?"

"The General." I answered.

"And how did you come up with him as a suspect?" Abberline asked, leaning into the table after catching his interest.

"Honestly I did not. I really have not had time to work out the intricate relationships within this house. If someone wanted the man dead, I certainly could not name them. I only mentioned the General as the man was his batman for years and likely had intimate knowledge of every black decision ever made within the walls of Stamford House."

I took a deep swallow of the whisky, allowing its fire to run down into my belly. Though not calming the drink at least gave me something to do and a moment to get my thoughts organised. Not having Abberline attack me as a possible criminal from the start was a situation I was unused to.

"And your attacker?" The Inspector asked.

"I have no idea. I can't say I have done nothing to warrant such an effort as I have certainly asked enough questions of enough of the household to cause suspicion if someone was paying close attention to my actions. I cannot imagine that is the issue though as it is not like I am getting close to uncovering the truth of what is going on here, even if someone possessed the knowledge of who I really am and the reason why I am here. The attacks indicate desperation to me."

"Desperation?" Willkie asked.

"Someone was clearly trying to pin Charles's murder on me. If I was then to die or disappear, perhaps with a little evidence planted in my room, then the other murder could be pinned on me as well. This would effectively hide the true motive for either man's death."

"That doesn't sound very desperate to me," the Sergeant commented, more to his commander than me.

"Desperate because they had not really thought it through. Certainly there would be evidence pointing towards me for those deaths, but then if my body showed up, who killed me and why? My murderer would still need to be caught, meaning the murderer of the other two still had a problem."

Willkie nodded in understanding and wrote something in his notebook. Abberline did not move, as though he had already come to this conclusion by himself. "And what of Vulk?"

"The last time I saw him he had a pretty maid on his shoulder, which means he is likely up in the girl's quarters even as we speak. The man is a true dog."

"How does he do it, it's not like he's the most handsome bloke around," Willkie noted, a little mean-spiritedly I thought, though not without reason. Vulk's face showed the map of a long, hard life, which only seemed to heighten women's attraction to him.

"Animal magnetism," I suggested with a shrug.

Once more I was set free to roam and investigate, though this time with a warning to keep an eye out for muggers with maces hiding in the shadows. It was so pleasant to see that Abberline and Willkie cared. I would be moved if I believed for a second that they were not trying to have a little fun at my expense.

Deciding it was time to catch up with Vulk and get his report; I headed towards the front door. It was only as I stepped outside that the realization hit me that I had absolutely no idea where the gardener's quarters were on the estate. Rather than ask someone and run the risk of the murderer overhearing and discovering my destination, I decided to just stroll about the few areas I had not explored as these most likely contained the staff quarters. I was also no longer walking defenceless, as I had collected my trusty sword cane from my room, while hidden deep in a coat pocket was my Webley pistol. Both had served me well in the past, though I admit to my surprise the Stamfords had not confiscated them when they originally found my unconscious body at their gate.

Almost immediately I found the Stamford House stables. This was a long, one-story building, which meant there was no room above for stable boys to sleep in. Instead they had their quarters at the far end of the structure, and upon inspection I found these empty. Most likely the lads were in the main house following the day's grand excitement.

The next building along my path was similar to the stables, but far smaller. This proved to be a washroom and well. Following this was the groundkeepers quarters and, unsurprisingly, they were deserted too. Most likely the entire house staff were all now talking to the police.

Peering into the gloom of the garden I decided against wandering down the dark paths contained therein, and was about to turn back to the main house when movement caught my eye. It was a figure; though the gloom was so impenetrable I could not tell if it was a man or a woman. What I could tell was it was coming on fast, so now was likely a good time to remove myself from its proximity.

I barely had time to turn when fingers with the strength of iron wrapped around my neck and I found myself physically hauled into the air. The grip around my throat was painful and the growing pressure in my head from the strangulation was intense.

No sooner had the attack began then it was over and I was dumped on the ground. Catching my breath, I levered myself up on one elbow and caught a glimpse of my saviour, an enormous shaggy beast that had sprung to my rescue and was fighting with my attacker. What little moonlight penetrated the garden's canopy illuminated both figures. Each fought with an unbelievable amount of energy and strength and their ferocity was startling as they tore into each other.

Claws and teeth caught what little light there was, while fur, flesh, and long, dark threads of blood ribboned into the air. The scene was bad enough, but what truly stuck with me was the noise. Standing in the dark listening to the guttural roaring and screeching as both creatures tore into each other, the sound of flesh being shredded and teeth clenching on bone and punching through skin, it was haunting.

The fight suddenly ended with a yelp of pain as one of the great beasts was violently thrown into a tree and landed with a heavy impact. My attacker took this opportunity to run off into the night at inhuman speed.

Fearful, I moved over to the where my protector had landed. Instead of the wolf-like monster lay the figure of Vulk…a very naked and unconscious Vulk to be sure. I leaned in and checked his vitals. Besides a few deep gashes that I noted were already closing, the old dog seemed to be healthy.

The noise and commotion of the battle brought men with torches running from the house and I made myself scarce. Vulk seemed fine and his wounds had already healed, and at this stage I simply could not afford to be found with a naked man in the Stamford garden. It was not that I could not explain the occurrence to Abberline; it was more living down the snide remarks that were sure to follow.

CHAPTER ELEVEN

Heading the long way back to the house, I dodged the yelling men and the policemen blowing their whistles and snuck through the house's rear door. I then made my way up to my room, with the throbbing in my head having grown to unbearable proportions.

From the sideboard next to the bed I fixed a concoction the staff had left there for the pain and drank it. Almost instantly the pain, not only in my head, but also in my neck where the second attacker had grabbed me, began to dissipate.

Toeing both my shoes off without undoing the laces as the act of leaning down would have encouraged the pain in my head to return, I dropped back onto my bed and, within minutes, was asleep...

...and almost immediate was wakened by someone pounding on my door.

It seed the day's unending troubles would ensure I got no sleep. It was one of the Stamford's men making all the racket, who beckoned me to follow. I knew he was an employee of the Colonel's and not one of the General's troopers by the simple fact the man was about thirty years too young.

"Do I need shoes?" I asked, pointing out my stockinged feet.

"Just going to the bottom of the stairs."

"All right then, lead the way."

I padded down the corridor like some grumpy penguin. The stairs proved tricky as, with no carpet on the naked marble, my feet slipped and slid anytime I did not put my weight directly over my toes. Having gingerly navigated down to the bottom of the stairs I was then greeted by a glorious sight. Willkie, Abberline and half the house staff standing around a naked Vulk, who was managing to remain decent thanks to a strategically placed blanket. I did my best to hide my grin; I really did, while those around him were laying on a nice round of scowls—all that was except for Willkie, who was unashamedly smiling from ear to ear.

"Is this the man who attacked you and stole your clothes?" Abberline asked Vulk.

"Him, no, never, I doubt he could hurt a flea. No, the guy who jumped me was a big fella, all muscles…and with a really big club."

"A really big club," Willkie repeated as he wrote down verbatim the werewolf's statement in his notebook.

"Can I go back to bed now please?" I asked, feeling the pain creeping back into my head.

"Ahem," the man who had collected me subtly coughed. "Colonel Stamford would like a moment if you'd be so kind."

"Certainly." I tentatively followed the man to the office where the interviews had been carried out earlier. I had been correct with my earlier assumption. The office was the Colonel's. Dominique Stamford sat behind his desk, fiddling about with some paperwork.

"Sit, please sit." He gestured, so I sat. "How are you feeling?"

"Well, since my initial arrival I have been hit in the head two more times and have been questioned about two murders. I certainly hope you do not believe I had anything to do with them? I assure you, I did not."

"Not at all. The attack on yourself I believe proves you are innocent of those crimes."

"My thanks, I can only hope the police feel the same way. That inspector seems to not share your opinion."

"Well allow me to alleviate some of your concerns; this is more of a mercy call. I was wondering if any of your memory had come back yet?"

"Very little. When I met your father I recalled seeing his picture in a newspaper, but so far that's about it."

"Pity, I was hoping to get you on your way."

"I apologise if I have been an inconvenience and overstayed my welcome. I can be out of here shortly, it may just take some time to work out where I could go."

Horrified at the suggestion the Colonel blurted: "Lord no, please do not feel I am throwing you out. I only meant if you have an inclination who you are we may be able to get you out of this house and home, away from any further peril."

"Ah, I see. Well unfortunately I still have no idea, though with all these policemen around I have asked them to make enquires about any missing person reports. Hopefully it is only a matter of hours before my family finds me."

"I certainly hope so. To lose so many members of my household is bad enough. To lose a guest would be unthinkable. I was contemplating perhaps we could put you up in a hotel to help keep you out of harm's way."

Trouble. I had not considered the over-the-top civility of the British gentry might have them sending me out of danger in such a way. It was time for a bout of reptilian sneakiness.

"Your kindness and concern is most appreciated, but for now I would like to stay if I could. Though I barely know any of you, at least you are familiar faces, and after talking with the General and regaining even that sliver of a memory, I have hopes being here will be far more beneficial than sitting around in a hotel surrounded by complete strangers would be."

"Of course, you are more than welcome to stay. I just wanted to make the offer, just in case you were feeling somewhat vulnerable and imprisoned by your situation."

Getting up from the chair I offered the Colonel my hand. "I do appreciate all you have done for me and intend to pay you back in kind, but for now if you do not mind, the bed you have so graciously supplied me is beckoning and my headache has grown worse. I need to put myself away before I collapse."

The Colonel gave me words of encouragement, sympathy, and regret as he escorted me out the door, but I recall few of them now. I was more interested in sleep, so allowed myself to be shepherded into my room and put to bed. I do believe I was asleep before the door to my room was even closed.

CHAPTER TWELVE

And all too soon I was awake again.

The clock in my room doled out its long chimes denoting that I had been asleep for all of twelve minutes.

Sitting at the footboard of my bed was a very disturbed looking Vulk. I was unsure how he had crept into my room, but the old dog had his ways.

There should be something very disturbing about finding a werewolf sitting at the end of one's bed, even a friendly one. The knowledge that, while asleep a creature of horror and nightmare had found its way into your room without you ever being aware of its presence was enough to cause you never to sleep without a crucifix or a string of garlic over your bedhead.

Clearly there was an issue as Vulk had risked the wrath of the police to pass on his report.

"He's gone, and when I say he's gone, I mean to say they have all gone."

Such a riddle in my pain addled, sleep deprived condition was always going to cause confusion. My head was throbbing and the siren call of that wondrous pillow kept insisting I lay down and let the world spin on without my paltry interference for the next day or three.

"I am sorry, what are you babbling about?"

"I don't babble," the old werewolf snorted.

"Babble, prattle, pick your verb."

"I report...enthusiastically," he replied, lifting his chin to the sky in fake outrage that did nothing to help my darkening humour.

"Please, for all that you hold dear, make your report so I can get some bloody sleep."

"Our young friend in the hole is gone, and I don't mean he was dug up and discovered."

"You're saying De Gois is missing?"

"I'm saying there is no scent of anyone around that hole other than us. I'm saying the only scent I could find was our own. There is not even a scent of anyone other than us in the vicinity of the hole, which is impossible if someone had discovered the body and dug it up."

"So what are you are saying here is … he just got up and walked away by himself?"

The werewolf sitting at the end of my bed gave me a raised eyebrow suggesting a man with a werewolf sitting at the end of his bed did not have the right to suggest anything was impossible.

"Wait, either my head wound is worse than I think and my brain has been turned to scrambled eggs, or you said something about 'they' have all gone. Other dead bodies?"

"In my search of the grounds I found two more holes like the one we found. Both until recently had bodies in them, and both are now vacated."

"Just how big are the grounds of this house?" I asked, though clearly dumbfounded by the idea that bodies could just be lying about, undiscovered.

"At least twenty acres. They were buried in the wood running along the back of the property. I don't think they were dead servants, at least not dead servants from around here as no one has reported any missing recently."

"I am starting to think this may be a job for Abberline. We will need to find out if anyone has been reported missing from the surrounding properties." Tired as I was, my mind was engaged now. A tiny thought had begun to creep in and it refused to be removed.

I swung my legs over the edge of the bed and began to dress. As I had not actually undressed yet from the night before, this really just meant I had to put my shoes on and head for the door.

"Where are you going?"

"I need to follow up on something with the police…wait…do you have any money?"

Unhappily handing over a handful of notes and coins, Vulk asked: "Anything I should do while you're spending my cash?"

"Try and find out what happened to the General's batman. Despite our current predicament a body simply cannot vanish from a room with no trace. His death also seems to have been different from the others, so perhaps it was done in a rush and the murderer made a mistake."

"I'm on it, and Amun…?"

"Yes?" I paused at my bedroom door.

"Watch your back, lad."

Picking up my sword cane, I gave Vulk a wink and was out the door.

CHAPTER THIRTEEN

An old saying goes there is never a policeman around when you want one.

Supposedly Abberline had left men stationed at both entrances to the house, with another down at the front gate, but these men were nowhere to be seen. Leaving the house and passing through the unlocked, unmanned front gate, I had to walk a number of streets before I found a cabby, who took me to Scotland Yard.

As the hansom cab bustled along the cobbled streets into the city, I sat and watched as ghostly, skeletal trees with naked branches clawed at the thickening fog and the night sky slowly transformed into rows of houses with dark windows resembling dead eyes. As London grew out of the dark and enclosed the road I turned over what few facts we had uncovered so far.

Bodies with no blood, vast amounts of blood with no bodies, bodies buried like springtime tulip bulbs, then those same bodies disappearing with apparently no assistance—there was definitely something strange and amiss occurring at the Stamford estate.

Arriving at the Yard, neither the Inspector nor Willkie proved to be on duty, but I did find one of the officers who had been out at Stamford House earlier.

"I need to talk to Abberline, it is most urgent."

"I'm sure it is sir, but if you could return tomorrow when the Inspector will be on duty."

"This cannot wait as I believe people are in imminent danger. If it is not possible to get Abberline a message, could you at least tell me where the body from the Stamford House murder was taken?"

"Well sir that would be the city morgue of course. I have to inform you though that the morgue is closed until tomorrow."

"What, so they just pile up the bodies from the previous night on the back step until the morning shift comes in and packs them away?" I asked incredulously.

"No sir, the office of the morgue is closed, not the morgue itself."

"Thank you." And I was off again.

The morgue was only a few blocks away and, rather than waste time hailing down a cab I decided to stretch my legs and get the blood flowing to better empower my thought process. Even at this late hour the streets of Westminster were alive with the clop, clop, clop of horse drawn vehicles going about their business. Bakers, rubbish collectors, transport vehicles using the empty streets to move their goods before the day's traffic choked the thoroughfares snaking through the world's largest city. Heading away from the Thames and towards Victoria Station, I had the strangest feeling I was being followed. A few quick corners and a close inspection of a large display window to catch anyone within its reflection revealed nothing, so I moved on. I could not think of any reason to keep someone from knowing I was headed towards the morgue, so cared little if there was indeed someone following me.

The desk-sergeant at Scotland Yard had been correct. The Morgue office was indeed closed, but the rear door proved a boon ... eventually. Here I found two men on station, and after five minutes bruising my knuckles on the door to get them to move from behind their desk and answer, a pound each had them chatting like a couple of gin-freaks.

It would seem I had just missed all the excitement. For the last three hours the staff, along with a handful of policemen, had been searching the building from top to bottom for a corpse that had gone missing. Not only had it gone missing, but also a number of other bodies appeared to have been attacked by some sort of savage animal.

I kept it to myself that a suspicion of this, or something similar, was what had brought me out into the night to try and circumvent. A quick investigation revealed the missing cadaver had been Fortey, the man found exsanguinated in the Stamford's hallway. The other bodies were not related to the house in any way, though they all seemed to have similar wounds as the Stamford man's. All had been bitten, as though by a dog, wolf, or perhaps even a large serpent.

Leaving the two morgue employees behind to their toil, I re-entered London's night air and walked headfirst into a man who seemed to have been waiting for somebody. His stammering and awkwardness suggested he had in fact been waiting for me.

"Abraham Stoker...of the London Daily Gazette. Could you tell me why a man staying at Stamford House, a location where there have been a number of murders by the way, has just been visited both Scotland Yard and the city morgue in the middle of the night?"

It would seem there was little doubt he had been waiting for me.

"I have lost my dog. Have you seen him? He is about this big," I asked, horizontally placing my hand at the same height as the reporter, "...wet nose and an annoying habit of pissing on the sidewalk."

"Very funny Mr...?"

"...Wales, Mr Prince of Wales."

Walking down the street towards a row of cabs, the reporter followed close behind. At least I now knew the sense of being shadowed did not mean I was going mad. I should have realized a reporter might have begun staking out the police station to see who they could catch entering or leaving the premises.

"Mr Wales, could you please answer the question?"

"I believe I did."

"Then could you tell me why a man with an injury to his head has left Stamford House, where there has been a prolonged police presence over the last few days, and has taken a midnight stroll to Scotland Yard and then the city morgue? I'm sure my readers will be asking the same question when I print this in tomorrow's edition."

I opened the first cab's door and, after a moment's hesitation, gestured for the reporter to join me.

As the cab bounced its way towards Stamford House I pondered my next move. Clearly the young man seated next to me knew far more than he should, but did he know enough to be a danger, or could he be fobbed off with a simple and all-encompassing lie?

The fact that he sat next to me in silence said more than any words could have. He clearly knew he was on to something and felt comfortable enough to allow me to come to that conclusion by myself. He was a fisherman with something hooked ... something big and he knew it; it was now just a matter of being patient and reeling in the catch or becoming too aggressive and losing whatever it was on the line.

"Tell me what you think you know?" I demanded.

"Nice try, but no, I don't think so," Stoker said, watching the dark streets fly by. "It's hard to learn more than you know by admitting how much you already know. People generally don't talk if they think they have gotten away with something."

"A valid point, and you have also just given yourself away. I really could not care less what you reveal in your little paper, and you clearly do not have enough to print anything interesting or else why would you be here? I believe you have snippets of what you think may be a story, but little more than that. You need either conformation, information, or a source which you can track like Hansel and Gretel through the forest."

"Certain of yourself, aren't you?" The reporter asked, warily.

"I am certain you do not have the story you think you do. I am also certain you will now tell me what you know, and what your intentions are so that I can ascertain if I should bother bringing you into my confidence or simply boot you out on the street right here."

Sitting back in the cab's seat, I left the reporter to ponder his thoughts and to plot his next action. If I was wrong, I lost nothing, as he would still likely have the information to barter something out of me. If I was right, however, and he was as intelligent as I figured him to be, he would see the hopelessness of his situation and agree to my demands. He had the tail of an animal and was determined to hold on and find out what it was. If that tail belonged to a tiger he could have a ferocious story, though there was always the risk of having his hand bitten off. If, however, the tail belonged to a donkey, well I think you can see where my analogy was heading. What felt like an eternity later, the reporter finally spoke.

"One body has been taken out of Stamford House and I believe someone else was murdered inside, but that body is missing. I know Scotland Yard is involved, which isn't all that remarkable for such a high profile family like the Stamfords. What is surprising is that Inspector Abberline is on the case. I also know of at least five other people that have been found murdered or missing around the countryside surrounding the Stamford grounds. A lot of feral cats and even a pet or two have gone missing too."

Of course I could not be sure, but I had a reasonable idea of what had been happening to the cats at least. As to the other bodies, well that was the growing mystery. "So why follow me?"

"I wasn't, well, not directly. I was following someone who was following you. It proved surprisingly easy as they were solely intent on watching you and they never bothered to see if they were being followed in turn. They disappeared at the morgue though and I thought I had missed you leaving, so I was sneaking about the building to see if there was another exit you could have left by when you walked out."

"Someone else?" I said, more to myself. "Who else could have been following me? Do you happen to have a description?"

"None whatsoever. Though they were easy enough to follow, the person did seem to always find the best cover to hide in or behind. It was next to impossible to see any features, and I certainly never saw a face…"

"You said he … he never looked back…?" I began chewing this over. "So someone else is interested in my movements?"

"It would seem so. Why would they be interested in you and your movements?"

"You know as much as I do, Stoker. Sadly, I took a hit to the head a few days ago and am yet to recover my full faculties."

"You have…amnesia, I believe they call it?" He sounded sceptical.

"I do."

"No you don't," he said, smugly.

"I don't? And how have you come to that conclusion?"

"A man with amnesia does not catch a cab to Scotland Yard, then walk to the city morgue without knowing where he's going. A man who knows where he's going is not therefore a man suffering from amnesia."

I believe I must have sat there a beat too long trying to think of an answer, as he held out his hand and said before I could respond: "You know who I am, now it would be rude if you did not share your true name, Mr Wales."

"Amun." I answered automatically.

"Pleased to make your acquaintance Mr Amun, now if you could be so kind as to inform me what's going on inside the walls of the Stamford estate, well I'd be greatly appreciative?"

"You can be as appreciative as you want but I cannot give you an answer that I do not possess. I can confirm there have been two murders in the house, or at least one murder and one suspicious disappearance."

"I knew it."

"As for the Inspector's presence, I have no inkling as to why he has been called in. Perhaps someone in the home office owes Stamford a favour and has placed the good Inspector in charge of the entire affair. I have no knowledge either way."

"But..."

"I really cannot tell you anything. I have been either in bed with a broken skull or staggering from one interview to another with the police. I really do not know much more than you do at this time, though I did hope that would change by my trip tonight."

"I see. Since you know I will continue my enquiry why not just share what you found out tonight now?"

"Nothing really, well, what I did learn was that I need someone who has contacts with the London spiritualism community. I feel that some of the answers about what is going on here may well lay with them. Do you know anyone?"

I had hoped the strange question would somehow derail the reporter by disguising the fact that I really did need to talk to someone who knew about spiritualism. Instead Stoker took me by surprise.

"It would seem that, indeed, I might be of service to you. I know of such a man and would happily make the introductions."

Well, I hadn't expected his reply and now I was in a bind. I had an inquisitive reporter who was capable of helping with my own investigation, but in doing so he could uncover why I was involving myself in the affair before I was ready for anyone to know the truth. The question was simple, take this man into my confidence or shun him and turn a possible ally into a certain enemy.

After a number of long, silent minutes the cab pulled into the bottom of the path leading to the Stamford's front gate. I levered myself out of the confines of the cabin and, before he could follow, placed a resisting hand on the reporter.

"If you could meet me here tomorrow at one o'clock with your friend, I will make my decision to inform you further then." A helpful acquaintance at the time seemed to be more valuable than a troublesome, antagonistic rival. "Perhaps we can help each other out, perhaps not."

I gestured for the cabbie to move on, and once I was sure his passenger intended to remain a passenger, I made my way back to the house and my waiting bed. Vindictively, I noted as I walked back into the house that, as sharp as young Stoker was, he had not noticed I had left him to deal with the cab fare.

CHAPTER FOURTEEN

W alking up the short path to the estate's front gate it became clear something was not right. The few gas lamps lining the street, along with those positioned to illuminate the gatehouse, were all extinguished. The garden path beyond the gate was also too dark, and I could see little light bleeding across the grounds from the distant house. When I had left, though the policemen supposedly on duty had been oddly missing, the path at least had lanterns illuminating the way from the house to the gate. The fact there was now no policemen and no lights indicated something was terribly wrong.

Unarmed except for my razor wit, which many would argue made me totally defenceless; I crept through the gate and immediately turned off the path. Here I found one of the missing policemen. Like a blind man I ran my fingers over the dead man's body in the dark until I found what I was looking for, his whistle and his club.

With no time to come up with a better plan of action, I put the whistle to my lips and 'peeped' for all I was worth. Within seconds I heard the answering call of other whistles and knew help was on its way. Like some Indian smoke signal in the New World, or the famed African bush telegraph, the whistle was being repeated throughout the vicinity, beckoning any Bobby within earshot to head this way.

Hefting the policeman's baton, I gave the whistle one last blast to help those coming to locate me, and then headed towards the house.

My whistle had done some good as I could see lights flickering to life in the top levels of the house. I was too far away to call out a warning and did not want whoever was skulking in the garden to know my whereabouts, so decided not to issue any further warnings. Sticking to the shadows I moved uphill in a crescent shape trajectory to keep myself out of the clutches of any villain lying in wait along the path. Using what little light filtered through the gloomy night from the weak moon above and its deathly, foggy halo, I kept as low to the ground as possible, allowing myself to catch any movement and restrict any watcher's opportunity to see my approach.

With the truncheon strap wrapped firmly around my wrist I ducked under the small tree the gardeners had been planting yesterday and halted. Before me a figure was lurking behind a hedge running along one side of the garden's main path, his right hand held above his head in some strange martial pose I did not recognise. I recalled having watched the movements of the Wǔshù martial artists in China during the Xia Dynasty, and I completed my own training under Baqet III at Men'at Khufu during Egypt's 11th Dynasty, yet never had I seen anything like this.

From the side of the house came voices, followed by two men carrying lit torches. One broke off and walked towards the front gate, calling loudly, I assumed, for the policeman who was supposed to be on guard there. The second figure turned out to be Vulk, and he was heading down the path towards me, the tree, and the shrub hiding the oddly posed villain.

Rising as quietly as possible I crept up behind the assassin. I was unsure of my timing, but did not believe I could reach him in time to stop his attack on Vulk without speeding up and giving myself away. Luckily the old wolf began supplying enough covering noise as his large booted feet crunched their way down the stone path, so I sped up.

Judging by the shadows cast by the torch, Vulk was just beginning to walk along the other side of the shrub when the statue leaned back to give his strike all the power his body could muster. Even in the dim light I could see his hand was sheathed in some sort of gauntlet, though what that would be used for I could only surmise.

Under the cover of Vulk's trudging feet I sprinted forward and brought the truncheon down on the man's exposed wrist in a way that would have put a smile on old Baqet III's face.

With a wail of agony the bushwhacker spun about and took a large step backwards, moving straight into a very surprised looking Vulk. Both men tumbled to the ground, and before either could react to their situation I stepped in and bopped the mysterious figure in the head with the club. The satisfaction of someone getting hit in the head, and that someone not being me, was supreme. To reinforce my enjoyment I gave the man a second blow, just in case, I then blew the police whistle again to allow the approaching policemen to triangulate in on our position.

I offered Vulk a hand up. "I believe we are in real trouble old friend."

The man that stood before me removed his shirt and shoes, and then his features began to melt away before my very eyes. In his place was a creature I would describe as half bear, half Vulk. The metamorphosis unnerved me, but not as much as when the Vulk part of the creature gave me a wink before it loped away into the night.

The grounds and the house were soon ablaze as torches and lamps were lit across the estate. Running into the garden were a number of policemen, their night lanterns casting elongated shadows across the pathways.

Picking up Vulk's discarded clothes and torch, I placed the flame near the befuddled figure at my feet. I inspected his right hand and its large metal gauntlet. The thing resembled those the knights of yore once wore, though with a slight difference. In the middle of the steel fists palm were two protruding, razor sharp spikes.

Underneath the black hood I found a bearded man staring back at me. The blood running freely down the side of his head was evidence of my ability with a truncheon. The assassin's entire outfit was black, except for around his neck where I found a silver chain holding a large, intricately carved medallion.

I was so focused on this pendant that I did not see the two similarly dressed men sneak up behind me and hit me on the head before it was too late.

I may have mentioned earlier in my journal how life at times can be so satirical.

CHAPTER FIFTEEN

Vulk's face swam into focus, replacing the vison of Aphrodite I had been happily dreaming about. He had reverted to human form and was dressed again, so, at least I didn't wake up to the vision of a monster.

"What is it with you and gardens?" he asked. "How's the head?"

I gave him a smile to confirm I was at this moment the second most sarcastic person in the garden and sat up. My vision blacked out briefly and the pain in my head went from agony to excruciating. What permanent damage had been done I had no idea. I did notice through eyes forced almost shut by the pain that I was alone on the ground.

"I think your bandages softened the blow," the old werewolf said, inspecting the top of my head with a prodding finger. I batted his hand away.

"You find anything?" I asked.

"I don't think there was ever anything in there to find," he answered, indicating my head with a smirk. "As for whoever hit you and the guy you hit, I know where they came from, I know where they went, well, I know where they met a horse and cart, and I followed their scent until I lost it with the rest of the morning traffic closer to town."

Morning? He was right. The sky was filling with the off-pink hue of the day's first light.

"And what about you, did you learn anything before your nap?"

"Well..." I said, getting to my feet with his help. "...I do have this."

The silver pendant twinkled in the lamplight as it spun about at the end of its long chain.

"Is that a dragon?"

"A dragon biting its own tail under the cross of St George."

"What does it mean?" Vulk asked, prodding the medallion with the same finger and in the same fashion as he had my wounded head.

"It means we have serious trouble old chap."

We made our way back up the path to the house's main hall, which was bustling with activity as policemen inspected and questioned the household staff, most of who were busy trying to continue with their duties for the start of the day. Everywhere there were pots of steaming hot tea and I helped myself to a cup, discovering as I did so my great thirst. As I downed a third cup Sargent Willkie found me and beckoned for me to follow. Vulk trailed behind and I figured I now had a permanent shadow until this danger had passed.

Inspector Abberline was seated with Colonel Stamford and his wife. No one at the table seemed pleased to see me.

"Sit down, Amun, before you collapse." It took a beat for me to realise the Inspector had just said my name in front of the Stamfords. I guess my ruse was now over. "You look like death warmed over."

"Then you can only imagine how I feel?" I agreed, weakly lowering myself into the proffered chair.

The inspector indicated another to Vulk with a look. The wolf indicated he would rather stand with a nod. You could almost feel the pent up frustration emanating from the werewolf after twice failing to come to grips with our foe.

Abberline went on. "Colonel Stamford, Mrs Stamford, It's not so much my pleasure as my duty to introduce you to Amun Galeas and his associate Sebastian Vulk. Both men have been in your house under false pretences; and as dishonourable as this may sound I must admit to my own culpability in the ruse as I was aware of their chicanery."

Before I could voice a complaint, Abberline headed off any protest I might have issued with the simple explanation, "Two men died last night, both of them my own, and another two now lay at death's door. This has gone from a simple murder investigation to a monstrous crime of the worst kind. Anyone capable of killing so many policemen is capable of doing anything."

I nodded my agreement at this assessment and looked at the Colonel. His eyes seemed to bore directly into my soul, so it was probably time for an explanation.

"I was hired by the family of Jerome De Gois to find out what happened to their son."

"He ran away with that girl," Mrs Stamford answered a little too quickly.

"He most certainly did not. My investigation has revealed tickets were purchased, travel was arranged, but nowhere could we find anyone who ever saw the couple together. We also know no one had actually occupied the berth on the ship you all claim they left on, and before anyone says anything, we know Jerome De Gois never left the grounds of this house."

"And how could you know that?" Abberline asked, leaning forward in his chair.

"Because we found his body in a shallow pit at the bottom of the garden," Vulk explained.

The anger that passed over Abberline's face was only there briefly, and those who did not know the man well would likely have missed it completely. The fury that hardened his eyes, however, was there for all to see. "And you kept this to yourself?"

"We kept this to ourselves as there is a problem. The corpse vanished, and it is hard to report a murder when you have no evidence of said murder, and that everyone likely associated with the crime continually repeats the same story that the man in question had sailed to America."

Abberline thought this over for a moment than gave me a nod that what I had said was likely true. He was not happy with me for holding something back, but he was calming down a little. The good Colonel on the other hand was far from finished with the matter.

"You sir, are the vilest of human beings! You take advantage of my family, my hospitality, and my sympathies by lying to me, and then under false pretences you scuttle about my home under some delusion that one of us had something to do with that poor boy's death, if he even is … really dead. How can I know this is not some part of a further ruse, or worse, that you killed the boy yourself and are now trying to pin his murder on us? I want the both of you out of my house this very second!"

Stamford screamed this last part as he stood and pointed at the door, and while his face went from crimson to a deep maroon as he took a deep breath, likely for some more yelling, I took the opportunity to reply.

"I could care less about what you think of me, Stamford. By my count at least six people have died in this house, with another half dozen or so dead in the surrounding grounds." I gave Abberline a look saying I would explain that one later. "This affair has become extremely dangerous and I believe the Inspector here now has the right to impound this house and all those in it for questioning and their own safety. A curse has been brought down upon our heads, and until this matter in concluded I do not think anyone here is safe, whether they physically remain here or not."

Abberline gestured for me to remain in my seat. "Though I am displeased with Amun's methods I cannot help but point out he is the only one who has gathered any information about what is going on here. If his actions tonight are any indication and to be believed, his presence has time and again foiled a much large plot."

"Oh, I have more than that," I grinned, holding up the silver dragon talisman. "I believe we are in far more trouble than any of us could have conceived earlier. This house has caught the attention of an ancient and bloody society and I fear we will not be rid of them until they have what they are seeking, that or they have been exterminated from the face of the earth."

"What is that?" Mrs Stanford asked, studying the medallion I held.

"It is the symbol for 'Societas Draconistrarum', an old European association that seems to have landed on our shores and taken a special interest in the Stamford family."

"And why would they do that?" The Colonel asked, sceptically.

At the room's door a policeman waved himself in. "Sir, Mr Amun has two visitors at the front gate. They say they're expected."

Abberline gave me a quizzical look.

"If we may?" I asked, rising and indicating Vulk. "The two of us have a little research to do. If we could report back later today, maybe this time tomorrow at the very latest, I suspect we will have answers to all your questions."

I tossed the dragon medallion to Abberline. "We will be back. Look after this Inspector, it is of vital importance."

Turning the dragon over and over again in his hands, the

Inspector gave a single nod and I headed for the front gate, with Vulk not one step behind.

CHAPTER SIXTEEN

At the front gate sat a hansom cab with my stalking shadow from the previous evening. Sitting beside Stoker was a fellow of a similar age with an impressively waxed moustache that stuck out further than his ears, giving him something of a bullish appearance. Introduced as Stoker's cousin, Dr Arthur Doyle, I began our meeting with an apology to the man.

"It would seem I have brought you both out here under false pretences. What I thought was a case of spiritualism has become more about assassination and fairy tales."

"Oh dear," sighed the doctor, crestfallen with losing his chance of a little adventuring. The life of a doctor it seems was not exciting enough for some.

"We had an agreement, so do not for a second think I will take kindly to being brushed aside like this," the reporter growled.

I held up my hand in a placating gesture. "Nothing of the sort is going on, I assure you. The situation has become far more dangerous than I had realised last night, and I just cannot in all good conscious put two fellows like yourselves in harm's way for no reason."

"Let me assure you a good story is never a poor reason," Stoker said, puffing up like some lizard under threat from a dog. "I have a sense there is a wild tale to tell here, so I am in this until the end."

"Me too," exclaimed Doyle with, if not equal, than substantially enough bravado to perhaps convince himself of joining in whatever his cousin was talking about.

"I figured this may be the case so I took it upon myself to come bearing gifts," said the reporter and he handed me his notepad. The top page said, 'Corpse Discovered in Office. Not stolen. Fear of further misadventures cause morgue to bury body immediately.'

"So this is about the missing body from the morgue?"

"It is," Stoker beamed. "Before picking up Doyle here, I checked in with the Morgue and found out the body you were oh-so-subtly enquiring about turned up this morning. Unlike many of the others, this one hadn't been touched and only misplaced, but as the man had no family and there is no reason to keep him, the city coroner has sent him on to Brookwood Cemetery for immediate burial."

"What do you mean 'sent him'?" Vulk asked, not sure who 'him' was, but curious about the idea of corpses being shuffled about.

"I don't believe we've met sir. May I enquire—?"

I interrupted with a quick introduction before the reporter's slightly caustic ways angered Vulk. "His name is Vulk and he is my closest associate. Vulk, this is Abraham Stoker, ace reporter of the London Daily Gazette, and his cousin, the honourable Dr Arthur Doyle."

"Pleased to meet you Mr Vulk. Now to answer your query, sent him by the Necropolis Railway. Surely you've noticed there isn't a lot of room in the city for burial grounds."

"Not something I have ever thought about, but now that you mention it…"

"Bodies have been shipped out to the large plot at Brookwood for years. The lack of space in London's established graveyards means churches have been having their older 'contents' relocated to make space for new occupants to be put in."

"It is also to save us from ourselves," Dr Doyle added. "Space has become so cramped in some places with all the rotting bodies being in such close proximity to those who live here that it has caused outbreaks of disease. The bodies are even starting to bleed into the water table, so a dedicated train line called the Necropolis was built to carry all the bodies and their funeral parties out to the new cemetery. The trains can then bring the mourners back at the end of the day."

"That's quite clever," Vulk admitted.

"Clever and necessary, Anyway the body was removed this morning and sent on the first train out. He's likely already in the ground," Stoker said.

An idea dawned. "Well gentleman, it would seem we have to catch a train."

"And I know where we can buy a ticket," Doyle volunteered, catching on.

While Vulk found a second buggy, I ducked back into the

house and bundled up a few things I thought we would need, then the four of us headed to Waterloo Station to catch the train of the dead.

The cab ride to the Necropolis station at Waterloo Bridge gave me the chance to ponder our next move. If my suspicions were correct, well, we would have to return to Stamford House and report our discovery and the danger. And if I happened to be wrong, well that would be problematic. When you know what a villain is after or intends to accomplish, then his moves and actions can be predicted with a certain amount of accuracy. If, however, you have no idea what their plan or goal is, then it's all but impossible to plan ahead and you end up reacting. In life, as in chess, if you react for too long you will find yourself at a great disadvantage and the game is done. If my suspicion turned out to be wrong, we would have to find some new way of determining what was going on and how it was connected to Stamford House.

It also occurred to me that having a licensed physician along was not such a bad thing. I had us swap cabs and asked Doctor Doyle to change my bandages during what remained of the trip and make sure there was nothing wrong with my head...other than the obvious. Doyle could also prove useful with inspecting the body of General Stamford's footman.

I was a little disappointed when the station for the Necropolis train did not live up to my expectations, though in the cold light of reality the building could never have achieved what my over-active imagination had dreamt up for what the railway would be like. I had pictured some ghoulish building, all misty gloom, with skeletal figures stalking through its shadowy interior as a phantom steam engine screeched like a dying horse as it pulled into the station with a blast of steam and a cough of smoke from the fiery, hell-like depths of its smokestack. Instead the station was, well if not cheerfully upholstered, than respectfully so. Flowers and sectioned off seats so that groups of mourners could occupy a corner of the waiting room without the need to mingle with the bereaved of other parties. The train itself was a surprise too as it was neat and clean, with both first and second-class cabins.

Having little money on me, we got Stoker to pay for our fare, as it was he who wanted the story, after all. We caught the midday service out to Brookwood Cemetery in Surrey, a journey that took around an hour, leaving the four of us plenty of time to get better acquainted. We had learned the cemetery closed at six every evening thanks to a brochure we found at the station, and this would have been a problem if any of us were strict, law-abiding citizens. Instead we unanimously decided to hide out in the enormous cemetery until after closing and then find what I hoped would be Fortey's final resting place. We could have located it during the day, but just in case something went wrong it would be handy to deny having been anywhere near the grave.

Luckily at Waterloo Station we had the foresight to obtain food and drink enough to last us the entire day and partly through the next, all paid for by the London Daily Gazette of course. Too our overall betterment, Stoker was proving very desperate for his story.

The warm day passed slowly and I finally caught up with some sleep on a bed of green grass under a well-canopied tree in one corner of the manicured graveyard. Doyle and Stoker proved themselves useful by locating the grave without actually approaching it, while Vulk sat guard over my prone form. The hungry mutt also managed to eat at least half of our supplies.

We had picked our spot well. Seated as we were, our profiles were invisible behind the dozens of tombstones surrounding us, yet the field of stones allowed us to peek over them and inspect what was happening about us without giving our position away.

A hand reached down and patted my shoulder. Unhappy about being awakened, I levered myself off the grass on one elbow and grumpily asked, "What?"

The two men sitting before me eating sandwiches grinned over their half-eaten meals.

"You snore," Doyle smirked.

"You snore like a demon from the seventh level of hell," Stoker added.

Vulk shrugged a shoulder that said, "They are both right, you do, but who cares?"

Feeling better than I had in days, I fought back a yawn and

asked, "What did you find out?"

"We have located the grave. He was buried after all the other funerals had taken place. There was no real ceremony and certainly no one from the Stamford House was present, just a priest who said a few words over the coffin before it was lowered into the ground. It's in a rather open spot so we will have to wait until well after the cemetery closes and its dark, or else we could be spotted."

Enjoying the cool evening breeze, I lay back to ponder why no one from the house had gone to the burial, and why it had been rushed. Finding no answer, and after eating one of the few sandwiches left from the once mountainous pile I told my fellow sentinels, "Keep your eyes open and wake me when it gets dark. I am going catch up on my sleep."

The day's warmth had been replaced by the evening's sharp chill, something London with its paved roads and claustrophobic, canyon-like streets rarely felt anymore. Instead the city seemed to have developed its own weather system that was impervious to much of what Mother Nature produced. This made the city a little nicer during winter and brutally hot during summer. Even the city's renowned fog seemed to have been replaced these days by an impenetrable haze, fuelled by a million fires and gas lamps, not to mention the steam and smoke belched out by the city's trains and factories. Once beautiful white buildings today were slowly being stained black, and I did not even want to think what was happening to the city's drinking water after the rain washed all the soot into the rivers and creeks.

Spending a day sitting in the sun in a wondrously green field, even one dotted by the bone white headstones of a graveyard, reminded me just how squalid life in London has become. Yet there is no other city I would live in, and believe me, I have lived in a few.

My companions woke me as the last sliver of sun dipped under the hills lining the distant horizon. Already it was becoming hard to see details in the lowering light of the graveyard.

With the cemetery empty we picked our way to the location where our two new friends had watched Fortey go into the ground. The grave was freshly dug and as exposed as both men had noted. Obviously the more picturesque spots in the park-like setting were kept for a clientele of a greater social standing. Fortey had not rated one of those spots. Even in the growing darkness we could see the location of the grave was weedy and sparse of grass.

"So what now?" Vulk asked, toeing the fresh dirt.

I sat on the ground and made myself comfortable. Then I took the bundle I had been carrying from Stamford House, opened it, and lay its contents out. Before us lay a number of swords I had taken from the estate's walls. "Take a seat and a sword gentlemen as this could prove to be a very long night."

I lay on the scraggly grass covering an older grave and looked up at a sparkling night sky.

I had assumed one of two things would happen at the gravesite. Either the men dressed in black with the proclivity for dragon jewellery would show up and dig the poor man out of his grave for the same reason they had taken the other body away, or something of a more supernatural nature was about to occur.

After a few hours everyone was getting restless. Vulk continually sniffed the air, freezing like some bloodhound whenever he thought he had caught the scent of something unusual, before returning to scanning our surroundings and pacing. At some point Doyle curled up and fell asleep. Stoker wrote notes, even in the dark, though what he was writing I had no idea as nothing had happened since our arrival.

I was starting to consider the possibility that I had totally misread the situation when, just a few hours before dawn, Fortey's grave began to tremble and we were all up on our feet. The rational mind is a fascinating thing and I listened with concern as the others tried to explain away what we were seeing. There are areas where the Underground Railroad caused similar tremors, and the three men began wondering about the possibility of a train line somewhere under or near the cemetery. Doyle suggested the possibility of a localised earthquake, and I was happy to point out an earthquake localised to just the grave of Mr Fortey seemed a little improbable.

Stoker raised the possibility of a safety coffin; the type where people concerned about being buried alive had a bell installed in their grave. The bell would be placed by the gravestone, connected to a cord that the recently buried non-corpse could yank and ring to alert anyone topside they were still alive and in need of assistance.

Was it conceivable Fortey had been alive when they buried him? We all looked at each other, the possibility catching in our imaginations like a hooked fish.

When a hand breached the topsoil Stoker screamed, Doyle looked vindicated, and Vulk jumped back, ready for action. As for my reaction, well, I suspect I displayed none because I well knew what we were seeing was likely to happen, as fantastic as it may have been.

We all watched as what had once been the Stamford's footman dug his way out of his own grave. With unnatural strength and vigour, Fortey soon managed to work his upper torso free, and almost comically sat there with his head pivoting from side to side to take all four of us in. I approached carefully and asked the man if he needed a hand.

Instead of taking the offered help Fortey, exuding great force, broke free from his tomb and, without even shaking off the grave dirt, attacked.

Caught by surprise, the creature's first blow sent me flying backwards into the graveyard. As I re-gathered my wits and struggled to get my feet under me, Doyle, screaming like a banshee, darted forward and stabbed the former Mr Fortey with a sword. When the creature shrugged the Doctor away, Stoker stepped forward and emptied the revolver he had brought with him into the beast. Once the gun clicked on an empty chamber he darted back to reload.

The bullets had torn large holes into Fortey's chest, with one having torn a large chunk away from the side of his head. None of the wounds seemed to slow him down.

Instead of renewing their attack, the cousins stopped and were now gaping at the melting form of Vulk, who was in mid-wolf transformation by the time I staggered back to the gravesite. I could tell by their nervous glances that Doyle and Stoker were wondering which of the creatures they were sharing the graveyard with was going to kill them first.

"Ignore Vulk and get on with chopping Fortey to pieces!" I yelled, diving into the knees of the creature just as it seemed to regain focus and moved towards the two men. Though the impact was like hitting a stout tree, I managed to topple him over and the former footman crashed down on top of me.

With a blood-curdling roar the metamorphosed Vulk leapt into the fight and his great shaggy head bit into Fortey's shoulder with a sickening crack, snapping the clavicle. The bite also allowed Vulk to keep both arms free, and claws as large as a lions soon had parts of the undead creature flying through the night air.

As much damage as our combined effort had done, the unnatural stamina of the creature that had just clambered out of Fortey's grave was even greater. Despite the fact most of its torso was now gone, what remained continued to claw at Vulk, trying to break the werewolf's grip and free itself.

"Give me that!" I yelled and snatched the reloaded revolver from Stoker and rushed forward. I waited until the creatures head turned towards me, slammed the weapon into the creature's open mouth, smashing a number of its teeth in the process including one enlarged canine it had grown since climbing out of the soil. I then emptied the gun entirely into its head, making sure to avoid the werewolf on the other side.

With a snuffle, Vulk released his grip and stepped back, gore dripping from his enormous jaws and clawed hands. Even with its head ruined, the creature continued to writhe, as though trying to stand.

Stoker gave Doyle's shoulder a shove forward. "The head … Cousin use your sword and cut its bloody head off!"

The Doctor stepped in and swung at the beast's exposed neck. The creature continued to struggle until the sword severed its spinal cord and the unholy monster's head rolled away. Immediately the body sagged to the ground, its unnatural energy gone.

"Now that's the way to spend an evening," Stoker grinned, taking back his revolver and reloading it. "Are you going to tell me what's really going on now?"

CHAPTER SEVENTEEN

Saying the word made it no more real.

"Vampire...that was a vampire?" Now that I think back I can see that Doyle was making more of a statement than asking a question.

I shook my head. "Fortey's body was more the shell of a vampire as it had not yet fed since it turned."

"The mutilated corpses in the morgue..." Stoker said with a snap of his fingers, "...the one from Stamford House."

"The dead have no blood, at least not the type of body fluids creatures like this feed on. That explains why it did not rise while still in the morgue. It had not turned yet and having no blood of its own, it took time for it to build up enough strength to escape its grave. It then had to wait until night so that it remained out of direct sunlight."

"And this thing became that strong after just lying there for a day, imagine if it had fed," Doyle said, turning over one of the beasts hands.

"We may be in serious trouble gentlemen," Vulk admitted, returning to the gravesite after washing the battle gore from his body in a nearby pond. "I can think of at least two missing bodies that are out there somewhere and, if bitten, have had time and opportunity to feed. We may have a true battle on our hands here."

Back in human form the werewolf closed his fists and stretched his arms. Huge muscles like steel bands flexed and a big wolfish grin spread across his face as he reopened his fingers in a predatory manner. "This is going to be fun."

We fed the pieces of the vampire back down the hole it had climbed out of and sealed it. Unsure if such things were necessary, we had driven a stake through its heart before we did so, and the head, we took with us, just in case.

Walking out of the graveyard I moved over to the nearby Basingstoke Canal and reared back to throw our trophy in so that it would never find its way back to the body, but as I prepared to release Doyle yelled out for me to stop. I pulled up short and listened as the Doctor explained that it would be unwise to throw the head into the water as vampirism may be akin to a virus, so dropping the head in the canal could potentially spread the infection. I thought it unlikely, but this view was the reason I had thought it wise to have the doctor along in the first place.

Instead of disposing the head in the canal we walked back to the railway station and waited for the morning's first Necropolis train heading back into London. The dark engine of the train already sat in the station; pumping and belching steam and smoke as the fire inside its bowels grew. While the engineers busied themselves feeding water into the beast, Stoker snuck on board and threw the head into the engine's furnace. Nothing biological could withstand the heat generated within the fires of the stove that heated the massive machine's boiler.

When the driver tooted the engine's whistle, announcing the train was ready to depart, the four of us took our seats in the carriage and rode all the way back to London in exhausted silence. The energy that had fuelled our fight last night was all but gone and some of us were really starting to feel our bumps and bruises.

It was subtle, but I also noticed as we rode back that the two cousins had left a noticeable space between themselves and Vulk. Though nothing had been said, they both occasionally sent the werewolf quizzical looks. I interpreted these as wariness, wonder, respect, and fear as the two entertained private thoughts that they were riding a train after having fought a battle to the death with a vampire ... and having done so with a flesh and blood werewolf. The cousins had just discovered in the vampire and in Vulk that the world was far more dangerous and a lot stranger than they ever could have imagined. Oft times, it requires a little time and some quiet introspection in coming to terms with things like that.

After the train pulled into Waterloo Station we parted ways, promising to meet up again the next morning at Stanford House. Vulk agreed it was going to be handy having others to corroborate our eventual tale to Abberline, or at least most of what we could tell the Inspector without being ridiculed. So far the two gentlemen had proven most useful in our quest, and I felt their further involvement could only enhance our chances of success. I was also of the opinion that if things became as bad as I believed they were going to be, two extra sets of eyes and hands could prove useful.

Vulk and I staggered back through the Stamford gates after arguing with the three policemen stationed there as guards. Luckily a forth policeman, who had been patrolling the grounds, recognized us and let us through.

Unsure of our status in the house now, we both retired to our original rooms. I was pleased to see the Colonel had yet to follow up on his promise of having me thrown out, so after a quick wash and change I blissfully slid into bed to catch a few hours sleep.

This time nothing and no one intruded upon my slumber and I awoke the next day to bright sunlight streaming through my room's windows. My watch told me it was nearly nine am, so after a wash and a shave I dressed and headed down to the dining room for breakfast.

Once more the main table was piled high with food for both staff and the police guard. I loaded a platter with eggs, toast, and bacon, and with a mug of tea, sat in one of the few unoccupied chairs in the room.

With my feast balanced on one knee and a mouthful of egg, a policeman I recognised, and who more importantly recognized me, strode over. "You're required," he said, then at my gesture towards my lap added, "...and yes, you can bring your plate."

The three of us (the policeman, myself and my breakfast) strode out of the hall and into the Colonel's study. In attendance were Abberline, the Colonel, a dishevelled-looking Vulk, and the bright and alert figures of Dr Doyle and Bram Stoker.

"It appears you had something of an adventure yesterday?" Sergeant Willkie said from the wall he had been leaning against. I had not noticed him there before he spoke.

I gave everyone a well-balanced bow, sat, and scooped another forkful of egg into my mouth. Normally one for the niceties of a civilized meal, in truth I was damned hungry and was afraid this could be the last food I would be seeing for a while.

"Your two friends here have been filling me in on their involvement so far. Amazing stuff, but they refused to tell me what this is all about. It would seem they don't think I'd believe them," Abberline said. The two cousins looked sheepish.

"I can barely believe it myself," I admitted around a mouthful of bacon. Placing the now half empty plate on the side table next to the chair, I faced the Inspector. "It is the work of vampires, though why they are focusing their attention on this house still eludes me."

"Vampires?" The Colonel stammered, dangling the fetish I had taken off the intruder yesterday…was it yesterday? So much had happened in such a short time I was having trouble recalling the exact timeline of the last few days. "I thought this was about some European religious cult?"

"I had honestly forgotten all about them," I admitted. "The answer Colonel Stamford is yes and no…or both. Yes to both is probably a better way of putting it."

"You're losing us," Abberline said. He had not queried the possibility of vampires as the policeman had worked with me before and knew of Vulk's little secret. I still recalled the first time he had seen the wolf change. Like the two cousins the Inspector's world had suddenly expanded at that moment to include not only the possible, but also the highly improbable.

"Let me tell you what I know," I said, indicating what the Colonel had in his hands. "That medallion came from a group of men that I believe are about to cause a lot of mayhem, not only for us but for the city of London, perhaps even the world if we do not stop them here.

"'Ordo Draconum.' The Order of the Dragon was a thirteenth century Holy Roman order of knights, first created and placed under papal decree to protect Europe from the Muslim hordes of the Ottoman Empire. They mostly employed knights from the old German states and the surrounding region, men who had been on the front lines against the Islamic nation for years. Perhaps because of such experiences the order was often all that stood between the Christian West and the Muslim East, and their battle ground was the state of Wallachia," When this name earned me a room full of blank stares I added, "or as we know it today, the Kingdom of Romania."

Reaching across the table I took up the pendant from where the Colonel had left it. "The Order of the Dragon was a secretive order, though it was never as large as the Templars or the Teutonic Knights. There are few descriptions of them and even their emblem, the dragon swallowing its own tail under the cross of their patron St George has only come down to us through second hand stories. What we do know is the holy order ended when Vladislaus Draculam took the throne of Wallachia and began a wave of terror against the Turks, and controlled his country in a way that is still remembered until this day."

"If he was so famous why have none of us heard of this Vladislaus Draculam then?" Stoker asked.

"Because most of us know him by another name, Vlad the Impaler."

Even I found the stillness in the room a little disquieting as everyone pondered this information. "Because of the atrocities Vlad committed, not only to the heathen Turk but the Christians who stood against him, the Holy Roman Emperor disbanded the Order of the Dragon—not that it mattered much as Vlad ensured the order lived on. It became what you would call a cult of personality as new recruits who committed themselves to the Order agreed to serve their leader, even from the grave. These men have gone on to terrorise the provinces of Wallachia and Transylvania for half a millennia, protecting the secrets of their order and their mysterious leader, even after his death. This included the whereabouts of Vlad's tomb."

"I thought Vlad was killed by the Turks and buried?" Stoker asked as he took a break from his furious note taking.

"He was, but when his enemies later dug up his body they discovered the grave was empty. It is assumed the Order of the Dragon had removed it earlier, and even today are keeping it safe."

"So what does this have to do with us?" Stamford nervously queried.

"I really have no idea," I admitted. "But judging by what has been happening, there is something drawing them here, and I sense they are on some sort of shortened time line, meaning we will be seeing them again very soon."

"And the vampires?" Abberline asked, getting us back on track.

"That I admit was a total surprise to all of us. The bloodless corpses we have been finding of course suggested vampires, but who honestly would have considered they were real?" No one in the room raised their hand.

"If they are … real," the Inspectors said, though without a lot of conviction. Though we were not exactly friends, the man knew me well enough to trust I would not invent such a fantastic story.

"What I did notice was the man I took this from," I said, holding up the pendant, "and he was wearing an odd gantlet with two large prongs in the palm area. I believed they use these gloves to simulate a vampire's bite as a way for them to keep the terror of night stalkers in the minds of those they live amongst."

"So you're saying we are not dealing with true vampires?" the Colonel asked.

"I most certainly am not. What we saw, what we had to deal with last night, that was most certainly an undead creature, and I believe there are more about. By my calculation there are as few as nine vampires in this area alone, and lord knows how many more have been created in the last few days."

"What do you mean 'what you dealt with last night'?" Willkie asked, catching on before anyone else.

"On a hunch the four of us," I explained, indicating myself and the other three, "we followed the corpse of the Stamford's footman Fortey to the cemetery at Brookwood. There I assumed we would encounter some of the Order of the Dragon, who I assumed would have an interest in the body. As it turns out the danger came from the grave itself."

I indicated one of the two men seated with me to carry on the tale. It was Doyle who spoke first.

"Out of the grave came a nightmare. Within seconds the creature pulled itself out of the hole, knocked Amun here for a loop, took a number of sword thrusts from myself, along with the entirety of Stoker's revolver into its chest without slowing one bit. The only thing that really saved us was the unique assistance from Mr Vulk here. Thanks to him we managed to lop the vampire's head off." Doyle gave the werewolf sitting patiently at the other end of the room something akin to a nod of respect.

Abberline looked at me as if to ask if this was the entire story. I nodded it was.

Taking up the thread, Stoker continued, "We buried most of the body back in its grave if you'd care to take a look. As for the head, that's hopefully now little more than ash in the belly of a train's furnace by now."

"And you expect us to believe this rot?" Stamford spat,

standing up from the table and stalking to the door. "That my family has somehow come under the curse of an ancient Roman death cult and a horde of ungodly night creatures. Well I for one refuse to hear any more of your rubbish and lies." The Colonel stomped out of the room.

"It's all true," Vulk yelled after him helpfully. "And they're from Romania, not Italy!"

CHAPTER EIGHTEEN

The meeting went on for a while longer, though little more was achieved as it devolved into a circular conversation about the possibility of real vampires and plots concerning forgotten European cults of death. The one thing to come out of the conference was Abberline's insistence on a larger police presence at the house for the foreseeable future, along with better armaments for his men. There was even a suggestion of calling in some grenadier guards stationed nearby, but the Inspector allowed himself to be overruled on this by the outraged Colonel, who claimed this would be overkill. Recalling the fight with a weakened vampire last night, I did not agree with the Colonel's line of reasoning.

It was also agreed that the policemen and house staff that had died the other night would have their bodies tied up and be left under guard by men with very sharp axes. I did not believe these bodies would be coming back to haunt us any time soon as they had been killed by assassins from the Order of the Dragon using their funny gauntlets, but you never knew and it was far better to be safe than have your neck bitten later and be sorry.

After the meeting dispersed I found out that Vulk had headed back to bed. We would need his help tonight if things were to go as bad as I feared. I was also in need of a nap, but decided to try and hang on until after lunch. During all the excitement I had forgotten the General, so figured I could kill some time by heading back to the greenhouse in order to check in with him and ensure he had survived the Dragon's assault on the estate.

I crossed the estate's garden under a darkened, overcast sky and found the General asleep in his chair. The hothouse was as stifling as ever and, though the General looked as feeble as he had earlier, there seemed a little more colour to his complexion. This was not really saying much as he was still a grave shade of white, but at least he did not seem translucent as he had before.

I sat down in the same chair I had occupied earlier just as someone dressed in white slipped out the greenhouse's rear door. It would seem not all the Stamford family had abandoned the old man.

I sat patiently for a few minutes before yet another batman

entered the greenhouse, checked on the General's condition, scowled a thunderstorm at me—though never presumed to enquire why I was there or have me removed—and then left.

After what felt like hours in that heat the General woke up, smacked his lips dryly, spotted me and asked apologetically, "I am sorry Mr Amun, did we have a meeting scheduled?"

So, he knew my real identity was as well.

"Nothing of the kind General, I felt someone should come down and see to your well-being after the excitement of the last few days."

"All is well, indeed I feel better than I have in weeks."

"Your colour has certainly improved."

"Has it? Perhaps I am on the mend at last."

"I did have a few more questions for you General, if you feel up to the task?"

"I am the very paragon of health at the moment. Ask your questions and I will do my best to answer them."

"Just a few things. When did you return from the Crimea?"

"Oh, many years ago. I believe it was 1856 or 57. I remember coming home on the *Dunbar*. We were all so excited to get back to England as the war had been a nasty one and many of our boys were suffering from fatigue."

"I know this must be painful, but can I ask what the source of the friction is between you and your son?"

The recently returned colour in the General's face drained away and he slumped back into his chair. "The death of my wife, he blames me for his mother's loss. I did everything I could to save her. I would have made a bargain with the devil himself if he could have taken me instead of her, but my Mary just could not hold on."

"What did your wife die from?" I asked, but the General was no longer listening. His gaze seemed to be focused on something in the distance, and I realised he was looking into his own past.

"When his own wife fell ill the lad's grief became too great. He needed someone to blame. His world did not make sense anymore and he needed to focus all that anger and bitterness on something to help him move through the grief. I became the bogeyman of his mind; that somehow the neglect of my own wife during my years of service overseas was transferred to his own. In a strange way I believe the two women merged into one, and he saw me as the villain who had helped kill them both. As a father, how could I not allow him this reprieve from his pain? I saw a chance to perhaps bring my son back from the brink of insanity. So what if he hated me, if it shook the grip grief had on his soul, well then it was a small price to pay. At least I could save one member of my family."

A voice that had been clear and strong grew more raspy and quiet, and then the General began to shake and cough uncontrollably. Before I could even get out of my chair his new batman returned and, without saying a word, wheeled the old soldier back into his rooms. I called after them, asking if they wanted a physician, as I knew there was one currently sitting up in the house eating the Colonels teacakes, but I received no response.

After a few minutes it was clear no one would be returning, so I left the greenhouse with the realization I now had far more questions than I had entering the infernal building. This was not the problem it would seem as questions had answers and I now had some threads to start pulling at. How had the wives of the General and the Colonel died? The answers to that question could prove most illuminating.

On my way back to the house I found my path blocked by Dr Doyle and Bram Stoker. Both men looked determined.

"You seem to be waiting for someone."

"We seem to be waiting for you," Doyle admitted.

"Time for some answers!" Stoker said, pulling his notebook like a gunfighter in the American West.

"You left us out in the wind with the police. I thought the Inspector was going to arrest us for withholding information." Though Doyle's manner almost suggested he would not have minded this as his desire for new experiences bordered on the manic, I did concede the point.

"And now you know why. In this case having no information was a far better shield from the police than too much information, and I do apologise for deliberately leaving you in such a state. If I had told you everything I knew, and you were then questioned by the police, an all too real possibility after you came to the gate yesterday morning and piqued Abberline's interest by the way, he would have known if you held anything back. He is a worthy holder of the title 'inspector' after all. It would also not have helped our cause if you had passed on any information about the knight order or vampires before I had the opportunity to do so as he would not have believed you. This information coming from me at least gave it a chance of credibility…we have a history working against such oddities you know." Stoker almost leaned into his notebook with the promise of this statement. "A past we will not be going into here," I explained, to his great disappointment.

The reporter, however, was not going to leave things there.

"What is the story of Vulk? How long has he been a …a…"

"…a werewolf?" I said with a broad smile at their inability to even say the word in bright daylight.

"Exactly."

"I am afraid that would be passing on a confidence."

Though I knew the werewolf's origin, in truth it was nothing much to write about. He had been a shepherd whose flock had come under the attention of a monster and he had managed to get bitten while trying to protect his livelihood. Even then he was a large lad, strong of heart and wide of chest, and this is why he likely survived the encounter with his progenitor.

"I can, however, tell you the story of how we met, though the story would most certainly not be for print but for your own education in what we face and why you are safe with the shaggy beast."

Stoker seemed ready to argue, but his cousin, with a nudge, encouraged him to put his notebook away. Once the task was completed the reporter made a gesture of showing me his empty hands. "All right, spill."

The three of us walked to a small garden gazebo and took a seat. Though there were house staff and policemen all around, the spot was secluded enough for my tale to be told and not overheard.

CHAPTER NINETEEN

"Vulk was probably two-hundred years old when I first met him.

Much like what was occurring around the Stamford Estate, people had begun disappearing from the countryside surrounding Corrour Lodge, a hunting estate located at Scotland's Rannoch Moor. Legend had it that a monstrous hound, that the locals called Cù-Sìth, stalked the Highlands and moors, hunting anything and anyone stupid enough to wander through the nightmarish landscape at night alone. The legend of the black hound, now tied with the mystery of the missing people from Corrour, had caught my imagination and I decided to find out for myself what was going on.

As there was no national constabulary like the Metropolitan police force, my first move was to locate a local magistrate called Henry Saint-Martin-de-Boscherville, and together we investigated the murders.

The small community around Corrour and Rannoch Moor was wary of outsiders, especially when so many of their own had gone missing. Things were not helped either by the presence of Boscherville, who was seen as an oppressive agent of the King and Parliament. It would seem the rural Scots still held some small resentment at the idea of joining the United Kingdom.

We spent our days exploring the local region, looking for any sign of violence or murder. Over the following weeks the natives did not warm to our presence by a single degree, yet despite their refusal to assist us in any way, we soon discovered what had happened too many of the missing. It would be our discovery of a canid, but not one of the great black mythological beasts often reported from the dark regions of the land, no—our discovery was little more than a fox.

We became suspicious after a number of consecutive days searching one part of the moor when we noted the little beast traveling to the same part of the landscape every day. Following the path of the fox, we soon found it feeding on the exposed leg of a man. Borscherville immediately used his influence and position to call in a troop of soldiers stationed some miles away, and an extensive search was begun of the entire moor.

This more-thorough investigation uncovered most of the missing had died and were either buried in the soft soil of the moor or had their bodies weighed down and sent to the bottom of the marsh.

We did not find all of the missing, mind you, suggesting there were likely more buried out there somewhere, they had just not been found. Taking the bodies to the local mortician, the only real place suitable for such grizzly blossoms of the wild land, we completed an autopsy. None had been killed by any sort of animal at least they were not killed by the four-legged variety.

During one late night expedition onto the moors I became separated from our party when a particularly thick fog rolled across the landscape. Normally I have a fine sense of direction, but night had fallen and there was simply no light to help guide the way. Not a moon, not a star, and it was impossible to perceive any sort of feature such as a tree, hill or building. I was soon reduced to prodding and tapping at the very ground with my walking stick to help find some sort of path. I soon after began calling out for help.

After what felt like hours of stumbling about in this manner, at some point something answered my call, and the noise sent a chill through my bones. What I heard was a howl, and not the howl of some feeble hound. This had been the call of a wolf, a very large, very hungry wolf, or so I determined by the hairs standing up on my neck.

Always one to take the offensive rather than sit back and be sport for those looking to take advantage of a situation, I decided to follow the ghost-like baying. Better to be heading towards danger rather than caught running away from it.

After bumping my way up the side of what I was sure was a mountain, and having fallen only a few dozen times, I came over a rise and found myself looking down on a remarkable scene, one I shall remember until the end of days. Less than one hundred feet away was an enormous shaggy creature, far larger than any dog, with disproportionally large shoulders and head. I watched as the werewolf gorged itself on a specimen of *Cervus elaphus scoticus*, or a Highland Red Deer to those who have not studied Linnaeus.

From my vantage point on high I watched as the monster

finished its meal. It then bounded away into the night, only to kill another deer. Once it had finished eating the second creature I followed the beast to its lair on the side of a craggy hillside. I then hunkered down to wait until morning. A few hours later, as dawn broke across the misty landscape, the figure of a tall man with a scraggly beard wandered out of the cave. Steeling my nerve, I walked down and introduced myself.

The werewolf turned out to be Sebastian Vulk, a Norwegian Úlfheðinn, who had been driven out of his homeland because the nation suffered a sudden bout of Christianity. The Úlfheðinn were berserkers, one of Odin's wolf dressed warriors."

"Are you saying Odin was real as well?" Doyle asked.

Exasperated at the interruption, I snapped, "No, I am saying in Norse mythology the Úlfheðinn were associated with Odin. Now may I continue?"

"Please, by all means," Stoker said, silencing any further questions his cousin may have been about to ask with a stern look and a gentle kick to the shin.

"Vulk had been in the Highlands for years, and yes, his presence and occasional sightings created not only the mythology of the Cù Sìth, but also another black-dog legend from Wales, the Gwyllgi. Unlike the legend though, Vulk does not entirely become an animal when he transforms into a lycanthrope..."

"...another name for werewolf, right?" Doyle asked.

"Correct, Doctor. I was prepared to kill the werewolf while it was just a man when none of its unnatural strength nor endurance could have been a help to it. With a pistol in one hand and the naked blade of my sword cane in the other, I cornered the werewolf and quizzed him about the murder.

"Instead of a monster, I found a man, a somewhat charming and likeable man who admitted to quarantining himself away from humanity in the remotest regions he could find. Humanity, however, had other ideas and had begun spreading and infiltrating even the wildest areas with their farms and towns, forcing the werewolf to continually move on and seek out even more remote regions to live."

"Why would Vulk move away like that unless he believed there was the chance he would kill and eat someone?" The reporter side of Stoker just could not help but follow up a lead it would seem.

"He wasn't afraid for them, he was afraid for himself. If the brothers Grimm have taught us anything with their tales of horror and fear, when humans and wolves met, things never work out well for the big bad wolf."

"So if Vulk was not the killer, who was?" Stoker asked.

"Well, two nights later another woman went missing, and this time Boscherville and I were on the case. The following night I took a gamble and gathered Vulk who had been shocked and distressed, not only by the murders of innocent people, but that he had been blamed for them. Using his astonishing sense of smell he helped track the girl from where she had disappeared to her resting place. The girl had been murdered and her body dumped in one of the deeper pools within the moor. Vulk managed to pick up the scent of who had done the horrible deed from there, and we three tracked the scent all the way back to a man called Richard Cabell.

Here was the true monster of the Rannoch Moor. Cabell's murder spree had begun when he killed his wife, who he believed had been cheating on him. He then murdered her probable lover, and through these murders the deranged man developed a taste for killing, one he simply could not control. I believe his finally tally was around fifteen dead before we finally put an end to his reign of terror."

"You arrested him?" Stoker asked.

"I did not. When we confronted him about his crimes, the man snapped and attacked us. The Magistrate was forced to kill him."

Nodding his head with appreciation, Doyle said, "A fine result then!"

"Not really. There is growing evidence that crimes like these are on the rise. Indeed there is a new science evolving to not only help trap such criminals, but perhaps to understand them and maybe even prevent similar crimes before they arise in the future. Though Cabell would no longer be killing anyone, science did lose an opportunity to explore and understand his demented mind and try to fathom why he committed such atrocities."

"A point the families of the deceased cared little about I would think."

"Punishment is not always about vengeance, my dear Dr

Doyle. Sometimes it is necessary to take a step back and explore all possibilities for the greater good."

Stoker seemed to step between us by changing the subject. "So the two of you have been together ever since this event?"

"Not at all. We are simply what you would call friends. I call on the old wolf at times to help out if I have a riddle that could use his special array of skills. It is also good to have someone who is not as short-lived as the rest of you. The world is a staggeringly boring place most of the time."

"And just how old … are you?" Doyle asked.

Stoker quickly followed this question up with one of his own, "And just who are you? What is your story?"

"That, my friends, will be a story for another day." I got up and left them with a smile, though I did note it was Doyle and not his cousin who, this time began feverishly writing down notes from our conversation.

CHAPTER TWENTY

Lunch was a tight-lipped affair. All the Stamford women were wearing some type of white garment, and as women's fashion is not an expertise I claim to possess, I had no idea who it was that had crept out of the greenhouse when I arrived.

Vulk joined us at the table, his status having clearly risen from gardener to houseguest. We sat by ourselves at the far end of the enormous table and quietly laid out our plans for the coming night. Though still treating us cordially, the family was clearly looking determined to limit its contact with us.

After the meal I headed to my room, drew the curtains and threw myself into bed. The ache in my head had lessened, but I was feeling drained by from the excitement of the last few days. The night promised to be a long one, so if I did not sleep now I would be of no use to anyone later.

Blessedly, sleep came quickly, and what seemed only minutes later but was in fact a number of hours, I was awakened by one of the house servants. A splash of water on my face, a clean shirt, a quick meal and I joined Vulk, most of the male household staff, and as many bobbies as Abberline could muster. We all gathered on the wide front lawn, and I noticed almost everyone had a weapon of some sort; I could just picture how bare the walls in the study and halls of Stamford House were now looking. Vulk threw me a wicked-looking sabre with a fine edge, while he hefted a Scottish two-handed claymore, and though he did not possess his unnatural strength in human form, the old dog certainly had the muscle to wield the monster blade. I made a mental note to make sure I was standing at least nine feet away from him when he began wielding that monster about.

Abberline sported a truncheon and a revolver, as did Willkie. The way everyone was organised, it was apparent that during my nap plans had been made. I was therefore unsurprised when one of the Colonel's men stepped up to take control of the troops, and by the way he barked orders, he had clearly been something like a sergeant major in his former life.

I asked Vulk what the plan was and he shushed me, as the man

I cannot think of but as the sergeant continued his organisation of everyone with simple, concise orders. I watched in silence as the largest group of men split into smaller teams, with the first ordered to guard the front door. A second was sent to watch the rear entrance, while the rest of us made up a third team and were asked to roam the grounds and be prepared to move in support of the others. The smaller group that had not been split up was mostly made up of the police, and these men moved down to watch the gates and patrol the streets and grounds surrounding the estate.

There were lanterns aplenty, with some long lasting beacons picketed along the paths and front gate. With all this it was unlikely anyone could get close to the house without being spotting by one of us.

The first hour passed with unnatural tension as we strained to hear any trouble approaching. By the end of the second hour there were snippets of conversations going on amongst the teams and alertness was on the wane. As the third hour ticked by, jokes were being thrown about, not so much to keep spirits up but keep everyone awake. As midnight passed we began allowing men to catch short naps in shifts. At least half the men were to remain awake at all times, as I was sure that if anyone was watching, this was the time they were most likely to strike.

High above us a small sliver of moon rose and fell with hardly a mention. Unbidden, Vulk began taking short trips along the ground's boundary. I was certain he was doing quick changes into his wolf-man form in the dark to use his heightened sense of smell, hearing, and vision. After a short time he would change back and walk into the lights we kept burning and shake his head. There was no sign of any intruder.

The night bled away and dawn burst upon the world in a chorus of birdsong and the open-maws of yawning men. The household staff with pressing duties began wandering off, while the police formed up and marched away when their shift ended. A new, smaller batch arrived to replace the bobbies who needed sleep, and even Willkie and Abberline wandered away, promising they would be back later with whatever troops they could spare for another night's guard duty. Vulk did a final circuit of the grounds, this time very much in human form, and after finding nothing, also retired. I decided to get some food before I went off to sleep.

Before they left I asked Doyle and Stoker if we could meet sometime in mid-afternoon at the reporter's office. I had questions that needed answering, and the resources of the London Daily Gazette could well prove beneficial in providing the information I required. A thought had entered my head while kicking rocks during last night's fruitless vigil, and this needed to be expanded upon. We all agreed to meet up again at three o'clock.

Entering the Stamford House while stifling a yawn and enjoying a wide stretch of the arms, I almost walked blindly into Robyn Stamford. She looked the picture of rest and relaxation, and I could only guess at the sort of dishevelled visage I was projecting. Gone was the malice and anger she had displayed at our previous meeting.

"And how was your evening's festivities?" she asked with a warm smile after taking a small plate of food and joining me at a table. My own plate was overflowing and I happily chewed my way through some bacon and a stewed tomato. I watched as the girl pleasantly picked at her plate and nibbled on a piece of fruit. Curious about this change in attitude, I swallowed a mouthful of sausage before answering. "It was a failure, I am afraid. No bat or owl did we see, much less a spookish apparition or a beast of nightmare."

"Well that is a shame. I was hoping we would have some more excitement like the other day."

"The other day?"

"When those men were killed…I mean it was certainly terrible for them, but my, what fun having all those policemen stomping around the place, asking everyone the strangest questions. Normally things around here are so very boring."

"Well, perhaps tonight they will show up and you can have some more fun."

"That would be marvellous," she beamed, missing entirely my sarcastic tone.

We ate and talked about minor things. A number of times I tried to find out if she had been the one in the greenhouse yesterday, but the girl proved as slippery as an eel. It was not as though she was being evasive; it was more like she simply refused to concentrate on any one thing for more than a minute. The smallest thing would distract Robyn and this would hold her complete and undivided attention until the next shiny thing came along to distract her. Eventually I gave up and returned to my plate, but could not shake the sense that I had just watched a wonderful performance.

Somehow I left the breakfast table having promised that Miss Stamford could attend my trip later in the afternoon to the London Daily Gazette. I somehow doubt she had an interest in how a newspaper was run as she claimed; instead, she was looking for any excuse to leave the house grounds. Robyn seemed to be the only Stamford family member who ever left the estate, and then only occasionally, and often by sneaking away.

Cocooned once more in my bed, it took sometime to fall asleep as my mind was ablaze with problems and possible solutions. I could not stop turning and tumbling around how the family had come under the notice of the Dragons and brought them to London. When sleep did find me, it was far from revitalizing, as the nightmares of my past, perhaps sensing my exhaustion, visited their terrors on me. After restlessly fighting my own subconscious, I awoke in a sweat, with the afternoon sun stretching across the bedroom floor.

I was at least as tired as I had been when I first lay down.

With no hope of further rest I got up and washed, dressed and headed to the front gate. I was hoping to avoid fulfilling my promise, but it would seem Robyn Stamford was prepared for such a move. There was no need for me to find a cab as the girl already had one, and was patiently sitting in it waiting for me. She was clearly determined to escort me to my afternoon meeting.

The journey took no more than half an hour, and we passed the time talking about London society. When I say 'we' of course, I meant Robyn, as the girl seemingly became more animated with each clip-clop we moved away from Stamford House. It was as though a great burden was being released and her inner fire was fuelled and stoked as it moved further away from hearth and home. For my part I listened dutifully and gave encouraging nods and grunts of disapproval at the points I believed warranted such reactions.

The cab pulled up in front of the newspaper office, and Doyle was awaiting our arrival by the front door. He introduced himself to

Miss Stamford, then led the way to the small office Stoker used at the rear of the building. Keeping my promise, I encouraged the reporter to find some junior lackey to escort Robyn on a tour of the Gazette, which the lad he found proved more than happy to do once he caught sight of the girl. He wandered away with Robyn in tow, barely containing the grin that threatened to split his face.

With the girl gone, the three of us got to work. Stoker took on the task of finding any other missing person reports from the area around the Stamford mansion, while Doyle and I began searching through older editions, looking for anything on the Stamfords, their house and the De Gois family. Though improbable, I had to make sure the family of the missing boy had not taken revenge into their own hands for his disappearance and death.

Nearly two hours passed before Robyn returned, shepherding a herd of young men, all hanging off her every word. Though clearly enjoying the company, she looked done with her newspaper experience so I suggested maybe having some afternoon tea before we headed back to the house. Before I knew it, the entire crowd had departed for a nearby coffee house.

It did not take Abraham long to come up with a list—well, two lists actually. The first consisted of names of the dead from the region, along with dates and a short description on the method of death. A quick perusal revealed most had died from what you could call natural causes, if only because an unholy one did not kill them. Three had been murdered by their spouses, and a number were clearly accidental. Two on the list warranted further investigation as they had been found just a few streets from the estate, apparently killed 'by animal attack.' What sort of animal could possibly be large enough and dangerous enough in the overpopulated streets of London to kill people and escape detection I could not guess? Certainly it could be a dog, but dog attacks were a common enough occurrence for a city coroner to spot.

Stoker's second list was of people who had gone missing. Though shorter, this was far more interesting as the majority were from locations very close to the Stamfords. By my estimation, if all those I considered a possibility had already turned, we were dealing with twelve vampires, and that number only included the ones we knew about because their disappearance had been reported.

It had been an effort to kill just one vampire, so if we had to deal with a dozen or more at the same time, it was doubtful many of us would survive, even with a small army camped at the house. It would seem our best course of action would be to start hunting the vampires down one by one and engage them one at a time, or in smaller, more manageable groups. Every other scenario I could foresee did not end well for us.

I ran everything we had discovered about in my head, looking at the information in every different direction I could contemplate. Clearly we were missing information, but it did seem that a pattern had started to form.

"Is it not time we should be heading back?" Doyle asked from behind a great wall of periodicals.

I pulled out my pocket watch and flipped it open. The gilded hands said it was just past six pm. Night was closing in, so I grabbed everything and headed for the office door.

"I may join you later," Stoker said, as he fell into the chair I had just vacated. "There is something I need to check on first."

"Don't dawdle, or you will miss all the fun," I said, and departed, followed closely by Dr Doyle.

Outside the newspaper we located the coffee shop where Robyn was entertaining a large crowd of men. Gathering her, we hailed a cab and were soon on the way back to the estate. The girl was flushed and alive in a way I had never seen before.

"Your outing today seems to have done you some good," I remarked sincerely.

"It has been sometime since I've been able to talk to a boy unchaperoned, and to have so many all at once—it was most delightful."

"I was under the impression you were out every night and had your pick of the bachelors in London society."

"I am indeed often out, though very often my trips have nothing to do with me, but are merely errands for his master's voice."

"You mean Beatrice?"

Robyn would not answer. Despite my best inquisitor's voice and a number of pointed questions, the Stamford girl refused to speak for the rest of the journey. She then leapt out of the cab the second we arrived at the gatehouse and, crying for some bizarre reason, ran off to her rooms.

"Was it something I said?" I asked Doyle as we disembarked. "Should I go and see if she is ok?" He shrugged, the motion explaining he knew as much about the mysteries and sensibilities of young women as I did.

Quick time, I marched after Robyn, when all I actually wanted to do was sound out the ideas that had been growing in my head. What had begun as a whispered memory was forming into an unending parade of images and ideas. My departure, at least, had the bonus of leaving Doyle alone to pay the cab fare.

Inside the grounds the troops were already marshalling. The household men seemed to number the same, but the police contingent was noticeably smaller. There were also far more torches set up, waiting to be lit.

Doyle caught up with me as I passed Abberline. "Evening," I said with something of a mock salute.

The Inspector looked at me as though I was late to something I had been the instigator of. With the sky above already darkening you could argue I was late, but if I did everything exactly when the good Inspector wanted me to, this would be a dull life.

"We seem to be light on numbers this evening," Doyle pointed out as the police officer joined us. An observant lad that one.

"The Chief has declared this entire affair to be a waste of time. It was only by personally promising the expenditure was necessary that I got this many men." This last was added by Abberline to silence the very question I was formulating. It would seem I was surrounded by a number of great thinkers that day. I then had a great thought of my own.

"I know where we can get a few more men."

Grabbing a lit torch, I headed down the darkening path to the General's greenhouse. Vulk materialised beside me and, walking side by side, we passed through the glasshouse's front doors.

"Thought you were going to miss the excitement tonight," he said, obviously fishing for information on what I had been up to all day.

"Abberline just made the same joke, though for him I doubt

there was really any humour in it."

"Always knew the man had it in him somewhere."

I thought I was ready for it, but once again the heat inside the building was shocking. As night was falling one of General Stamford's men was feeding a large brazier with coal. The orange fire inside illuminated the interior of the greenhouse and the underside of the larger plants, throwing spectral shadows across the interior of the building. In the middle of the heat and flickering silhouettes, sat the old man.

"Mr Amun, Mr Vulk, what brings you gentlemen into my abode tonight?"

Even in this hellish light I could see the General was looking even healthier then when we had last spoken. It was almost uncanny the change that had come over him. His voice was strong and constant, and he looked like he had put on weight. What really gave his improved condition away was the empty plate on the table next to his chair. It would seem he had started consuming food again.

Vulk noticed the same thing and shot me a look with one eyebrow raised. With those eyebrows, it was not what you would call a subtle gesture.

"We haven't quite got the force we need, General, and I was hoping we could borrow a few of your men to stand with us tonight."

The man pushing coal into the fire continued his work, but I could tell he had become a little more interested in what we are talking about.

"My men?" The General repeated, as though the idea had never occurred to him. "I am not sure that is possible, tonight."

"May I ask why?"

"Oh, it is nothing sinister. Most of them simply are not here at the moment. I had them go to Portsmouth to escort a shipment that just arrived, so they won't be back for a few days."

"Well how many do you have here at the moment?" Vulk asked, knowing full well we would need a battalion if things went badly.

"Besides Carver here, I have one more. He's asleep at the moment and is due to take over fire-feeding duties at midnight."

"Well I cannot strip you of your only help, but if we are still in need over the next few days, a handful of experienced old troopers like those working for you would be most helpful."

"They will be yours to command," the General offered with a snap-bow of his head. "Now, can I interest you gentleman in a drink before you take your post?"

Before I could answer Vulk moved over to the bar and poured himself a generous whisky. When he indicated to the General with an empty glass, the old man nodded an affirmative and asked for a whiskey with champagne. Interesting!

The cooling night air outside was a welcome relief and we both re-joined Abberline at the front door to the house. "No luck," I said, picking up a nasty-looking axe and, putting the head on the ground, leaned on its handle like a walking stick. "The General has only two men on hand at the moment. The rest have gone on an errand and will not be back until sometime tomorrow. We can have them out here with us then."

"With you," Willkie said as he walked out the front door carrying two steaming cups of tea. One he gave to Abberline, the second he took a sip from. "If nothing happens here tonight, we have been told the detail is to be pulled completely. There is only so long we can keep yanking men off the streets without some sort of an explanation, and somehow I don't think 'because we are fighting vampires' will get us a lot of credit from the Home Office."

Abberline peered over his steaming mug. "Things are not as bad as all that. The Colonel thinks he might be able to get some support from a local military base, though getting him to 'make' that offer was a fair amount of work."

"An issue for another day then," I said, leaning the axe against the wall. "If you do not mind, I may go hunt down something warm to fight off the chill of the evening air."

Once I had my own mug of tea, I returned and took up a station by the front door. I would like to report that the night passed with a grand battle between the forces of unholy darkness and the white knights of justice, but such a tale did not unfold. Much like the previous night, we stood, we got bored, we drank an unfortunate amount of stale tea, and we saw nothing of our foe. I was starting to lose heart, and even with the first-hand knowledge I had, I was starting to doubt myself. Had we overreacted?

With the Sun up, we called it a day. A few policemen showed up to replace those on station as the estate was still considered a murder scene, but it was only two men, and both were stationed at the front gate.

As tired as I was, I did one final inspection of the grounds to make sure nothing had changed from the last time I had done so. Satisfied there were no suspicious-looking holes in the ground or tunnels where vampires had been burrowing past our defences, I went to bed.

I was so tired that I ignored the food being placed in the dining hall and went on up to my room. The world could keep spinning without me for a few hours.

CHAPTER TWENTY-ONE

Apparently, the world just could not go on without me after all.

I was dreaming of walking Hadrian's Wall with Lucius Septimius Severus Augustus, when someone began shaking my shoulder. I was out of bed in a flash and had the man on the ground with my hand about his throat before my sleep deprived brain caught up with my actions and I realized a murderer would likely not be trying to politely wake me.

Under my hand was a wide-eyed Abraham Stoker. Helping the man back to his feet, I offered him a feeble apology.

"I thought I was going to die," Stoker said as he rubbed his throat and drank the glass of water I handed him. I turned and tossed my scattered sheets and pillows back on the bed and, finding I had once more gone to bed fully clothed, joined my visitor at the room's small table.

As he drank and stretched his neck, he handed me a newspaper. It led with the story of the *Dunbar*, a three-masted ship that had sailed from London on the Australian gold rush route, taking men and provisions to that distant colony to feed workers into the colony's growing insanity for the precious metal.

In January 1857 the passenger ship sailed from London after already completing a similar voyage and spending most of her earlier career ferrying troops to and from the Crimean War. Sailing into a north Pacific typhoon, the captain decided to re-provision in Madras, where he picked up a number of passengers looking to head home. This would of course be via New South Wales but as it would likely be months before another passenger ship appeared with an open berth to take these British citizens stuck on the subcontinent home, they decided to take the longer voyage via Botany Bay.

The *Dunbar* sailed south, and on the night of August 20th was approaching the entrance to Port Jackson through a storm, when the ship's captain, James Green, made a fatal mistake. Having made the same voyage many times before, it would seem Captain Green was of the opinion the ship had already passed through the famous Sydney Heads and into the harbor beyond. Instead of the wide waters of the largest natural harbor in the world, the *Dunbar* sailed at full speed into the rocky coastline along the southern entrance. The Blackwall built frigate shattered on impact and sank, taking with her all hands and passengers except for one.

James Johnson had been working the rigging when the vessel hit. The sudden stop of forward momentum as the *Dunbar* struck the coast, along with his own tenuous position above, caused the sailor to be flung forward from the mast as though from a catapult.

When the disaster was discovered the next day, rescue parties from Sydney began searching the shoreline for survivors and vessels plied the water around the wreck, hauling corpses and flotsam out of the rough seas. During all this nobody bothered to look up on the cliff face where, for two days, Johnson clung on for dear life.

"So what has the wreck of the *Dunbar* to do with our current situation?" I asked.

Stoker handed me a second paper. This one was a comparison shipping manifest from the company that owned the vessel showing who had been onboard and who had been lost. About half way down the page I saw what had caught the reporter's eye.

"This cannot be."

"It's real enough…I checked," the reporter said.

Right there on the manifest was the name of General Wilberforce Stamford who, according to the record had drowned with the others on the *Dunbar*. Stoker explained he had also found no trace of the General's arrival back in London. One day he was lost at sea, the next he was home safe with his family and retiring from the army.

It was all terribly mysterious.

There was a knock at my door and, before I could say anything, Colonel Stamford entered the room. He was brandishing a pistol and a sabre, and behind him came two of his men. "You're alive."

"Apparently..." I agreed, patting myself down as though I was surprised at the news and checking for holes. "...another death?"

"Two," answered one of the men over the Colonel's shoulder.

"Show me."

They were both in the house. Two maids; one the wife of the

man charged with managing the stables. Both were in the cellars, and both had been exsanguinated. I had one of the men fetch Vulk; we then stood back while the wolf gave the room a thorough inspection. He could find no trace of anything out of the ordinary. Later, when we were out of earshot, the werewolf mentioned he did not think vampires actually had a scent. He had only found the earlier burials by smelling overturned earth or by catching the aroma of something else carried on the body. If he was correct, then our greatest defence, the werewolf's heightened senses, had just been greatly diminished.

It took nearly two hours for Abberline to make an appearance. The bodies were then whisked off to the city morgue and, on instructions from the Inspector; they were locked in a prison cell for the night and autopsied the following day. Abberline pointed out on a Sunday it was doubtful any doctor would be on hand to perform such a task until the start of the professional week.

Sunday. It was Sunday! If the Inspector had not told me the day it would have slipped past completely unheeded. Why had such an upstanding family as the Stamfords not been on their way to church, especially after the last week? Would not kneeling in the presence of God be a natural balm to soothe the terrors and fears of such a disturbing time? Yet the entire family was buttoned up inside the house. This added to one more oddity on a growing list.

Eventually I sent Stoker home to heal and get some sleep, before heading for the greenhouse to check on something that had been nagging me. I found the General in his chair, though the space was unheated for the first time since I had arrived. Still chair-bound, the blanket was gone and I could see the old man occasionally moved his legs, as though life was flooding back into them.

"I have already heard," Stamford announced as I slid into the visitor's chair opposite him. "My men returned this morning and they will be standing post with you tonight. I have sent most of them to rest so they will be in some sort of shape to help should it be needed."

His voice was strong, with the timbre you would expect of a man used to commanding thousands of men in the field. His eyes were also bright and alert, and if I did not know any better I would say this was a completely different man to the one I had met just a few days earlier.

I had wanted to ask him about Australia and his time in the Crimea. For most, the idea that he had somehow died, only to later return from the dead would constitute an impossibility. Perhaps this was simply all the result of a clerical error; perhaps the General had never been on the *Dunbar*. Perhaps there had been more than one survivor of the shipwreck, or even another General called Stamford. Perhaps there was a simple, obvious explanation for all that had happened and was happening. I knew differently though.

I had been prepared to grill the old man on all, but at the last moment I shied away. The return of his vitality was something I had not been expecting, and could bring a new factor in the investigation.

Instead I talked about the most recent murders, as though I had only come down to inform and ask for any information he may have on the incidences. If there was a connection between the General, his health, and the deaths all around the estate, I did not want him suspicious that I was starting to think along that path. I needed more information and perhaps to even have a private look about the greenhouse before I started pointing a finger at the now far more vibrant old man.

After half an hour of verbally dancing with the General, I got up and returned to the main house. Having been up for hours already and with the morning all but gone, I grabbed a plate of cold food and retired to my room. On my table was a note from Abberline, pointing out he would return that night with as many men as could be spared. As they had already been ordered not to return, he was unsure just how many that would be; though with these latest murders he seemed confident it would be more than two. I considered asking the General or the Colonel to use their influence with those military units stationed near the city to bolster our numbers, but figured that would be pushing our luck. Having a garden full of armed servants and policemen was one thing, having trained soldiers marching through the streets would likely bring the ire of some of the more influential members of society living in the neighbourhood, all but guaranteeing any complaint would ensure we lost our government sponsored protection.

Fed, washed, and with a chair strategically wedged under the bedroom door handle to ensure my privacy, I slipped between my sheets and began running all the facts we had uncovered so far over and over in my mind. I made a mental list and started moving pieces from one to the other, hoping to discover if any connection could be made between them. What seemed like three of four separate jigsaw puzzles I was certain would when tied together create one image; we just needed to start matching the pieces together to create a clear picture.

I was so busy sketching all the possibilities and permutations of the facts onto the inside of my eyelids that I missed the assassin moving through the room. Hands behind my head and splayed out on the bed like a starfish, I was totally unaware of the man as he quietly rose over me and lifted a large wood cutting axe over his head. I assume he was about to bring the makeshift weapon down on my exposed neck when a werewolf crashed into the scene.

Vulk's roar was the first thing I knew about my impending danger, and my eyes snapped open to see an empty ceiling. Rolling out of bed with revolver in hand, I spotted two figures fighting in the dim bedroom light on the other side of the room. My would-be attacker seemed to have trouble seeing in the dark as he took a number of swings at the werewolf with his axe, but each blow missed by at least a foot.

Vulk had no such trouble in the low light and, ducking under a desperate blow, stepped into the assassin and, with a clawed hand, tore the assailant's throat out. Blood fountained into the air and I grabbed a bed sheet and ran forward, wrapping it around the dying man's neck to stop the spraying fluids from covering everything in sight.

The man-wolf looked like he was ready to eat the assassin, whose blood and gore splashed face I did not recognise. I pushed myself in between the two, a tremendously dangerous thing to do if the werewolf was in full hunting mode, but I felt safe enough or foolish enough in the heat of the moment. Once the dying man was on the floor and Vulk had begun to settle down, I searched the body and found little in the way of identification except for a silver medallion on a chain around his neck containing the now familiar dragon eating its tail under the cross of St George.

An inspection revealed my door was still locked, with the chair

I had placed under the handle still in situ. Vulk was now looking more Vulk-like as he reformed back into himself. Retrieving the assassin's axe, I hefted it in my hands. The long sturdy handle and heavy iron head gave the instrument a lot of weight, and at that moment it looked far more like a headman's axe than an instrument for felling trees. I was sure I had seen, if not this exact axe, then most certainly its twin down at the house's store of firewood during one of my inspections of the estate. The fact the assassin had not brought his own weapon, but had resorted to picking up a tool from the house was just one more fact entered into the 'how very strange' column in my head.

That list was getting so long I would need to write it all down at some point before some of the facts started slipping away. I have a grand memory, capable of retaining many facts and strategies, but it is not a completely infallible one.

"You alright?" Vulk asked, back in human form.

"I am fine, thanks to your timely intervention. How did you know something was wrong?"

"I had no clue. I was tracking our friend over there and followed him into your room."

That comment triggered an ice-cold realisation and I began spinning about, inspecting every nook and cranny of the bedroom.

"And just how is it both of you got in without using the door... nor the windows by the looks of things?"

"Follow me." The werewolf turned and seemingly walked through a wall. I realised in the dark it only looked like that is what occurred—in fact, a large wooden panel along the opposite wall to the bed lay partly open, and on the other side was a small corridor.

With eyesight far inferior that of the wolf's, I took up a candle from the bedside table, lit it and stepped into the murky void.

Narrow and dusty, the bare bones of the house lay exposed as we snaked our way through the confining space. I mentally kept track of our movements and calculated we had first walked along the corridor outside my room before taking a sharp turn down the main entryway's spiral staircase. At our feet was a continuation of the marble stairs on the other side, the wall clearly built over part of the much larger stairwell. This had been a clever way from whoever designed the house to create a stairwell for those using these nefarious corridors without building a new set of stairs.

At irregular intervals, there were doors cut into the wall, which I felt unsafe to try, as I had no idea who or what was on the other side. Occasionally there was a peephole, and a close inspection of these allowed us to locate where in the house a particular door or wall was and who was on the other side. The walls with peepholes were generally in unusual places where, I presumed, the viewer was most likely to be seen if they exited without checking to see if the area was clear first.

I now had a reliably accurate mental map of the house and decided to complete a quick experiment. The next time we arrived at a fork in the corridor, I quietly caught Vulk's attention and pointed out the direction I wanted to go. I did this twice more until we came across the part of the house where I believed Charles the batman had been killed in. Lowering my candle, I found a large, dry bloodstain on the floor.

Vulk tapped his nose and pointed at the dark, cavernous end to the hallway we were in. I nodded and we were off again. I would not have needed the werewolf's senses to track this path as the blood smears along the floor clearly showed the way the batman's body had been dragged.

We walked down another set of narrow stairs and by the growing chill I figured we were nearing the basement. The building materials had also transmuted from the brick, wood and marble of the house above to the cobble-like stones of the foundation beneath. Here was where the two maids had been killed.

The long stretch of the secret corridor at the bottom of the stairs was extremely cold and damp, and we soon found the source. An old well sat at the end of the passage, its wide, ominous mouth grated closed for safety. An inspection proved the grate was unlatched and slightly ajar. Lifting the lid, I peered down, but could see little in the abysmally dark pit. I stepped away and allowed Vulk to look.

With only the briefest glance the werewolf nodded, "He went down there."

"Can you figure out who it was that brought him here?"

Vulk took a big sniff and sneezed. "No good. There's just too much moisture and mould down here. To find any sort of scent I would have to turn into a wolf, and I could probably keep enough thought in my head to track whoever was here, but I doubt I would remember enough when I changed back to tell you who it was. Separating them would take a wolf's mind, but tracking them would take…well… me."

I had never given this much thought, but it made sense. Vulk did not just change physically, he changed mentally as well. While in man-wolf form he kept aspects of both, and though perhaps he did not keep the highest functions of a human brain, he retained enough control to keep simple thoughts in his head, and these certainly seemed to remain when he returned to human form. To go full wolf was a different matter and meant to do so he had to give himself up totally to the beast. The complete change made him great in a fight, but not the best companion to be around in a confined space.

My friend, as always, continued to surprise me.

"Do not concern yourself with this one," I said, slapping him on the back. "I have a fair idea how the body got here, and if need be we can try your way later."

"You going to tell me who it was then?" he asked as I turned and headed up the stairs. "Amun…Amunnn," he called out as I left the corridor. "You're not going to tell me, are you?"

CHAPTER TWENTY-TWO

It was too late in the day to get some sleep, not that there was much chance of that now anyway as I was abuzz with adrenaline and this new information. We now not only knew how the killers were moving through the house, but how they were getting into the building without being seen. Suddenly the affair seemed less supernatural and more strategic.

Instead of sleeping, I walked into the kitchen and took a cup of tea. The cooks were baking and stewing up a storm, and I assumed this meant they had received word the police would be arriving tonight in large numbers again. My hypothesis would prove to be incorrect as the amount of food the cooks were preparing was just what was needed to feed a large household every day.

I found a quiet space for myself in the house's library and sat down. Cradling the mug of tea in both hands and allowing its heat to radiate through my fingers and along my arms, I let my mind drift across what had been happening around the house recently.

I was so engrossed in the patterns of steam rising from my cup that I failed to notice Lucinda had drifted into the room and taken a seat opposite.

"Penny for your thoughts?" she asked.

I looked up from my cup. "Just pondering all that has occurred here recently."

"Exciting, isn't it? I have not seen so many young, handsome men in uniform since I watched my father march his troops off to the docks."

I thought about that. The Colonels last real deployment anywhere had been at least a decade ago. Lucinda must have only been a small child then.

"I was thinking more of the loss the estate has suffered. Husbands, wives, old friends, there has been a lot of death here recently."

"I suppose that is true, but honestly there has been a lot of death around this family for years. Uncles, grandparents…"

"Your mother," I said so she would not have to.

"We do not talk about her anymore," Lucinda said, her face

growing grim. "In fact we don't talk about much about anything anymore. On the day I lost my mother it seems I lost my sister as well; my blood sucking sister and all the men she chases after. Even when she was engaged to Jerome, she was always flirting with the men around here, so she never had time to talk to me."

"I will admit your sister does seem angry," I said with a smile, "was she like that before the death of your mother?"

"Not really." Lucinda withdrew into her chair, allowing the shadows in this deeper part of the room to hide the tears starting to well in her eyes.

"Your step-mother seems nice enough." I said, understanding there was likely not much more going to be said on the subject of her mother and sister.

"She is."

"Nice to have someone else in the house to talk to. How did your father meet her?"

"She was a hand maid to my mother and the one who actually explained to my father how she had died. Somehow they started to grow closer because of this, until before we knew what was going on they were getting married."

"I have seen you two together. It is good to have a friend like that." I was hoping to get the girl chatting about something more pleasant so I could get her onto a topic where I could learn something new about this mysterious family. "I have spent a lot of time walking this earth and let me tell you, it's a far friendly place if you have someone walking by your side. People you can talk to, can genuinely have a relationship with, well those people are rare and to be cherished."

I took a sip of my tea and sat back in my chair, watching the emotions play across Lucinda's face. This lovely young girl, seated with the mansion as a backdrop, looked lonelier then anyone I had seen in a long time. No matter its gilded edges, a prison is a prison, be its walls made of bars or an over anxious parent.

I was about to ask Lucinda where in London she would like to go for our dinner when one of the servant girls ran into the room, looked at me and said: "I was told to tell you they are here."

Abberline marched up to the front door with only five bobbies with him. Despite the two dead maids, the Inspector's superiors had decided that too much manpower had been wasted watching over the house, and so refused to sign off on any further expenditure. The men Abberline brought with him were simply those he had direct command over and did not have to ask permission to use. The policeman also arrived with a covered wagon, though when I tried to investigate I was told bluntly the contents within were none of my business.

More encouraging was the arrival of General Stamford's men. They showed up sporting their own weapons and looked a dangerous bunch to a man. Some of them were older, but clearly cut out of the military cloth one would expect from those who had served their country for a lifetime. What I did find surprising was the number of young faces amongst the crowd. I asked one and found out many were the sons of the more valued men the General had lost during their service, and Stamford had employed them to ensure their families continued receiving a wage and never suffered any financial hardship because of their loss.

The old man had grown even higher in my estimations, though I was surprised how many of them there were. What the General needed twenty or so ex-soldiers for was something that needed investigating…so I decided to investigate. I noticed none of the men were those I knew from the greenhouse, so I approached and asked a man I did not know in the slyest way I knew how: "What does the General need so many lads for?"

The man stared at me, his fierce eyes trying to boil through my skull and out of the other side, judging their sheer intensity. Someone's arm dropped on my shoulder and another of the men led me away. "Don't mind Vincent there, he doesn't even like his mother, who I'm pretty sure he killed and ate when he was just a wee baby."

I allowed myself to be steered to the periphery of the gathering men. My guide introduced himself as John Batten, the man who also had been taking command of the police and staff two nights ago.

"We don't want any of them catching word of what I'm gonna tell ya," the ex-soldier said with a nod towards a certain group of the household's men, men I assumed worked for the Colonel.

"The General has many interests. Family fortunes don't make

themselves you know," he said with a wink, leading me to assume he meant legal family fortunes do not just make themselves. "Most of these lads are from a warehouse the General runs, a few are from family interests outside of London. None of us here live at the house full-time."

"That is still a lot of men to be loyally serving the General."

"Loyal? Bullshit. We are here mostly for the cash."

My own raised eyebrow, though admittedly not as devastatingly efficient as Vulk's, proved influential enough to bewitch the ex-soldier to continue his tale. "When we all left the service and followed the General into retirement it was with the promise that, when the old man died, one-third of his fortune would be split amongst those who remained. The only problem with this was to get the money we have to be in his service when he dies. There were thirty of us when we first began; today there are only twelve of the original men left."

Could this be the reason why some of the General's men had been killed? Was someone trying to increase his share of the prize before the old man died? He had certainly been sick enough lately to suggest the end was near, perhaps forcing someone desperate enough to take such a step. No, the idea did not make sense. Why kill the maids?

"So that is why there are so many younger faces. Let me guess, they are the sons of the men who died in the General's service and have taken the place of their fathers to keep the family in the will?"

"Got it in one," Batten agreed, "and I don't wish ill of the old codger, but he does seem determined to outlive us all. Over the years, maybe eight of us just walked away, frustrated that we were all but enslaved to a house and home that wasn't ours and wanting to start our own families."

"Understandable. To be little more than slaves, with the only payoff for your labour the money that may or may not appear sometime in the future, that would be exasperating."

"Oh it's not as bad as that. We are paid a fair wage for a fair day's work. The General's money is more like our own retirement fund. The old man figured he would never have created his fortune if not for us, and seemed determined to see we are all looked after once he's gone. I can guarantee you the Lord-High-Almighty Colonel Stamford will toss us off his property the second his father isn't around to shield us anymore."

"He does not like you?"

"He blames us," the man said, than realised this was probably a sentence too far. He shut up completely after that and wandered back to the ranks of his fellows.

My mental list of issues was growing longer and longer. Blamed for what?

Though I had seen my fair share of battles, I would never claim to be any sort of warrior and was happy to leave the dispersion of the troops to those who knew their business. Batten again showed that, during his younger days when he still wore the scarlet, he had been an NCO of some merit. He took control of the men and soon had them standing at attention and presenting their weapons for inspection, and even the police got caught up in the spontaneous parade. Those weapons he deemed too ridiculous or ineffective were swapped for something far more lethal, until everyone looked like they could fight a bear if need be. We were also told where our positions would be for the coming night's surveillance.

The idea proved rather simple. The General's troops were to watch the back door and the greenhouse, as that was their purview anyway. Most of the police and household men would be with Vulk, myself, and both Stoker and Doyle, who had wandered onto the grounds just a few minutes earlier. Both were brandishing revolvers, and cutlasses from a Stamford wall.

We were charged with the front gate and the house, and a small squad would guard the main stairwell and look for any trouble inside. One final group included the boys of the house, and to keep them out of trouble they were assigned as messengers to make use of their younger legs. I noticed many of the household women had joined each other in one of the larger bedrooms upstairs, determined that no one would be left by themselves to fall victim.

All in all I found this a very satisfactory plan and was thankful to whatever entity was currently in charge of luck that the vampires or the Order of the Dragon had not attacked earlier. This new structure had me feeling rather more optimistic about our chances than I did this morning.

That optimism ended when the first vampire hit us.

CHAPTER TWENTY-THREE

I am not really sure how it happened.

Later I recalled we were all standing around, chatting amicably and looking at a garden illuminated by dozens of all-weather oil filled lanterns when, one by one, those lights went out. Two men, one holding a lit torch and the other a weapon held at the ready, cautiously moved down the path to relight the lanterns. We all watched like hawks as the armed man moved into position, allowing the second man with the lit torch to reignite the lantern. Even with hindsight it was hard to remember exactly what happened next.

One minute the men were there, answering our catcalls about hunting boogeymen in the dark with calls of their own that, if we were so brave, we should be down there with them, and the next minute both were gone. We were still watching closely when, within the instance of a blink of an eye, their torch went out and both men seemed to evaporate into the encompassing gloom as though the night had swallowed them.

"Throw a light down there," someone yelled. Instantly a number of lit torches arced through the air towards the location where the men had disappeared. What they illuminated was a true scene from Dante's inferno.

Both men lay beyond the path where we had last seen them, their bodies and limbs posed at such unnatural angles it was clear they were already dead. Looming over one body, fanged jaws dripping fresh arterial blood, was a vampire. Judging the gasps and murmurs from some of the men standing nearby, they had recognised the monster as one of the missing household staff.

Caring little if we watched or not, the undead creature picked up the body it was standing over and, with a single hand, lifted it towards its mouth. With an audible crunch the vampire bit and began to drink whatever fluids were left. The way the corpse twitched I realised that, somehow, the man was still alive. I decided to keep this gruesome fact to myself.

The feeding continued until someone regained enough sense to shoot the vampire. This first bullet hit the creature in the shoulder and seemed to hurt it, though not in the same sort of way if it had been a living man who had been shot. The vampire seemed to recognise being shot, but then it simply shrugged off the hit and began tracking where the round had come from. Once it had sight of the man with the pistol, it bared its enormous canine fangs, hissed and attacked.

Instantly a dozen pistols rose into the air and discharged. A number of rounds hit the vampire's body and slowed its advance, but they did not stop it. It is amazing how quickly six bullets can be spent, and when the pistols began clicking on spent chambers, the unholy creature took the opportunity to spring forward, arms outstretched and mouth agape in a ferocious snarl. The twin fangs jutting out of its mouth made the vampire resemble a venomous viper.

With all my might I swung the axe that had been used earlier by my would-be assassin in a two-handed blow that struck the creature mid-leap. Though the impact nearly jarred the weapon out of my hand, I held on for all I was worth as the head bit deep into the vampire's chest. The blow forced the creature to fall backwards into a nearby bush, and it almost pulled me with it. Before I could even attempt to regain my step the vampire had got back on its feet, despite my axe still buried deep within its torso. The creature was about to leap away when the cavalry arrived.

Spears, swords and more bullets lashed out at the creature, driving it to the ground under the weight of their impact. Behind this assault was Batten, barking orders to ensure those in the fight struck out at the beast and not each other. Their attack meant I got my axe back and even got in a chop or two whenever the thing's body came into view.

Gore and body parts flew, and the bloody work only ended when someone got in a solid blow to the filthy thing's neck, severing the spinal cord. Instantly the fight went out of the vampire, which slumped to the ground dead...again.

Breathing heavily and scared almost witless, I heard Batten still manage to order: "Re-light those damn lanterns." Without thinking of the danger I was running down the garden path with a lit torch and reigniting the extinguished lights.

With the garden illuminated again and the few policemen who had been stationed down at the front gates joining us out of fear, I realised how stupid I had been to run into the garden like that. I needed to wise up quickly as fate would not likely be so kind again if I lost my head in the future. I was supposed to be intelligent, so it was time to start acting like it.

Under instructions from Vulk the vampire was dismembered, with particular care paid to the head. This was removed completely, and then split in two with a few solid blows from an axe. The remains were then thrown into a fire someone had lit besides the main footpath.

Looking into the forest of concerned faces lit up by the firelight I spotted Abberline and gave him a look as though to say 'see'. He nodded an affirmative. Every one of us standing the line now knew the night indeed held unholy terrors.

The next attack was not a supernatural one, but carried out by knights from the Order of the Dragon. They were all dressed in black, with their right hands shrouded in the weird two pronged gauntlets we had seen before. These Knights were amongst us before we knew what was going on. They moved quickly and their clothing made it hard to keep track of them within those parts of the garden that were least illuminated. Some fifteen Dragons charged us from out of a group of trees, four were shot before they got within ten feet of the group defending the rear of the house. Things did not go so well for the rest when the survivors suddenly veered away from the rear door and charged for the front. The highly skilled martial artists killed three men, two from the house and one policeman in the garden.

It was Vulk who led the counterattack and, with axes, swords and a halberd likely last used during the War of the Roses, he and those with him drove away those attackers they did not kill outright. Though I thought it unnecessary, I said nothing when the men began dismembering these bodies as well. I doubted there was any chance the dead would turn into vampires, but I also doubted anyone was really interested in hearing about that at the time.

Out of the bloody carnage I managed to retrieve another of the dragon amulets and handed it to Abberline, who slipped it into a pocket. I shook my head and indicated he should wear it. I revealed the amulet I had taken to wearing around my neck to indicate just how good an idea I thought this was.

It was one of Colonel Stamford's men who noticed that the two dead men killed by the vampire were gone. I couldn't be sure, but I felt the attack by the Order had been a feint so that other members could carry out their main charge, to seek out the undead monsters made by their master and carry them away.

I had my suspicions that the Order had something to do with the appearance of the undead, and the amulets likely protected the wearer from either the vampires or from turning if bitten while dealing with a hunger-crazed beast. Besides stealing away the corpses, this attack was likely just to check out the strength of our defences.

I sent one of the lads acting as a messenger around to the back of the house to inform the General's men what had happened and to expect either another feint or a larger attack.

I then gathered as many of the survivors as I could in the garden and told them about my change of mind from my previous belief. "From now on if anyone gets bitten we are going to have to deal with them the same way as we did the vampire."

A few men argued as their particular religious beliefs either held it a sacrilege to abuse the dead, or they were required to be put into the ground as 'complete' as possible so they would remain whole in the afterlife. All patently ridiculous of course, but the middle of a war with the living dead was not the time to start a debate on individual philosophies.

Luckily Abberline understood, and his word carried a lot of weight within the group. "Sorry lads, but if you're bitten it's either that or you live the unholy life of one of these creatures, which unless I'm mistaken would be even more frowned upon by the Almighty." Most of the men nodded their agreement, even the ones who had been dissenting just a few minutes earlier. It would seem no one wanted to end up a creature of the night.

After our meeting, and to my surprise, the Colonel stepped up and proved his worth by reorganising the estate's defences. He had apparently watched the entire attack from a second floor window and, just like any good commander, had seen what we had done right and what we had done wrong. With the help of Batten he created fire teams out of the men with revolvers and hand-held weapons. Men with swords and axes stood on the outside of each group, placed there to protect those men with revolvers who stood in the middle. We all recognised the intelligence of his plan, as the revolvers had proven useful at stopping a vampire long enough to allow those with bladed weapons to finish it off.

Once we had completed some simple drills to help coordinate the new squad formations, two maids appeared at the front door with steaming cups of tea and some food. The men devoured the victuals; though we ensured two of these new fire teams were on guard just in case. There is nothing like a near-death experience at the hands of a vampire for the appetite, I always say.

The runner we had sent to the back door had not yet reappeared, and the maids claimed the General's men were still on guard there. I was about to enter the hallway and make my way to the back door when a maid's scream shattered the night. I whirled and watched as two vampires bounded up the garden path towards the front door, with a third close on their heels.

The first of our new fire teams stepped into their path and let loose with a barrage of pistol fire. Once their revolvers were empty, they crabbed sideways to reload while a second team stepped in and fired. I had run out and joined the third team, which was ordered by the Colonel to keep back and enter the fight only if absolutely necessary. Holding back proved exceedingly difficult to do as every instinct we had was screaming at those of us with revolvers to empty them into the hideous maw of the nearest monster, but we held our fire and position.

The first vampire took perhaps thirty rounds to the chest and head, yet it still managed to move forward, though it was now reduced to a slow, almost pitiful crawl. One eye was ruined and a large chunk of its lower jaw was gone, but what I knew of their curse informed me that almost any damage would be repaired after a decent feed.

The second vampire had been close behind the first, but it had changed its bearing and it now darted deeper into the garden. This part of the estate had been unguarded because there was little there to defend, and I had begun looking for Batten or even the Colonel to ask if we had a plan on what to do about this move, when a loud

SNAP brought me to a halt.

Down one row of bushes, the vampire's forward momentum had ended and it was standing in place, looking down as though figuring out why it could no longer move. One leg was tightly held in the clawed teeth of an old bear trap, and now I knew what had been on the covered wagon Abberline had brought in earlier.

"I really had not expected the thing to do much damage or even hold it for long," the Inspector said from behind me.

The vampire began striking at the contraption as though the snare was alive and could be killed. Built to hold a struggling, pain-enraged European brown bear, the trap could likely withstand this sort of punishment for a while, affording us time to deal with the other two creatures.

While our focus was on the ensnared monster, the third creature managed to reach the front of the house and tore into our ranks. Between men fighting for their lives, I managed to unload my pistol whenever I had a clear shot, while others hacked and slashed with their swords and axes. I saw one of our men go down under a nasty blow, another thrown what had to have been twenty feet into the air. He flailed about as though trying to gain the ability to fly, before landing somewhere in the distance with a wet, mortality-ending thud. I reminded myself we had to go find him later, if there was a later, and cut his head off, just in case he had been bitten at some stage during the fight.

Though we had been blindsided, the formation of small teams meant that one group was prepared to meet this threat, and they moved forward and brought the attack of the third vampire to a halt. While the blows and gunshots of one of the small teams whittled the monster down, Vulk and I decided to deal with the first vampire.

Despite its extensive wounds the vampire had managed to move another dozen feet towards the house. With half of its face missing we thought it wise to keep on its ruined vision side, thus keeping out of its vision. The creature snarled and lashed out at any noise, and turned to focus on Vulk as he began lunging in and out like a fencer in an attempt to slash its leg tendons.

I tried to swing my axe at its head, and though it somehow ducked the razor sharp weapon, thanks to a sizeable amount of momentum behind the swing the axe buried itself deep in the vampire's spine. Instantly, whatever movement it had retained in its legs was lost, although its arms seemed to have enough life in them to fight and still cause damage. I began chopping away at them like some demonic woodcutter as the vampire continued to crawl about, grasping for a victim.

After several minutes of hacking I stood back on my haunches, breathing deeply, my arms burning from the exertion of swinging the heavy axe around. Vulk joined me, wiping gore from his own blade and we watched as what was little more than a torso and head attempted to belly crawl its way towards us like a worm. Its progress was halted when a group of men jumped in and, with a flair for the dramatic; one stood on its neck and fired his revolver directly into its brain. The straggly hair on the monster's head caught fire from the muzzle flash from the gun and a black, oily substance began to flow out of the bullet hole. The ex-soldier barely had time to lift his foot from holding the vampire down before someone else brought their sword down on its neck, severing the head.

Taking stock to ensure nothing else had snuck up while we were engaged, when it was obvious the fight was over I called out to Batten and pointed out the pieces of dead vampire lying about and gestured back down into the garden. The old Sergeant caught on and began barking orders at everyone standing around not doing anything to start feeding the fire again.

The rest of us moved down the path to the vampire still caught in the trap. It had beaten the two metal jaws holding its leg out of shape with its bare hands, and had almost completely severed its snared leg in doing so. Believing the beast helpless, one man got too cocky over our earlier successes and charged forward with a spear. The creature saw him coming, ignored the trap on its leg and leapt forward. The chain keeping the trap in place pulled taut with the noise of a piano wire being struck, and although the vampire only moved forward a few feet, it was enough. Catching the spearman with both hands, the vampire yanked and twisted. I can still hear the man's neck snap when I close my eyes and picture the scene.

From around the side of the house stepped Sergeant Willkie who hefted a medieval shield that he must have taken off the Stamford's wall. With him were half-a-dozen men brandishing weapons. I grabbed Vulk and we followed close behind, shadowed in turn by Doyle and Stoker.

The vampire ignored our approach and began to feed on the dead man in its hands, tearing into his throat and drinking deeply.

"Look at that, he's forcing the man's heart to pump the blood for his feed like a bloody fountain!" Doyle called out. The doctor was correct and we watched as the creature held the dead man in a powerful hug and rhythmically squeezed his chest. The two looked like some demonic bagpipe player squeezing out a tune from its ungainly-looking instrument.

Once they were near enough, the men following Willkie struck at the creature from behind the sanctuary of wood and steel that he carried, slashing at the beast's eyes, throat, wrists, and ankles. An unlucky pike-man thrust his weapon into the struggling vampire's chest and his metal blade became stuck between the creature's ribs. With impossible speed and strength the vampire grabbed the pike's handle and heaved, levering its owner forward, over our heads and into it's waiting arms. Within seconds he was dead and the vampire was again feeding on fresh blood. I swear I could see some of its ghastly wounds healing before my eyes.

As we began to organise a safer way of approaching the last vampire the Order of the Dragon hit us again.

CHAPTER TWENTY-FOUR

Our attention was so focused on despatching the last vampire that a new wave of black clad assassins managed to slip into the rear of our group and attack us from behind. Within seconds a number of our men lay dead and the rest of us were franticly fighting for our lives. Understanding that things were desperate, Vulk shifted to man-wolf form and leapt at the still feeding vampire, landing on its chest and driving it to the ground. As he tore one of the creature's arms off, I gathered the few men about me and formed them into as tight a unit as I could. We still had the shield Willkie had been carrying and it was now on the arm and shoulder of someone who seemed to know how to use it. We lined up behind the man and the shield, thrusting swords and pikes out at the new attackers. The longer weapons kept the Knights at arm's reach, while those of us with revolvers struggled to hastily reload.

I flicked my own revolver's barrel closed with a loud click as a scream of rage cut across the battle. I spun about and watched as Vulk's enormous body was hurled through the air and into the side of the house. He hit with a sickening impact that would have killed anything mortal.

"Grab him," I bellowed to Stoker, who was now standing directly behind me, "and the rest of you, hold this formation and start moving us back into the house."

We needed to get something substantial at our backs and force everything to come at us from a narrow, confined space so we could concentrate our strength. Several millennia ago I had been standing on the Persian side of Thermopylae and watched as the Greek leader Leonidas and his men tried to break the horde trying to invade their country. Though losing that fight, I did learn from Leonidas the strength of a good defensive position.

Physically pulling men into position, we began shuffling them sideways, calling out to keep them in formation whenever anyone tried to make a break for the apparent sanctuary of the front door. As the little island of humanity crabbed its way to safety, we picked up stragglers and wounded along the way. Three of the Order worked out what we were up to and tried to cut us off, but a volley of gunfire left one dead and the rest of them in retreat.

Stamford House was unusual for London as it was built at a time when homes were literally considered a man's castle. The building had been constructed to withhold a siege, with lower floor windows built at least ten feet in the air, and all were built with shutters that could be closed for further protection. Thankfully, some forward thinking employee had already battened all the shutters on the lower floor. The two main doors had large oak frames with enormous brass hinges and could be bolted firmly shut from the inside, meaning they could withstand anything short of a cannonball. As the last of the surviving men from the attack stumbled through the massive doors, both were slammed shut and a large beam slipped into place.

After ensuring the unmoving Vulk was still with us, I ordered four men to head to the back door, lock it, and gather any of the General's troops stationed there if they had survived. There had still been no reply to the message I had sent there earlier—in fact I could not recall ever seeing the young boy after he had run off to make contact with the men stationed there. I had to assume the worst, and if the General's men had been as unlucky as us, they could be in real trouble, perhaps even dead.

I found Inspector Abberline helping the men with revolvers to reload them, while Willkie and others were trying to find weapons to replace the ones they had lost in the fight. Though there was little noise coming from outside, I had to believe whoever was left from the Order had freed the ensnared vampire and we could soon be under attack from some direction we had not yet thought of. Though the house could withstand a siege from ordinary humans, a creature like a vampire could easily scale a wall and enter from some other direction. With this in mind, I ordered the fires in the house's chimneys to be stoked with as much fuel as they could take to keep the blaze as high as possible and hopefully stop something for entering down the chimney flues.

"Burn the furniture if need be," I called out to the maids who were assigned the job. "We need to get those fires as hot and as high as possible."

The front door had only been locked for a few minutes when a scream burst from the floor above. Taking the stairs two at a time, with Doyle right behind me, I raced into the family's private corridors and found Mrs Stamford in the clutches of a Knight. Unable to tell if the she was alive or not, I charged into the pair, hoping to break the man's grip on the woman. We all tumbled to the ground, though the Dragon recovered quickly and was already getting back to his feet when Sergeant Willkie arrived and kicked the man in the head. Once the Knight was back down Doyle fired a single round from his pistol into the man's chest, killing him instantly.

I took the doctor's offered hand and got back to my feet, giving him a nod of thanks. He returned this with a wink, before following Willkie to check the rest of the floor and the windows to make sure we had no more nasty surprises hidden inside. While they were checking, I leant down and inspected the limp body of Mrs Stamford. Not only was she dead, her throat had been torn out as though she had been fed on. I inspected the duel spikes on the dead Knight's gauntleted hand, which revealed no blood, indicating it had not been the weapon used to cause the wound. This meant we likely had a vampire in the house.

More men arrived and I asked them to carry the bodies downstairs and behead them before they could turn. I then stalked with some trepidation to the far end of the corridor and, without waiting for permission to enter, kicked in the only locked door on the floor.

On the other side were the two Stamford girls and their father, who must have come up earlier to check on his family.

The Colonel was horrified to hear about the death of his wife, and seemed genuinely upset to the point that he took a swing at me when I refused him permission to see her body. I did not think there was anything to be gained by informing him we had just beheaded the woman to stop her transformation.

The two girls looked almost disinterested in the death of their stepmother. They also seemed to care little about the news that a vampire likely lay in wait somewhere in the house, though I did notice the Colonel had picked up a revolver and looked ready to fight.

We ushered the family downstairs to a room with only one

door and no windows. Here we also herded the rest of the female servants, all of our wounded along with three armed men, making sure at least one of them had a shield and a pistol. These archaic pieces of armour had proven their worth in giving a normal man the chance of surviving a vampire attack as long as he had some fellows around to help out. I did not even bother asking the Colonel if he wanted to join our defensive efforts, instead preferring that he remained with his family and out of our way.

One of the policemen I had sent to check on the General's men stationed at the backdoor found me and asked that I follow. The rest of the men we had sent had set up a barricade at the rear door, and I was surprised to find them with only three of the men from those that had been stationed there. These men reported the vampires had attacked them in number, and the fight had moved into the furthest parts of the rear garden, triggering a trap set by the Order of the Dragons.

I carefully snaked my way through the barricade, opened the rear door and stuck my head outside to have a quick look for myself. The garden was pitch-black, with every torch extinguished. Realising that leaving the door open even this long was asking for trouble, I leaned back inside and barricaded it once more.

With the doors locked, the windows shut and fires burning brightly in every fireplace, I had officially run out of ideas on what to do next. Luckily Abberline was on the case, and his ability to command men came to the fore. He ordered water to be brought, allowing the men to get a drink, and it was not until this was mentioned that I realised how thirsty I had become.

Next, Abberline ordered everyone to begin inspecting those standing next to them, specifically looking for wounds. It took me a few second to realise he was looking for anyone who had been bitten and escaped our notice.

When everyone proved to be both bite and fang-free, we took stock of what resources we had left. We had five revolvers with plenty of ammunition, so a sentry was stationed at each door with one, with the remaining three left in the hands of a firing squad stationed in the connecting hallway to both doors and the stairs upstairs, leaving them ready to lend their support in whichever direction they were needed. At least two men with shields were at each post, along with two men that carried either swords or axes. In the confined spaces of the house, the defence of the shields and the reach of both the guns and the edged weapon should be enough to hold off a vampire or any number of the Dragon knights, who strangely seemed intent on using their spiked gauntlets as their primary weapon. I could only assume this method of murder was something historic or religious, rather than any belief that they were a more effective weapon than a pistol or sword.

I had used the time while Abberline organised everyone to gather whatever men were left and, pulling one of those with a revolver out of the middle group, armed myself with another shield and a sword and commenced a room-by-room search for the vampire that had breached the inside the house.

None of us had seen it, but I had to figure this was the same one that had been caught in the bear trap on the front lawn just before we pulled inside. If so, the creature was wounded and likely looking to feed again. This could explain why we had found the Dragon with the corpse of Mrs Stamford. He had likely been carrying a meal to the vampire. Feeling I now had proof there was a definite connection between the vampires and the Order of the Dragon, I figured that while we had the time it was prudent to find and kill the creature lest it attack at some future, inopportune time.

I had four men with me, and we quickly worked out the safest routine for checking a room. The one with the shield would push through the door and hold firm, then someone with an edged weapon would move in close behind, ready to slash at anything that moved. Next would be the man with the revolver, followed by the last man, watching the rear so we did not get jumped from behind. At all times I made sure the dragon medallion was around my neck and within easy reach. If it had any power over the creatures, its presence could prove the difference between death and survival.

Room by room we searched, scaring ourselves silly as we burst into an empty room, before steeling ourselves, pulling open a new door and charging inside like a troop of screaming monkeys. A slow, thorough search of each room found nothing.

When we ran out of rooms upstairs we began searching the few unoccupied areas on the ground floor. This took no time at all, so we then proceeded down into the dark of the basement, the one area I was sure a hungry vampire could be lurking.

Brandishing weapons and a watchman's lantern, the team moved down the stairwell leading to the lowest floor, ready for anything. We first checked the wine cellar, before moving on to the cold room food pantry. If it was at all possible we grew even more frightened when we found nothing. Certainly fighting a vampire was scary, but at least you knew where it was but a hidden vampire, was proving to be downright terrifying, as every shadow or blind corner could be holding death with big teeth.

Despite our search, we found nothing, so together we made our way back up to the ground floor, making sure every pool of darkness we passed had a weapon thrust into it or shield covering it.

CHAPTER TWENTY-FIVE

Upstairs I received the welcome news that Vulk had awakened and had begun helping search the house for any sign of the vampire. Someone had also thought to lay out some food, so I greedily stuffed a chunk of bread and some cheese into my mouth. The men stationed at both doors reported there was no sign of any activity at either entrance, suggesting our fight was over for the night.

Taking a quick headcount, we had lost at least nine men by my count, though the number could be higher. I had figured during the chaos that some of our troops may have simply run out the front gate, and just as likely they had not made it. We had killed ten or so Dragon knights and at the most only three vampires. On paper it would seem we had come out ahead, but any death on our side of the ledger was one too many.

Vulk returned from having looked about the house and reported he could find no trace of the vampire who had made it inside. He gave me a subtle look, and then none-too-subtly mentioned he had made sure to look 'EVERYWHERE', which of course meant the secret passages inside the house walls. I had been concerned that the vampire could have made it into one of the hidden passages, but could conceive of no way how it could possibly know about the passages. I had also not wanted to search them earlier as it would have been suicide without the support of the werewolf, and in any case I was holding the existence of the passages as an ace up my sleeve. Anyone else who let it slip they knew of their existence would instantly be added to my 'I-need-to-know-more-about-this-person' list.

I found the Colonel and Abberline deep in conversation inside the Colonel's office. They were busy planning what the family intended to do once the sun rose in the morning. Still hours away, I felt it was a little premature to be making such plans that far ahead. If we were not on our guard there was still time enough for us to meet a nasty end well before dawn.

"Any sign of them?" Abberline asked, indicating he meant inside the house.

"None," Vulk said as he grabbed a glass of water from a pitcher and downed it in a single swallow.

I looked about the room. "Where is your shadow?"

"Willkie is back with the wounded. If any of those boys are capable of even sitting up, he will bring them back here and arm them with whatever he can. That should free up a few more men to guard the doors."

"And the stairwell," Batten called out from his position at the front door. Damn…that man had great hearing.

I nodded my approval at the plan. We were running out of men to fight, and we still had no idea exactly how many vampires and knights of the Dragon we had to deal with.

"Has anyone questioned the General's men yet? How many vampires did they see? How many did they kill?" A universal round of head nodding had me back on my feet and making my way to the rear door to find the few surviving troops stationed there.

Vulk came with me. In silence we walked down the corridor connecting the front room to the back, and through to the rear entry. Even during this short journey we made sure to keep an eye on any shadow or dark corner, refusing to be blindsided again by one of those monsters.

I stepped into the kitchen behind Vulk, who stopped suddenly and whispered: "We need help here."

Peering around the werewolf's glacier-sized shoulders I could see that the door was wide open, with no sign of any of the men that had been posted there. Vulk pointed to his nose and mouthed the word 'blood'. Hefting my pistol and wishing I had brought the shield and sword I had foolishly left behind, I crept forward slowly, hoping to close the door before something could get in. It was only as I got closer that I realised that something was most likely already in.

As I put my shoulder into the hefty door and began pushing it shut, I spotted the corpse of one of our men lying on a patch of grass about ten feet outside. With a small shift of position I increased the area I could see and spotted two more bodies. None of them seemed to be the General's men.

Ignoring a snarled warning from Vulk, I leaned forward, stuck my head outside and, with the immediate area seemingly free of danger, crept over to the bodies. All three had their necks torn open, with duel puncture marks that I assumed had been created by the gauntlets worn by the Dragon Knights.

"Are you thinking what I am thinking?"

With a start I turned and faced Vulk, who had silently moved out of the door and was standing behind me. At the door a number of men that Vulk had retrieved stood about looking confused, so I put a finger to my lips, begging them to be quiet. Vulk gestured for them to hold position at the door.

I stood up. "This could be bad, but if it helps I think I finally know what's going on!"

With a few quick, and then one long sniff, the werewolf pointed towards the far end of a sculptured hedge. Together we crept that way to have a look.

I estimated at least eight black clad Dragons were there, along with three of the General's men. All now wore gauntlets and seemed to be planning how they were going to take the rest of the house. This was all an assumption on my behalf, I admit. Though we could hear them talking clearly, I did not understand a single word they said. This in itself was troubling tome since there are very few languages that I do not at least have a passing knowledge of.

Having seen enough, I pointed back to the still-open house door and we made our way back. My first thought was that we needed to prepare what few troops we had left for a new onslaught from the enemy, but by the time we got back to the house, another idea had dawned.

"Leave the door open," I whispered as we ducked inside. "Can you hold here until I go fetch more help?"

"Are you planning something sneaky?" Vulk asked.

"Very," I answered, with the first smile I'd cracked in want seemed like ages.

"Well, off you go then."

CHAPTER TWENTY-SIX

Fearing we had very little time before the enemy began pouring through the rear door, I moved into the house's main corridor and gathered the walking wounded Willkie had been dealing with and one of the healthier men. I left as many as I could stationed at the front door as possible, just in case whatever the Knights were planning was a diversion for a larger attack there. That meant there were eight of us, me, Vulk, one healthy man, and five wounded, to stand against at least eleven of them. This number was of course optimistic as it assumed they would not be coming at us with the assistance of one of their pet vampires.

Outnumbered and trapped … even Leonidas had his Thermopylae.

To my surprise the Colonel and Abberline joined us expanding our number to ten. I explained my plan, and the retired officer suggested a few improvements to the position of our troops, with Stamford determined to be the first to meet a renewed attack head on. I was unsure if the Colonel could be trusted as it was his father's men who had turned out to be the enemy, but the determined look on his face, likely fuelled by the death of his wife, helped silence those doubts.

With the men stationed the way the Colonel had recommended, I hefted my retrieved sword and shield and moved into a pool of darkness opposite the open door that I had been designated too. It had been several centuries since I carried both weapons into battle and I was surprised at how comfortable they felt. It would seem you never forget some things.

Though we were blind to the movement of the Dragon Knights, Vulk was not so hindered after he turned into his wolf form. The werewolf stood directly behind the open door and acted as our eyes, ears, and nose. He was also ready to slam the door shut if events got away from us.

From my position, I could just make Vulk out, and I do believe we all collectively held our breaths when he raised a furry hand and began counting down by lowering his raised fingers slowly.

A beat after Vulk's last finger fell the first black clad figure crept through the door. The Dragon Knight stopped and looked about, then nimbly slunk up to the edge of the corridor and looked. Seeing no one, the figure lifted a hand and more of the Order came inside. Brazenly taking the lead were three men dressed in the General's livery. I assumed they were at the front not only because they knew their way around the house, but also to relieve suspicion if they happened to meet any of the house staff before they were ready to strike. By the time the person realised there was something was up, it would likely be too late.

That was perfectly fine by me, as it placed them under the blades of Abberline and the wounded policemen with him, who I was sure would appreciate a little revenge on the men who had just butchered their friends who had earlier been guarding the rear door.

The tension and fear was palpable as the Knights filed in one after the other. I counted ten men, and to say I was relieved there was no vampire with them would have been an understatement. I noticed I had been holding my breath, so I quietly began taking in a fresh lungful of air. This was, of course, exactly when all hell broke loose.

Vulk smashed the back door closed, signalling two of our men to open the shutters on the lanterns they had been holding. This sent two streams of amber light piercing the hallway and rear door, catching the knights in perfect silhouette and temporarily blinding them.

With a thunderous roar, those men with revolvers opened up on the massed assassins, with short, insanely bright bursts of fire leaping out at the men and knocking them down one at a time like the childhood game of sticks and stones. Those of us with bladed weapons held back until the first pistol's hammer struck an empty chamber, meaning it was now our turn to do what damage we could to the surviving knights and allow the fire team time to reload.

Charging forward with a bellow, I struck the first Dragon I encountered hard with my shield, throwing him violently into the wall behind. Before he could recover, another of our men darted forward with an axe and hit him in the chest that sounded like a loud, wet thud.

I swung around looking for another opponent, making sure I led with the shoulder sporting my shield in a way I am sure would have pleased my old tutor, Xenophon. What I was not expecting to find was that the fight was already over. The few Dragons who had survived our initial gunfire had not been able to recover and had been overwhelmed during the second assault by the men with bladed weapons.

With no one to vent my rage and nervous energy on, I decided to inspect the knights who had been shot to ensure they would not be a problem in the future. I noted all had been strategically stabbed a few dozen times to ensure none of them were faking.

Once we were sure all the invaders had been dealt with, Vulk opened the rear door and loped out into the night. With one man who held a revolver and another with a sword and shield on guard, we started dragging bodies out into the night air and piling them up like sandbags to create some protection just in case another attack was to follow.

One of the men squawked and pointed deep into the dark where the stables and staff quarters where located when he saw two deep, green, glowing eyes moving towards our position. Men with revolvers soon took aim and I only just managed to stop them before they began firing. Out of the night ran Vulk's half-werewolf form. I was pretty sure the bullets would have done little damage to the werewolf, but why take the chance on angering the beast?

"I can sense no one else in that direction," Vulk said in his deep, rough voice.

"And what about the front garden, did you check what has been going on around there?" Abberline asked.

The werewolf just shrugged his shoulders.

With the rear door as secure as we could make it, and with men we could trust, Vulk, the Colonel, Abberline, and myself ran through the house to the front room. We needed to be ready for anything as the attack may have been a feint or part of some other nefarious scheme, so we charged into the front foyer with a whoop and weapons drawn. What we found were the men we had left still at their posts, happy to report nothing had happened during the fight at the back of the house.

It would seem the night was finally ours.

CHAPTER TWENTY-SEVEN

The dawn's first spear of sunlight in the sky ended the terror of the previous night. Unless one of us was foolish enough to get caught in a deep dark hole with a hungry vampire, that particular danger had passed for now, and I did not believe there were any more Dragon Knights hidden around the house to worry us.

With weapons drawn and from behind the safety of shields, the front door was unlocked and we emerged, blinking and grinning into the morning's warmth. First job was taking stock of what we had just undergone. There was blood everywhere; some of it dry and brown, while here and there red puddles of arterial blood pooled where someone had recently bled their life away. Wherever we had missed a small piece of a vampire from the fight we found only dark black smudges, evidence that the undead creatures did indeed burst into flames when hit by sunlight.

Here and there were the bodies of our dead, hidden away in lost corners of the estate where they had died in terror or with a curse on their lips, fighting to the very end with the hope someone, anyone would come and rescue them. Once again the remains of any Dragon Knights were gone, likely carried away by the men we had ambushed.

The second he was sure it was clear, Inspector Abberline sent a runner to the nearest police station with orders to bring back more men and doctors. Meanwhile the Colonel marched back inside the house and told the women to build a makeshift hospital and organise some hot food and tea. Sadly, the meal would be far smaller than the one required just ten hours earlier due to our numerous losses.

With everyone either busy or too exhausted to move, I gathered Sergeant Willkie and we both moved amongst the collected bodies of the dead, cutting the heads off anyone who hadn't already had the grisly act already done to them yet. This macabre work also gave us a chance to count everyone.

"We are missing three men," Willkie said when the final tally was completed.

"Are they the men who had originally been stationed at the back door with the traitors?" I asked, wiping gore from the head of the large axe I had been using.

"Damn, we are missing six men," the policeman sighed. "To tell the truth I had forgotten to add in the troops the General had supplied us with."

This was a good point and one that needed further investigation. Not all of the General's men had sided with the enemy. Many had stood and died with us, and others, such as Batten, were still with us. Did that mean they had been just as surprised when their former comrades had turned traitor, or were they part of some even more complex and nefarious scheme? Just who could we trust now, that we knew some of those who had been amongst us were not with us?

Soon hot tea arrived. It is amazing how optimistic one can become holding a mug of hot tea. Next came hot buttered rolls and plates of bacon and fried eggs. The men fell on the food like starving dogs and soon, the horrors of the night began to fade a little. Barely a word was uttered during the entire process of eating, just the occasional sigh or moan as the warm food entered an empty stomach, or an exploding flavour hit a tongue. The simple act of eating something so simple and familiar meant this meal was soon elevated into one of the greatest of our lives. I certainly know I have never enjoyed anything like that breakfast.

Food always was and always will be the great comforter in this world.

By the time servants had appeared and removed all the empty plates and mugs, the first bobbies Abberline had asked for began to arrive and reported directly to the Inspector. He sent them to guard the front gate and the lower level of the house. Though I was sure no vampire or Dragon had survived entering the house, it was far better to be safe than later sorry.

Two doctors arrived and soon after, an ambulance. The worst of our wounded were going to be hauled away to a hospital for care, but Abberline and the Colonel stepped in and made sure the instead stayed in the house and were well guarded. In my weary state, it took me a while to realise they did this for their protection as well as everyone else's. If anyone of the injured had received a bite during the fight they would likely be turning into ravenous vampires by nightfall and would need to be dealt with before they could do any harm. This explained why at least two of the policemen who had been with us during the night stayed with them. They at least knew what to do and would act if needed.

To my surprise, the Colonel also came through for us. He had sent a message to the local army barracks, commanded by a man he referred to as a near and dear old comrade. Not only did we have the police to protect us now, but two squads of infantry, armed with the latest, highly accurate and powerful Enfield rifles. There was also a small troop of Hussars, commanded by a young second lieutenant, who seemed a little too excited at the prospect of action.

It was obvious their overall commander, Captain Timothy Givens, had no intention of believing our story when we explained about our night's adventures, but he was under orders to follow the command of the Colonel.

Givens grumpily placed his units where the Colonel ordered, and allowed the cavalry to be stationed closer the house. From here they could be quickly deployed to any spot in or outside the estate if needed. I was not sure exactly when it was the young second lieutenant in charge of the horsemen had planted himself amongst us. Unlike his commander, he was clearly thrilled to be where there was the possibility of action, and did not want to miss a second of it.

By midday, the sun was high in the sky and everyone had caught their breath and most were starting to feel the aches and pains of the previous night's adventures. We had used the morning to sketch out a strategy for the rest of the day, and with the sun now at its highest point it was time to execute the next part of our plan.

CHAPTER TWENTY-EIGHT

Lt. Winston Churchill of his Majesty's 4th Hussars could barely contain his excitement at the plan we had come up with.

"Do you really think there is a nest in there?" he asked with a wide grin.

The time had come for me to lay my cards on the table … all of them. The few speculative threads I had been following at the start of this venture had begun to coalesce into near certainty with recent events. It was no longer fair for me to keep this information only to myself; at the very worst I could be killed, leaving everyone else involved in the dark as to what was going on and the entire world in real danger of being overrun by a plague of monsters. At best, I was wrong about everything and would be proven foolishly hysterical and laughed out of London. However, life being what it is and me being a man known for taking risks, this would not be the first time this had happened and I doubted it would be the last.

Abberline, Doyle, Stoker, Vulk, Willkie, Lt. Churchill, Colonel Stamford, and myself stood before the mansion's greenhouse with trepidation. About us streamed groups of men, all moving with purpose as Batten barked, threatened, and screamed out orders at them. Building on how we had tackled the enemy the previous night, small groups of men were placed at strategic locations about the greenhouse. Each group had at least two men carrying shields, others with modern weapons, and were further backed by troopers with edged weapons.

As our small army prepared to assault the greenhouse, I told those about me what I suspected had recently occurred on the Stamford estate. Inside the glass building was the General, who I was sure had been turned at some stage into a vampire, partly explaining his recent health recovery. This almost miraculous recuperation had been fuelled by the monster feeding at first on some of the bodies that had been recovered from around the estate when he had first been bitten, then more recently on those bodies, such as poor Jerome De Gois, that had been found during my time at the house.

Through what I already knew, along with the research we had

completed at the London Daily Gazette, I felt it was most likely that, during the Crimean War, when he was stationed in the former kingdom of Wallachia, General Stamford visited the island of Snagov.

Stamford was the fifth son of Captain Thomas Frederick Stamford, and after his schooling he accepted a second lieutenant's commission in the Royal Engineers. Stamford's first posting was to British-controlled Canada, where he carried out a survey to help solve a dispute over part of the border between that country and the United States.

Promoted to captain, Stamford returned to England and accepted an instructor's position at the Royal Military Academy. Later he was appointed the Inspector of the nation's railways in 1847, and here Stamford was involved in a number of investigations into railway accidents. Between all this he also managed to meet and marry his first wife.

It was as the Secretary of the Railway Department in the 1850s that Stanford helped organise an entirely new transportation system out of London, one that was very much needed to help relieve the pressure of the city's growing problem with graveyards. This would become the London Necropolis Railway.

It was while on leave from his position with the railways that Stamford had been traveling through Constantinople, just as Turkey declared war on Russia, triggering the Crimean War. Stamford immediately presented himself to the British Ambassador to the Ottoman Empire, Lord Stratford de Redcliffe, and offered his services.

The ambassador accepted and organised for Stamford to use his professional eye to report on the Turks defences against a modern military such as the Russians deployed. Awarded a captain's commission, Stamford was also offered the position of British commissioner to the Turkish army, and more specifically was asked to pass on military advice to the Ottoman general, Omar Pasha.

It was as the commissioner that Stamford assisted the Ottoman defence of Silistra, and during the following year he used his position to bring in a small core of men he knew and trusted, and these men became the nucleus of the well trained and thoroughly modern Ottoman army that Stamford took control of, and scored an important victory with at the Battle of Giurgevo in 1854. Here the Russian army crossed the Danube, catching the Ottoman army by surprise. Stamford rushed his troops into the breech and, leading from the front, charged the Russians. The fighting became so ferocious it eventually settled into hand-to-hand fighting, and a number of the British officers Stamford had brought in to lead this army were killed in the fighting. Despite these losses the Russians were eventually defeated and Stamford moved the army to join with the Pasha in time to fight at the Battle of Eupatoria, and he remained with them until the Siege of Sevastopol.

For his service, Stamford received the British war medal with clasp, the Turkish gold medal, the Turkish medal for Silistria, the third class of the order of the Mejidie, the Turkish Crimean medal, the French legion of honour, fourth class and the Sultan of Turkey presented him with a sword of honour and made him a major-general in the Turkish army.

After the war, Stamford was promoted to general as well as Commander of the Royal Engineers at Aldershot. Later he was named Inspector General of Fortifications, which likely explained why the Stamford estate looked so much like a fortress. He also returned to find his wife had died, and though the circumstances of Ellen Lintorn Stamford's death were not reported, the anger their son clearly felt suggested she had committed suicide.

Soon after his arrival home Stamford came down with a mysterious illness that had him bedridden and at death's door. Everyone assumed he had caught something from one of his numerous travels, or when he passed through the Pacific on the return voyage from the war, but I believed the truth to be far stranger than that.

It was in a newspaper from Australia that Stoker had found the single piece of evidence that possibly explained all that had occurred and why. The Hobarton Mercury, dated October 25th, 1854, carried a small story about the Crimean War. Australia was a major supplier of food and horses for the allied troops fighting in the north Pacific, so stories often reached this distant outpost of the Empire long before they were printed in London.

THE BATTLE OF GIURGEVO

The following details of the battle of Giurgevo will be read with interest: The news of the severe defeat which the Russians had sustained before Silistria appears to have fired the whole of the troops, and made them anxious to attack the enemy, who occupied Giurgevo, on the right bank of the river, with a force of about 25,000. The presence of several English officers, Captain Cannon, Captain Mansell, and Captain Stamford, Omer Pacha's aide-de camp, animated the troops still more; and they are reported to have earnestly petitioned to be led against the Russians

The intelligence which came in that the latter were in retreat seems to have determined Hassan Pacha and the English officers on a forward movement, and accordingly preparations were made for forcing the passage to the river, and giving battle to the Russians on the following day, Wednesday, the 5th. The Turks had only three large boats of which they could avail themselves in transporting their men to the other shore; but even with these slight facilities the passage was commenced at an early hour on the morning of the 5th. The enemy, by some means or other appear to have been aware of the intentions of the Turks, and only a few boat loads of troops had been carried over when they opened fire, both upon those who had landed and the reinforcements which were coming in. Not daunted by the discovery of their plan, though the Turks who had passed over were a mere handful as compared with the Russians, they gallantly returned the fire and strove to cover the landing of their comrades. For more than three hours the un-equal fight continued, the Russians principally directing their fire upon the boats of Turkish soldiers which were coming over, and among the crowded freights of which their bullets told with fearful execution.

It is said that at this time no less than 19,000 of the enemy were drawn up in line to oppose the landing, and at no period on Wednesday were there more than from 5,000 to 7,000 Turks opposed to them, counting even those who were firing from the boats on their passage across the river. The English officers, who were present all through the action, displayed the most consummate coolness and bravery; and the Turkish troops, having a confidence, which nothing could shake, hastened to follow them wherever they were led. From all that has been seen of the regular Turkish troops in this war, it is evident that they will follow English officers literally anywhere.

Their confidence in our courage and capacity nothing can shake, and I am certain that 5.000 Turkish soldiers, under an English general and officers, would cheerfully give battle to 30,000 of the enemy, and be themselves certain of success. It was in leading a charge against the Russians that poor Captain Stamford, of the royal engineers, received his death wound. His loss is very deeply deplored, as he was an officer who was both loved and respected by all the members of his profession. Only about a fortnight ago he had set out to assist in the defence of Silistria.'

The newspaper reported that Stamford had been killed at Giurgevo, yet somehow he had returned to London as healthy as the day he had left. Of course the Hobarton Mercury was not the largest newspaper in the world and it often printed stories told to its reporters by sailors and other visitors to that most southern of islands, so of course it is possible they had got the death of Stamford wrong. But what if the article was correct? What if the General had been killed, or at the very least grievously wounded in the Crimea? How did he then arrive home the paragon of health?

This was where my own knowledge helped highlight what may have occurred. I knew that the grave of Vladislaus Draculam had been raided just after his death, and that the Order of the Dragon had taken possession of the warlord of Wallachia's coffin. Years ago I had also noted the Order had suddenly become very active within Europe. The growing Crimean War seemed to have created a disturbance in the usually discreet order, and now the reason for this seemed clear. My understanding was someone had stolen the Impaler's coffin and the Order had been desperately trying to retrieve the holy relic.

It was my supposition that, while leading the attack against the Russians at Giurgevo, Stamford was gravely wounded. His men then returned to their camp in Wallachia, specifically near Lake Snagov, where they likely discovered the story of Vladislaus Draculam, and the possibility he had been reburied under the ruins of a monastery built on a small island there—a monastery Vlad himself had commissioned by the way. Following rumours about a number of miraculous recoveries of sick and dying people visiting the church,

Stamford's desperate men took the dying officer there, either for a miraculous recovery or to have the last rites read over him.

Something miraculous did indeed happen on that island and Stamford recovered. Most likely the men found Vlad's tomb and, as soldiers often do, they broke in to see if there had been any valuables buried with the former leader of Wallachia. What they found was the body of Vlad the Impaler who, though not strictly alive, was certainly far from dead. He was also very hungry.

Stamford and his men likely stole Vlad's coffin and shipped it home in 1857, via Australia, before being forwarded to England. At some point during this long journey, likely on the *Dunbar*, the coffin had been opened and the vampire inside escaped and decimated the crew before being recaptured or killed.

There was of course another possibility. It was not Vlad that had killed everyone on the *Dunbar* but the General himself. His body wracked by the burning need to feed that all vampires suffer from; he had escaped and begun feeding on the crew and passengers trapped on that tiny wooden island of horror struggling across the wide Pacific. By the time the *Dunbar* was approaching Port Jackson, there was not enough men to sail the vessel properly and she hit the rocky Sydney coastline, killing everyone not already dead except for a single sailor. The shipwreck had the added bonus of hiding the true carnage that had occurred on-board.

I took a breath and allowed the men listening in to my theory the chance to ask questions or add any information of their own. Most just stood there, mulling over what I had presented. I noticed both Doyle and Stoker were busy scribbling down something in their notebooks.

None of them had picked up the oddity of my address to the group, who seemed to doubt the General was involved. We now had two pieces of separate information that told us Stamford had supposedly died, during the war and as a passenger on the *Dunbar*. As shaky and unreliable as this evidence was, it was still evidence, and so could not be totally ignored. The Colonel remained adamant his father was sick from some tropical disease, so could not possibly be the vampire.

To be fair I also had some doubts myself, as there was a glaring problem with the theory. Why was the General all but an invalid when I first saw him in the greenhouse? Surely an illness caught in a wild corner of heathendom would not affect one of the undead, so likely there was something else going on.

Perhaps the General had not completely turned and even now the effects of the vampire's bite were wearing off, sending him back to the state he had been in before being bitten. Perhaps Draculam had not been released, and was laying in his coffin, awaiting the arrival of his sworn protectors, the Order of the Dragon, to retrieve him. These men could have found the General and somehow weakened him to the point of near death, perhaps using their medallions to capture or keep him under control. They could then have occasionally fed him, just enough to keep him alive and controllable, then searched the grounds for Vlad's coffin, or until the General finally gave up where he had hidden it. If this was the case, it would seem Vulk and I had arrived before they could find it—and thanks to our intervention the Brotherhood had retreated to the one place where they so far had found absolute privacy.

I was sure the Brotherhood had been incubating vampires to use as weapons. These they had collected inside the greenhouse through some ancient art, again possibly the silver amulets or some other arcane method, preparing to control the beasts to then eventually unleash upon us. Having failed with their main attack last night, I was positive this was the exact fate the Knights had planned for us once the sun fell in a few hours.

Despite this being mostly based on speculation, with my information we managed to come up with a plan of our own. Half the hussars dismounted their horses and pulled what weapons they had, mostly sabres—though a few had revolvers—and these men joined us outside the greenhouse. The rest remained on their horses, with orders to ride down anyone who tried to escape.

Once everyone was in place, the largest group of men, made up of soldiers, policemen and housemen, moved towards the front door of the greenhouse. This left the smaller group to move around and cover the rear.

As the large group moved closer to the structure, Lt. Churchill spoke up from behind his own sword. "If we all go in together like this, won't we just get in each other's way? Could I suggest we break into two groups and enter a few minutes apart? That way the second group can react to whatever circumstance the first group encounters, and either back them up or help them withdraw."

Accepting the suggestion, we split into two groups, with the first approaching the front door. Most of the Hussars, myself, and Vulk were with the first group as they were the most rested; Abberline, Colonel Stamford, Willkie, and the surviving men from the previous night were in the second as they knew what to expect and so would likely not run. Not a single man had refused to join us again. Clearly they wanted a chance to avenge their fallen friends against the creatures who had killed so many of their friends and colleagues.

"It comes down to the triarii," I whispered to myself, recalling the Roman tactic of leaving veterans to back up the younger, less-experienced troops in battle. Napoleon had used the same tactic with his famed Old Guard. It would seem young Churchill had a fine grasp of classical warfare tactics.

With everyone in place, Vulk raised an enormous axe over his head and bellowed a war cry I had not heard in centuries. Though not understanding the language, the first wave of men clearly understood the meaning of this challenge and charged into the greenhouse.

Once through the door the troops spread out, weapons pointing at every corner and shadow that could hold or hide a nightmare. Though the atmosphere within the plant room was still warm, it was no longer stifling, indicating we were only feeling the remnants of the heat that had once seemed to fuel General Stanford.

After ensuring the main potting room with the unlit coal blazer was assassin free, I ordered the large curtain that had always hid whatever was behind from view pulled down. As this occurred the second group of men entered the space and spread out. Sunlight lanced into the room through the open front door as these men entered, illuminating the glass panels at the rear of the room. Oddly, no one in the main house had ever noticed that the windowpanes in this part of the room behind the curtain had been painted over. I know I certainly had not, and I had specifically been walking that garden a number of times looking for anything out of the ordinary.

Nothing living stirred here either, though that was not to say there was no one there. Lying on the floor were two Dragon Knight corpses. Their bodies lay straight as arrows and their arms were folded over their chests. The silver amulets that normally hung around their necks were held in their cold, dead hands, perhaps to act as a talisman in the afterlife.

I removed my own amulet and tossed it to the Colonel, gesturing at him to put it on. I then removed the two amulets from the hands of the corpses to replace mine and to hand off to someone else—and immediately upon removal of the amulets both corpses came to life. The first awoke with something of a bewildered look on his face, but the second had no problems at all. He sprang off the floor, hands grasping and fanged mouth agape. I found myself staring at the monsters enormous canine teeth and could not shed the thought of how ironic our situation was. Just as the creature was about to wrap its hands around my neck, a steel shield was shoved between us. The former Knight collided with the weapon, and the momentum slammed us both to the ground.

The owner of the shield was a man called Bruce, one of the survivors who had been with us last night. I later confirmed at he had been ordered to shadow me, and was to go wherever I went and be ready to pull me out of whatever fire I inevitably fell into when needed. It would seem my friends were looking out for me.

Some of the new men still unaware of the danger charged into the fight and tackled the vampire. The creature reacted to the new threat by grabbing the first man and throwing him through one of the glass windows, and the second was killed when the monster just lashed out with a back fist, hitting him in the head at a strange angle and snapping his neck with a nasty, audible CRACK. The soldier's body went unnaturally stiff, before falling to the ground as limp as a marionette with its strings cut.

The vampire grabbed a third man and pulled him close. With powerful hands he forced the hussar's head back and, despite the soldier's struggles, bit deeply into the exposed neck and it began to feed.

While this was happening I took the opportunity to get back to my feet with the help of my new shadow, Bruce. Once I had my weapon at the ready I yelled at my saviour, "Try and pin the thing down with your shield, I'll go for the neck."

Bruce nodded he understood, then with a bellow he charged into the fight, throwing his full weight behind the shield and launched himself bodily like a child tucking their legs up and diving into a river. He hit both the vampire and the body of the dead soldier, and the impact managed to break the monsters right arm. The thing screamed and struck out with the ruined appendage, which simply flopped about like a wet fish. Bruce managed to keep the shield between himself and the vampire, allowing me to step in and take a swing with the sword I had retrieved from the floor. The blade cut through the air and stopped with a sudden, wrist-jarring thud into the creature's shoulder.

Bruce gave me a dirty look, as though I could do nothing right. "Want to try again Princess?" he growled as he struggled to keep the vampire in place.

"Sorry," I said, agreeing with his critique on my head-severing capabilities. I pulled at the sword, but it remained stuck, so I kicked at the vampire's head, and as the blow landed I yanked, freeing the blade.

"Now if you are through toying with the creature...?" Bruce grunted as the vampire's broken arm, already beginning to heal thanks to its recent feeding, began feebly swinging about and striking at the man's back. Fortunately it had no angle to wind up and do real damage.

"I am working on it...if you would just show a little patience..." I snarled back, hefting the sword over my head like some ancient statue depicting St George slaying the dragon. I then brought the weapon down with a noise similar to chopping into a thick cabbage. Blood fountained across my chest and face as the vampire's head rolled to the side, not entirely severed from the body. I lifted the sword again and finished the job, then returned at least one favour by helping Bruce to his feet. While I stood there, dripping in gore, the man barely had a mark on him, and the bastard grinned his approval at the situation.

Wiping blood from my face, I looked past the dead vampire and saw that the others had managed to kill the second vampire before it had even got off the ground. They had chopped it to pieces were then directed to do the same to the one we had just killed, so

Bruce and I stood back and watched them to get to work. A few quick strikes from the axes and the vampire was quartered, and the pieces were carried away to a fire someone had started in the garden. Like before, we were not taking any chances with the remains of these creatures.

From the floor of the garden shed, I retrieved the two dragon amulets and hooped one over my head, placing it clearly on my chest. I threw the second to Lt. Churchill, who looked at the amulet in his hand, then back at me with a questioning eyebrow. I told him to put it on, explaining many of us who had survived the recent attacks already had our own amulets, collected from the Dragon Knights we had killed earlier. I showed him the one I was wearing, and he wordlessly put it on. A smart lad that one, he'd go far.

To make sure there was nothing else in the room, in small groups we began fanning out to prod every corner with something pointy and sharp. It took less than five minutes to discover the entrance to the nest.

In the furthest corner of the room was a heavy wooden table, overturned and with all the legs broken off except one. We discovered the remaining leg could be used to help lever the table up, and underneath was a yawning black hole, wide enough for a man carrying something large to fit through. What light we could get to penetrate the chasm revealed crudely crafted wooden steps dropping down deeper into the abyss, one stride at a time.

"After you," Willkie offered with a flourish and a snappy bow from the waist. "It's your show, after all."

Collecting the shield from Bruce and making sure its strap was nice and tight on my forearm, I took the first step down into the nest. Directly behind followed two hussars, their sabres gleaming brightly over my shoulder as they caught the daylight streaming through the front door.

Trying to keep as much of my body behind the shield as possible, and wishing my vison would adapt to the dim light of the stairwell quicker, I gingerly took the steps one at a time. Though my vision is far better than those following—one of the few advantages from my long, chequered past—it proved so dark down the hole that I was determined to ensure my footing underneath was secure before levering my weight forward and down.

As we steadily crept further downwards in this slow, ponderous manner, behind the three of us came the rest of the hussars followed by Vulk, who for some odd reason had not seemed all that keen to be in the front line during this little excursion. Only later did I realise he had little intention of changing forms with so many new faces about, almost all of who were heavily armed. A werewolf did not live as long as Vulk had without being a little cautious in certain situations.

After eight or nine steps down my eyesight finally began to adjust and I could make out what we were walking into. Before me stretched a railroad tunnel, one that ran directly underneath the Stamford estate. The Order of the Dragon had clearly tapped into this tunnel to help them move about and keep their vampire charges out of direct sunlight. The simplicity of the plan was stunning, and I felt something of an idiot for not thinking of it before, especially after scoffing at similar suggestions made by my companions in the Brookwood Cemetery.

At the bottom of the crude stairwell those of us first down the hole gathered around and set ourselves to move forward. The cool dark tunnel running both to the left and right was beyond unnerving, and I thought we were going to need Vulk's heightened senses to help us find the path the assassins had taken. This idea was proven wrong when, of all people, Sergeant Willkie pointed the way. As a unit we moved on, and it took me a few minutes to see what sign the policemen was following to ensure we were on the correct trail. Though there were no footprints, there were faint lines in the dirt indicating where something, most likely a body, had been dragged.

The faint light that bled into the tunnel from the hole behind us, as well as through a junction and a distant access gate was extremely weak so, for the most part, we made our way along in the near dark by feeling our way with hands outstretched and feet prodding forward like the tentacles of some deep sea cephalopod. More than once we all jumped in fright at the shrieking crash of metal hitting the ground as someone caught a toe and pitched forward, dropping their weapon during the desperate attempt to catch themselves before they hit the floor. Needless to say, we were not the quietest secret attack force I have ever been part of.

These difficulties were confined to the human elements of our party. Once Vulk had entered the tunnel he walked through it with an envious assuredness we all envied him for. You had to know him well enough to see he had undergone a slight transformation, only enough so that his senses were heightened, but not enough for anyone in the dark to notice he was a werewolf. With brashness he stepped out in front and picked the path for us to follow, making sure we gave the worst obstacles in the tunnel a wide berth. With his heightened eyesight, the werewolf could see into the darkest shadow, and kept rumbling quiet assurances that we were still alone. With Vulk with us I knew we had no real cause to fear the dark—but the others did not have this assurance. Regardless, my inside knowledge did little to stop even me from being frightened of these creatures of the dark.

CHAPTER TWENTY-NINE

Only a dead man could have missed it, and even then I really doubted it.

Despite the pitch darkness, it was obvious when we began approaching the nest. It was the smell, … that fetid smell of rot and death that assailed us mercilessly.

Many of us tied handkerchiefs over our faces and tried to breathe solely through our mouths, but this only offered the smallest relief from the odour. My nose began running and my eyes teared up as though I had cut up a thousand onions, though, in all honesty, the atmosphere was nowhere near as pleasant as that.

As bad as it was for us, for the hypersensitive werewolf it was far worse. I had never seen Vulk ill, but his miraculously good health took a real beating down in that hellish pit. He even vomited at one stage, and he made it clear that such an unknown sensation did not agree with him at all. Who knew a werewolf could behave as a child?

Willkie signalled for us to stop, as we had arrived at a position in the tunnel where it had grown colder and the darkness, if at all possible, had become even blacker. Here we also found our first corpse.

Willkie struck a match and in the dim flickering light we could see the body was covered with insects. Rats and whatever else was crawling or skittering around the nest and our feet had also clearly feasted upon it. Unsurprisingly, the body was missing its head and that helped confirm my suspicions.

Though the Dragons seemed to worship vampires, or at the very least were keen to retain control of them through the use of their silver amulets, they did not seem to want the creatures multiplying and running loose. They seemed happy to select vampires that they could control, explaining why any bitten victims had been dragged away before they could turn. This was likely to keep them a secret weapon solely under their control. Vampires on the loose would destroy their monopoly.

Moving on, we soon found two more bodies, each in as bad a state as the first. Both were also missing their heads, yet despite this, a Stamford man pushed forward and claimed to recognise one of the bodies as a neighbour that had gone missing from just outside the estate a few weeks ago.

In the gloom Vulk spotted a side tunnel that had a steep downward grade to it. We completed our inspection of the main tunnel before heading down any further, ensuring no nasty surprise could sneak up behind us.

Entering into the second tunnel, it was clear this was not part of the original train line. It was much narrower and the walls and ground were more rudimentary in their definition. To me it was obvious the Knights had been busy digging more tunnels to expand their access about the estate. As we walked deeper it also became obvious that this part of the tunnel had some slight form of illumination, one that began to grow with intensity the deeper we went, until a definite halo of light could be seen before us. It was an odd form of illumination, and my brain had to work overtime to determine what it was we were looking at. I finally realised we were looking at a bend in the tunnel, with the light source still situated on the far side of the curve.

Weapons were drawn, shields were presented, and pistols appeared in hands as if by magic. The soldiers drew their sabres, and those wicked-looking long knives twinkled as they reflected what little available light there was, casting weird flashes across the wall in front of us and scaring the hell out of everyone on more than one occasion. The mind can be a real bastard at times. The horrors it can produce are often more devastating than the real horrors that populate the world. Unfortunately that was not the case here.

One of our number managed to creep up to the edge of the curve in the tunnel, without giving us away, to take a quick glance around the bend. He then signalled back to us and, though his gesture was not very clear in the inky blackness, it seemed like he held up five fingers indicating that there were at least five men on the other side of the curve.

For a second I thought we were in real trouble until the realisation struck it was doubtful many, if any of the five, were vampires. Those creatures did not seem to retain much intelligence, so I could not envision a scenario where a number of them were standing around having a chat.

It was Churchill who slipped forward and managed to get the first decent look, and he came back to us with a plan. Gathering most of the men about him, in a voice barely audible, the Hussar informed us there were five Dragon Knights in the room. A few seemed to be working, while the rest were standing guard over a number of large crates. He said they appeared big enough to house at least one vampire within each crate.

We had found the nest.

Churchill's plan was simple enough, and even now I am not sure how it eventually went so wrong. Vulk charged into the room in man-wolf form. I can tell you it was certainly a treat to stand next to Churchill and his fellow Hussars as they watched their first werewolf transformation. To give them their due though, they stood, watched, and remained willing to follow the werewolf into battle. Those men had the discipline that helped the English Empire span the globe.

In man-wolf form, Vulk quickly bounded the distance that spanned between our group and the five Dragon Knights. He then managed to keep them occupied long enough for the next line of men to move into the space and follow him into the battle. These men were to engage those Knights not already dead and help cover the next group containing the men with revolvers. The group with revolvers was to ignore the fight and keep an eye out for vampires. Bringing up the rear were those of us who were exhausted and or wounded. Some of us were getting a little tired of fighting the undead, the newly dead, as well as any ancient European cult hanging about and we were just happy to let others have a go for a while. In other words, Abberline, Doyle, Stoker, the Colonel, and myself brought up the rear of the contingent.

By the time the Hussars reached the battle, it was almost over. Vulk had leapt into the midst of the Knights, knocking them over like a game of rugby with the Knight's heads used in place of a rugby ball. Almost faster than the eye could track, he then grabbed the first man's head and twisted, breaking his neck. He was then on to his next victim before the first had even hit the ground.

The soldiers took over, surrounding the few Dragons who remained and cutting them down with raining sweeps of their long blades. As an assassination tool the gloves the knights wore were good for creating fear and paranoia and spread the legend and myth of vampires, but against trained soldiers with revolvers and swords, they were next to useless.

When we were sure all the Dragons were dead and beheaded, we moved on to the crates. One soldier gingerly reached out and took hold of the lid to the first, while the rest of us surrounded it and prepared to strike at whatever was inside.

When we all gave him a nod of readiness, the man took a deep breath, let it out slowly, then opened the latch and swung the crate lid open.

ourselves in the more confined space. The men with shields stood at the front, those with sabres behind followed by more men with shields. Those with blades included Stoker and Willkie; the latter looked grim and determined as he hefted a retrieved Hussar's sword. Behind them stood Abberline, the Colonel, Vulk, and myself ready to leap into the fray wherever we could do the most good.

This plan was a good one while we were in the confines of the fresh tunnel since it was so narrow, and likely it would have worked if the vampires had not been ready for us when we came out of it. As we exited the narrow tunnel and began the slow retreat back up the main tunnel to the stairs, an unseen vampire that I assume had been waiting for just this move hit us from some dark recess and attacked Batten. The former soldier had been instrumental once again with keeping us in formation, so Vulk was on this new threat in an instant. Both werewolf and vampire were soon entwined in a vicious battle, though not before two of our men lay dead after getting caught in their fight.

As the two monsters tore each other apart, Abberline called out to the survivors on the shield wall to concentrate on the danger before them. I heard something moving behind us and, as I turned about to investigate, was hit from something that felt like it was made of iron. Hands gripped my shoulders and hefted me into the air and I felt something cold on my neck. Another vampire had been in the tunnel and had attacked as the confusion in our ranks spread.

This initial hit had scrambled my thoughts, though I do recall feeling the beast holding me in its unbreakable grip, its teeth piercing my neck and it beginning its deep drink of my own blood. I could do little but struggle and flop about in a fruitless attempt to escape its clutches, yet within seconds of the attack the vampire withdrew its teeth and screamed in pain. I used this opportunity to wrest myself free and to regain my footing.

Spinning about, I looked into the face of one of one of our own men known as Willie the Dandy, though the eyes of this creature could not be confused with the man I had met earlier in the day. These eyes belonged to a wild beast, and Willie's cold, unblinking stare showed no warmth of intellect, only the emotionless, unthinking quality of a mindless predator.

Clutching at his throat with one hand, Willie the vampire's

other hand pawed at his mouth as though trying to remove something distasteful from his tongue. The gurgling noise from deep within his throat was evidence that he, rather, it was in great distress.

I pushed the creature a few steps back with a hard shove, then, by way of an explanation, said, "I am the punished." I then swung my axe in a wide arc up, and then brought it down, striking Willie in the knee. Though it felt like I had just hit a rock, the blade was razor sharp and carried enough momentum to sever the joint. Willie the Dandy would have been mortified at the state this left his expensive trouser leg if he was capable of thinking about such things anymore.

Willie the vampire crashed to the floor, thrashing about not so much in pain but more like a lion with a leg caught in a trap. Ignoring the poison that now seared its way through his body, along with his own ruined limb, Willie flayed about in an attempt to clutch at anything within reach to draw it in to kill and feed upon. Fresh blood meant rejuvenation.

I stepped away and gingerly touched my neck. Already, the fang holes had closed and the bleeding stopped. With care I wiped the blood off my hands, improving my grip. I then took up the axe again, raised it over my head, waited until the vampire overextended itself reaching for me, and then let loose with another blow. The heavy blade caught the vile creature across the back of the neck, severing the spine with a wet thud. Instantly, Willie the vampire slumped on the ground, its his body twitching, so I struck again just in case the thing's unnatural ability to recover from injury healed this wound as well. A third blow removed Willie the vampire's head entirely from the body, and as a final indignity I booted the severed head further down the tunnel.

Turning back to the main fight, I watched as the men on the shield wall pushed forward and struck at the vampires that had trailed us from the coffin room. These had obviously finished with the men we had been forced to leave behind and were now searching for new victims. I looked about but could find no sign of Vulk or the vampire he had been fighting.

I caught Abberline's attention and shrugged my shoulders as though to ask 'Where is he?' The policeman pointed to what I had taken to be a solid wall, but instead found another corridor hidden by shadow. This is likely where the two vampires who had attacked us in the tunnel had been hiding.

Retrieving a discarded lantern that had managed to remain alight, I entered this new side tunnel and immediately slipped on skin, fur, and more blood than I thought possible for a body to contain.

Inside the space I found Vulk, who was still in man-wolf form. He was covered in a dozen cuts and had a large piece of flesh torn from his right forearm, in what I took to be a bite. His other arm was wrapped around the vampire's chest, his clawed hands digging deep into flesh while holding the creature in place. The werewolf was also biting the vampire's throat, and if I did not have first-hand knowledge of how unnaturally vital these vampires were, I would have though it improbable for the creature to still be alive. It was missing its right arm, and the left hung limply by its side, broken. It was missing a foot, and I found myself wondering how Vulk had managed to do that? The clean edge of the cut suggested one of our men had got in a lucky strike with a bladed weapon, perhaps trying to help the werewolf defeat his foe.

The creature's remaining limb seemed to be in working order and, as I lifted the lantern high to throw light across this part of the tunnel, I watched the leg twitch and flap about, trying to gain some purchase on the ground or the wall. If it could succeed in this, I predicted the vampire had a chance of levering itself free from the werewolf's grip.

With few alternatives, I placed my foot on the leg to keep it in place and hit it with the axe, as though cutting firewood. The blade cut through meat and bone, and buried itself in the tunnel's dirt floor beneath.

The shock of the wound and the loss of even this small amount of leverage gave the man-wolf the opening needed to end the fight. Vulk quickly repositioned the vampire in his powerful arms and began to literally chew the creature's head off. It was one of the most impressive and disturbing sights I have ever seen in my long, eventful life.

Knowing there was little I could do to help, and knowing the werewolf's inhuman metabolism would have him back on his feet in no time, I headed back into the main tunnel. Our line was still holding off the remaining vampires with weapon thrusts whenever they approached the wall. I moved in behind and added my blade to the fight. "We need to hold here until Vulk can re-join us."

"He's still alive?" Doyle called out. I had been unaware the doctor was still with us and had feared he'd been one of the fallen.

"Very much so, and he took another vampire down for us. That just leaves the ones here, though the Order may have one or maybe two more hidden somewhere."

"Let's not forget the General and Draculam, if what you suggested is true," Abberline growled, as he swung his sword, halting a new vampire charge. I should have figured the Inspector would be keeping track of all suspects and victims. "And don't forget those men who have just been bitten. I am sure there must be a chance some of those we left behind will likely turn, I mean it's not like we have had any other sort of luck other than bad luck so far, is it?"

"Alright, there are likely a lot more vampires then these. You really know how to ruin a man's sunny disposition, don't you Inspector?"

I thrust my axe over the shoulder of the man bearing a shield before me, catching a charging vampire in the cheek, forcing it to take a few steps back. I then jumped when a bloody hand fell on my shoulder. Turning about, axe at the ready to decapitate the devil himself if I found him standing there, I only just managed to still my swing when I recognised Vulk.

Barely standing, the werewolf sagged against the tunnel wall, so I moved and ducked under his shoulder, heaving him to his feet. Even in human form, the werewolf was incredibly heavy, but still I was made of some stern stuff myself, and I began carrying him down the tunnel, calling out behind me, "Let's get out of here!"

Abberline and Churchill barked orders, and Batten made sure the shield wall retired in good order so that the two surviving vampires could not break through our defensive line. The move was reminiscent of Roman legionnaires travelling across a battlefield with linked shields, or perhaps even Spartan hoplites. Having actually seen those men in their red cloaks and bronze shields and helmets creep across a battlefield was an image I would never forget.

Without another incident or ambush, we reached the stairs

leading up to the Stamford greenhouse. After careful manoeuvring, we managed to get everyone upstairs without anyone being bitten. The sunlight streaming through the hole forced the vampires to remain in the depths of the tunnel so, for now at least, we were safe.

"Any sign of my father?" Colonel Stamford asked.

"None, I think he somehow escaped before we even got down there. I would have bet he was in one of those crates. We need to question all of his men and find out if he owns any more properties within the city. If he does, maybe the Knights moved him there."

"Sounds like a job for Scotland Yard," Willkie said, before stalking off to question the Stamford household again. Abberline wordlessly followed his sergeant, and the rest of us tried to barricade the tunnel mouth as best we could. There were still a number of hours of sunlight left in the day, so we had little fear of attack from here until nightfall. Still, always better to be safe than sorry.

While our Scotland Yard representatives tried to figure out our next move, I took a walk with Vulk into the garden. The old wolf was looking the worse-for-wear after our adventure, and though his stamina was beyond anything even remotely considered natural and his body capable of recovering from even the most fatal of wounds, I could tell he had reached his limit.

I was contemplating asking if he wanted to leave, but the werewolf pre-empted me.

"This has gone beyond a job. Those things have almost killed me three times now, and twice they got close enough to worry me. I think while we have this opportunity to rid the planet of such an evil once and for all, we need to."

His revelation came as something of a shock to me. Had the werewolf been thinking such things about his own curse on the world?

I never looked at him, just continued to walk alongside Vulk in the delicious sunlight. I had not been so glad to see the sun and so scared of the night since I walked my own garden all those years ago. It was amazing how different things can feel with a friend by your side.

CHAPTER THIRTY-ONE

We were happy to sit in the afternoon sun and take a breather. Batten and Churchill appeared from out of a work shed, spotted us, and headed over.

"Thought we had lost you down there," I told Batten, who I was sure had been killed a number of times during the fight.

"Me? It will take more than a toothy weasel like those buggers to knock me off," he said as he pulled one of the Knights silver medallions from under his jacket brandishing it. I suddenly thought that if this vampire problem were to continue for much longer I was going to have to investigate those medallions and try to uncover their secrets.

"How can we help you, Sergeant?"

"I assume we will not be going down there again today?" the old soldier asked, indicating the greenhouse and the tunnel it contained.

"Not if we can help it."

"Then I can assume we will likely get a few unwanted visitors again tonight?" Batten asked.

I thought about that for a second.

"I would say so. Whatever it is the Order is looking for I do not think they have found it yet. Judging by how much work has gone into these tunnels and the access they provided I don't think we have seen all of the Knights either."

I was also certain the Order would return with a new crop of vampires from those men we lost down the hole, and that they would set them loose on us.

"Well, I have a few ideas to create a warm welcome for them, plus we can dust off some old tricks that I have learned over the years, most admittedly the hard way." I was sure there was an interesting story behind that last statement, but Batten did not look like he was going to expound on this further, though I did offer a suggestion.

"I think you talk to the Colonel then, this is his house after all, and any help I believe would be appreciated and necessary."

Churchill was also keen for a rematch. "I need to explain to my commander what happened to my men. Hopefully, I will be back with more troops and a few surprises of our own later."

"You are seriously going to tell your commanding officer that the men he left in your charge were killed by a vampire?" Vulk asked, unable to hide the wry smile on his face.

"I am—luckily Captain Lent was a former junior officer under Colonel Stamford, so a letter from him will go a long way to smoothing that particular issue over," he said, patting a shirt pocket where I assumed the letter was hidden away.

"We will see you back here later then," I said, not quite dismissing them. Both men walked away to complete their missions and I returned to enjoying the afternoon.

Refusing to head back into the gloomy house, I eventually found a shady spot under a tree in the garden. With the day's warmth acting as a blanket, I fell asleep on the manicured grass. I have no idea how many hours I slept, but when I awoke the tree's shade had shifted and my legs lay in bright sunshine. Feeling hot and thirsty, I got up and went searching for a glass of water or three. If I found something stronger in the meantime, well, all the better.

The house was quiet, and I assumed everyone was catching some much-needed sleep. There were few bobbies on guard to ensure there were no nasty surprises from any surviving Dragon Knights. I recognised none of them, indicating Abberline was still on the case to get more men. The policemen let me enter the house with just a nod of welcome, so they had been told who I was.

Inside I found Vulk devouring a feast of sausages and an entire roast chicken. He looked far more alive than when I had last laid eyes on him. A bit of food and a little rest seemed to be doing wonders for his recovery.

"Where is everyone?" I asked, sitting next to him with a mug of hot tea laced with honey.

"Most are asleep. Stoker and Doyle went home."

"I can't believe they both survived again. They are both remarkable young men."

"They did very well, even managed to take one of those damned bloodsuckers out by themselves."

"It would seem we are becoming quite band of cutthroats."

"You would know!" Vulk said, hinting at my dark past.

Refusing to take the bait, I pointed out: "If we come under attack tonight, we will need better weapons than last time." The loss of the men with handguns had cost us during the fight. Once the vampires took those away from us, we were all but defenceless. "This time, everyone needs to be armed with at least a revolver…"

"…and a shield—did you ever think you would pick up a shield again?"

"It has been centuries. I think I was with the Pendragon the last time I used one in battle."

"The more things change," said Vulk. The line meaning so much more to those of us who had seen centuries pass as though they were months.

I managed another nap after cleaning myself up. It was good to get the previous night's gore removed. Rested and in clean clothes, I tried to locate the Stamfords, but could only find the Colonel, who was with the household men. Many of those who had stood with us carried wounds, and a few of these were grievous, perhaps even mortal.

I seemed to have misjudged the good Colonel. He had brought in a doctor to ensure the wounded were getting the best care possible. He had taken over earlier from Dr Doyle, who had been working non-stop on the men's injuries until he was almost to the point of passing out from fatigue.

When I asked about getting more weapons, Stamford explained it was all under control. I assumed the old soldier knew what he was doing, as he would have professional contacts to acquire said arms. I enquired about his family, and he told me they were all safe and sound, though he would not expand on this. It would seem he still had not forgiven my original ruse when entering his household, so I left to see if I could find someone else to ignore me.

As the sun dropped lower in the sky, the Stanford estate became a hive of activity. Soldiers filed through the front gate and set up a camp more akin to something you would see during a campaign in Africa; camp chairs, tables, wagons, and a number of policemen and their senior officers. I was watching these men unloading some heavily laden carts when Stoker found me.

"Doyle will be here later," he said. "Apart from being exhausted, he said that he wanted to look something up. I also may have some news, though I may wait until Doyle returns before I pass it on."

Time is a strange animal when you are waiting for action. It creeps as slow as a snail, and then, when you think you cannot stand the waiting any longer, it suddenly speeds up like a locomotive at full bore. This phenomenon was no more apparent than when that moment while we sat there, eyes on the sun, which seemed to just hang above the distant horizon for an hour, before quite suddenly it dropped like a stone.

As the last sliver of sun disappeared behind the trees to the west, Batten appeared amongst the gathered men and began organising everyone once more. This time we would not rely on lamps to illuminate the estate's grounds, as they had proven too easily extinguished. Instead, the staff prepared large bonfires across the garden, especially around the greenhouse and its entrance. To keep the fires fed; the men had lined up large piles of firewood close by, ready to be fed into the flames. As the day died and the last sliver of sun dipped away, the bonfires were lit and the men took up their assigned positions—whatever their assigned positions were. I believe I slept through this part of the planning.

There must have been fifty soldiers lined up around the greenhouse, all wearing similar uniforms to the Hussars. I assumed that either Churchill or the Colonel's letter had made our case with whatever senior officers had agreed to send us the men. Batten had split the troopers into teams of fifteen; with five men at the front with shields that had been happily hanging on army barrack walls just a few hours ago. Most shields had similar symbols on their faces, either painted or embossed, that resembled the patches the soldiers wore on their chests. Behind the shield carriers stood another five men, with some sporting a bladed weapon such as a sword or pike. Behind this line stood men with Martini-Henry rifles slung over their shoulders. I had experienced what these new weapons were capable of in Africa, and was aware they could fell an elephant at some distance. This guaranteed they would leave a big hole in any vampire they hit. Every single man also had a pistol belted to his hip.

A corporal with an impressive walrus moustache handed us each a pistol from a wheelbarrow brimming with similar weapons. We filled our pockets with cartridges, and then made sure the weapons were loaded. I left Stoker to retrieve the shield and axe I had been hefting earlier; both had proven to be lifesavers.

I returned to stand beside Stoker when Abberline and Lt. Churchill joined us. The young officer looked unflustered from the day's preceding activities.

"Gentlemen," I said, propping myself against the wall to the house we all had been holding up out of fatigue. "What sport do you have installed for us tonight?"

"Pretty much the same as last night, though this time I think the odds are more in our favour," Abberline said, indicating the red-coated soldiers everywhere.

I had not noticed that Vulk had joined us until the werewolf added, "Depending, of course, on our foe. Perhaps we have hurt them to the point they will not be able to mount any sort of offence tonight."

It was only as the sky darkened and the orange light from the bonfires started playing across the garden that I noticed five small tents placed around the greenhouse and the main entrance. I was about to ask Churchill about these when I spotted Doyle entering the garden. Two soldiers flanked the doctor; men I assumed had been posted to guard the front gate.

There had been such a large, obvious soldier presence around the estate all afternoon that I doubted the Order of the Dragon would try anything, especially anything like last night. There were far too many men on guard for the Order to be capable of slipping into the compound the way they had earlier. Instead, I was of the opinion that if they had anything planned, they would come from the tunnels. Our defences reflected this belief, with the majority of our men facing the greenhouse, and a few keeping an eye on the rest of the grounds.

Of course, once again we had completely misunderstood the situation and underestimated our foe. The Order of the Dragon had more operatives than we had believed, and in the few hours since our retreat from the nest, the Order had been busy. Like us, the dozen or so survivors we had missed had spent the day collecting and preparing.

One minute there was joking and friendly banter as Doyle reached us and we assured his guards the doctor was with us, and the next we were all scrambling for our lives.

CHAPTER THIRTY-TWO

It had been a long, quiet afternoon since we came out of the nest, and it looked like we would have a long quiet night. The only activity was from the men charged with keeping the fires burning as they occasionally picked up a log and consigned it to the flames. Fatigue was tugging at my eyelids, and as the time ticked past midnight I considered heading to bed and leaving the younger men to stand guard. After taking a short walk, I approached my companions to let them know of my decision; however, I stopped short. Vulk was looking hard at the dark entryway to the greenhouse door; I don't think he even knew I was standing next to him. His focus was that intense.

I was about to say something stupid and annoying when the werewolf suddenly squinted, then bellowed, "TO ARMS!"

Before anyone could react to this the greenhouse exploded, as more vampires than I thought could possibly exist boiled out of the shattered doors and windows. It would seem the surviving Knights had spent the last few hours running through the darkening streets of London and stealing people who they brought to the few vampires we had not killed earlier. Then, using their medallions I assumed, they managed to get these beasts to feed, converting their newest victims into an army of starving, mindless killers.

I watched with something akin to awe as the first vampire sprinted forward and hit one of the platoons head on, only to rebound off the shield wall. It quickly climbed back to its feet and leapt forward again, reached under the shield wall and grabbed one of the soldiers by the leg. Instantly swords and pikes fell on the creature, pinning it to the ground. A volley of rifle fire followed this up.

Shattered, broken and bleeding, the vampire was easily despatched with a blow to the neck. Tragically, this was about as good as the night got for us.

Seeing the first squad attacked by one of these monsters, the others steeled themselves. This attitude helped them not one bit when a number of figures crawled out of a smashed window before them. Seeing these, the soldiers froze in bewilderment and dawning horror.

"They're kids," someone yelled.

Men trained to fight and protect ran forward, ready to scoop up these children and move them out of harm's way. It was only as the first soldier reached them that he pulled up and yelled. "Wait, they're…"

The man never got to finish his words as one child leapt up and tore his throat out. His body slumped to the ground like a ragdoll and was instantly set on by the children, who bit and tore their way into his body and began feeding.

The Knights had raided a spike. I could tell the children had come from one of these low-grade poorhouses by the uniform quality of their clothing. Where they had found a workhouse full of youngsters, I cannot imagine, but it is not as though they were short of choices in London. Why they had done so was also obvious. If their plan had been to spread chaos amongst our troops, they had succeeded.

Seeing the tiny children charging out of the greenhouse, the soldiers hesitated, afraid the cherubs were fleeing the horror and not actually part of it. By the time everyone realised they were monsters, the tiny vampires had killed eight men and had torn a large hole in our now less-than-organised lines.

"Churchill!" I yelled, taking a guess at what was coming next.

"Well this has gone to hell," the Lieutenant said, taking a shot with his pistol. "What is up?"

"I do not know about you but if I was planning this attack, right about now, while we are all running around like foxes chasing chickens, this would be a good time to hit us."

Churchill looked at me, looked at the scene before us, then back at me.

"Shit!"

Running to the tents, the Lieutenant barked orders, which were picked up and relayed by men throughout the garden.

As though on cue the real vampires, those who had fed and were stronger than a rhino, charged out of the greenhouse. I did not even have the time to yell a warning before the flaps on the five garden tents were pulled back, revealing not only their occupants, but also the little surprise that Churchill had been saving.

With a master-at-arms screaming, "FIRE", the fuses of two small swivel guns, normally found on the deck of a warship and used as anti-personnel weapons, were lit. Grapeshot - dozens of musket-ball-sized shot wrapped into a tight bundle—exploded out of both guns, and the effect was nothing short of spectacular. Both charges blossomed and expanded upon leaving the barrels, catching two of the vampires in a deadly firestorm.

Despite the grapeshot shredding their bodies, both creatures still had enough desire to claw at the smouldering earth around them with whatever appendage still worked in an attempt to creep forward and snag a victim to feed on.

The noise from the swivel guns had been so loud it took time for my ears to adjust, and when they finally did, I could hear a chatter-chatter coming from the second surprise the army had been hiding in those tents. With their three-man crews sweeping the weapons back and forth across the face of the greenhouse, large, multi-barrel Gatling guns that chewed apart a number of the smaller vampires, along with the remnants of the two caught by the swivels, whose own crews were taking this reprieve to reload.

Every thirty seconds or so one of these machine guns fell silent, its crew snapping out the now-empty magazine and ramming a fresh one home. The gunner would then start cranking the gun back to life with the big handle on its side. Beside each tent were small squads of men with an NCO, who directed the gun and then ordered small squads forward to decapitate any vampire that had been brought down.

I watched from the rear of the action as teams of men converged on the lonely figures of the incapacitated vampires, which often still had enough vitality to roar and strike out like a trapped tiger. One by one these monsters fell to the guns and blades of the soldiers and constables, who hacked apart any creature with even the remotest spark of life still in it. And with that the battle was over.

Batten and a Hussar sergeant stalked across the garden, ordering men to decapitate all the bodies they found and to search every shadow and hole, ensuring no vampire had escaped. The fires had started to die out during the brief fight, and now men returned to feed the flames until the estate was alight and flickering with elongated shadows.

Getting on with the grizzly task, the bodies of the dead were fed into the flames. After some time I noticed more than one hard-eyed soldier with tear-striped, soot-covered face tenderly carrying the broken body of a child. These too were dropped into the flames, giving them a last moment of warmth in what had proven to be a cold, bloodthirsty world.

After about an hour, the ghastly task was done and we reflected on what had occurred. Five more full-blood vampires lay dead, along with two dozen children. It did not lift anyone's spirits when Stoker pointed out, rightly or wrongly, that the children had been dead long before they ever entered the fight.

From out of the surrounding gloom, Dr Doyle appeared, carrying a number of papers and a notebook. He looked at me and the others standing about and said, "We need to talk."

CHAPTER THIRTY-THREE

Back in the Colonel's office, I watched Doyle and Stoker spread out the papers the Doctor had brought with him.

"I think I know what is going on," Doyle said, pointing to a large book he had brought with him. "I have an extensive library on the supernatural world, and as a spiritualist I have looked into the history of Vampyres. With all that has gone on in the last few days and my research, I have come to a remarkable conclusion."

"And that is?" Abberline asked.

"General Stamford is not a vampire."

"Well, that will require some explaining," I prompted.

"We have seen the unnatural strength and stamina of these creatures, even those that have either only recently been bitten, or have not fed for some time."

"True, but what has that to do with anything?" Churchill asked, not catching on.

"I have it," I admitted. "If the General had been bitten, why was he so infirm during our meetings? Even starving, he should have been far more energetic. He was infirm because he was not a vampire."

I mulled the thought over a bit more. "That effect could have been due to the Knights perhaps controlling him with their amulets." I pointed at my chest, my finger tapping the large disk I wore under my shirt. "Yet the fact that he was talkative and lucid, that is more than enough proof to prove your point. All the vampires we have seen seem little more than animals and incapable of stringing a sentence together, much less holding an articulate conversation."

Doyle nodded his agreement. "I have read a number of medical briefs from a physician called Richard Lower about the blood transfusion experiments he performed a century ago. Though these were only moderately successful in transferring blood between animals, and though he claimed to have never succeeded with a human, the theory seems sound. I am of the opinion we may be looking at a similar case here."

"Claimed?" Stoker asked, writing something down in his own notebook.

"There is a rumour Pope Innocent VIII fell ill and a physician called Giacomo di San Genesio completed the first blood transfusion to save the pontiff's life. Genesio transfused the blood of three ten-year-old boys, all of whom mysteriously died during the operation."

"And the Pope?" Stoker did not even look up from his writing when he asked this.

"He died too. Though there are rumours he did not die but became one of the undead, and was later killed."

Through all this something had been causing Batten to think up a storm, judging by the way his eyebrows were furrowed. Finally he asked, "They're transferring the blood of animals into the General?"

The houseman had entered the room to report that the estate had been cleaned of body parts, and the troops where back in formation. I had not even seen him enter the room. His interest in the conversation was clear as we were talking about the man he had tied his career and retirement to.

"Not quite. I believe the General, through either illness or more likely the wounds he received in the Crimea, found himself at death's door. While in Wallachia, one of his men, most likely an army surgeon growing desperate to save his dying commander, knew of the experiments Lower had performed, heard the local legend of the undying Count Vlad and got the idea to transfer blood from the vampire into General Stamford.

We all assumed he had brought the coffin back with him from the war, perhaps to sell it and rebuild the family fortune. I said, "I think Dr Doyle has cracked the secret, the blood of these unholy creatures holds the ability to sustain life without actually transforming the recipient into one, unless of course they are bitten."

"That's pretty good work," Stoker said admiringly, slapping his cousin on the back, "and it explains just about everything."

"This lifestyle would likely require constant transfusions," Doyle added. "I think this is also how the Order of the Dragon has lasted so long without ever really having their presence revealed. They never had to recruit new members to keep the Order going as, through constant transfusions like the one I just described, the members have been keeping themselves alive."

"You mean these Knights are the original members of the

Order? That must make them centuries old."

"At least four centuries," Doyle agreed, "though I have my doubts any vampire will do. Whatever it is in the blood that sustains life, I believe it must build up with long-term exposure. Newly bitten vampires have the bloodlust and some of the strength, but I doubt their bodies can achieve a total transformation in such a short time. Their blood would carry little of whatever it is in the blood that allows such longevity."

Doyle was obviously in his element as he stalked about the room. "It is a Methuselah factor, perhaps similar to the same pathogen a Russian biologist I know has been studying. Dmitri Ivanovsky is looking into a mysterious disease killing people in the Crimea, and I'm starting to believe there is no coincidence here. People are dying from a cryptic blood disease in the same location we have a holy order loosing a creature they extract blood from to sustain life."

Everyone at the table looked like this was perhaps one fact too many.

Backing him up I stated, "I think the Doctor is right. Once you exclude the impossible, whatever remains, no matter how implausible, must be the truth." Doyle gave me a look of thanks, though it was he who deserved the credit after his fine work.

"I believe the blood for such a transfer can only come from an old, established, totally transformed vampire. The quantity of blood required to keep a dozen or more men alive in this way would either have to be enormous or of great concentration." The doctor punctuated this by pointing to one of the pictures he had brought with him. It was a portrait of a middle-eastern-looking man in a turban and with an impressive moustache. I recognised the clothes he wore as a mix between Ottoman and Holy Roman attire, not that I could tell anyone at the table that.

Always the policeman, Abberline added his own insight. "This also explains why the Order is so desperate to find the coffin. Without whatever it is the General stole, they are all doomed to die."

Finally Stoker offered his own report, which he had been holding onto since earlier in the day. "I have some information on what is going on here—I was unsure if it would be helpful so I did not pass on earlier, but clearly it does have some relevance. I went through the archives of the newspaper and I think I found something that backs up what has been said here."

"What you found matches up with Doyle's findings?" Vulk asked.

"Yes, and it also may expand on them, as I found a report about the General being gravely wounded in the Crimea. It would seem his loyal men carried him off the battlefield at Giurgevo, but I am sure John could shed more light on that. "

Batten looked somewhat sheepishly at everyone gathered around the table. "To my knowledge almost everything you said is true. I was with Captain Stamford, as he was then, when he led the final charge against the Russian line. The man truly had no fear and he helped break a force we all believed unbreakable. His assault was so audacious those men who, just minutes before had been about to run, turned back to follow him and that turned the entire Russian attack into a rout.

"It was as we broke through their lines that the Russian commanders turned their cannons on us. The firestorm was dreadful. Grapeshot tore through our men and theirs—they didn't care who they were killing. I watched as Stamford, hollering at everyone to keep moving forward, was cut down under the barrage. I grabbed his batman, Charles, and together we dragged his ruined body back to our own lines. What happened next I couldn't tell you, as I was later shot trying to find a doctor. I spent the next few months in a field hospital before being shipped back home, where I received word from Charles that Stamford had offered us all positions at the family estate. I will admit I was shocked to hear he had survived his wounds."

As the old soldier's story wound down, Doyle took over. "I believe Stamford's men uncovered the same ancient legend about an order of monks that never aged. The men of the order never got sick and could seemingly recover from almost any injury. I believe these men found the Order, learned their secrets and stole the body of Vlad. They then brought the Vampyre back in its coffin, learned how to transfer the blood, perhaps from one of the Dragon Order, and began bringing their beloved commander back to life—though only ever doing enough to ensure that they got back to London and established the proviso in his will about them all receiving a share of his fortune upon his death. Once this was done, they kept him alive just enough to build up the story that he was a sick man, but never enough for him to regain his strength and flee."

"But why then did he not try to get a message to someone to help him escape their clutches?" Abberline enquired.

"He was reliant on the transfusions. If for any reason they stopped he would have perished from his original wounds. At least that is my understanding of the science of the process. I know of sailors who suffered from scurvy on long voyages, and their bodies became so ravaged by the disease that decade-old wounds once again opened up."

It was Willkie who picked up the one thread that had not been explained. "None of this explains the presence of the Order of the Dragon though."

No one had an answer to that, though eventually an idea did dawn on me and I set it forward to the group. "They were obviously desperate to get the body of Vlad back and so likely followed Stamford's men back here. At some point, I think they got to the General and made a deal, offering to help free him from the clutches of his men. They then set about building a new nest under the greenhouse in preparation for getting their own vampire back."

"Interesting, I'll admit but that does not quite work," Stoker said, leafing through his notes, "and I have one last piece of information that is a better fit. I think I just worked out who our vampire is."

"You mean where the body of Vlad is hidden?" Abberline asked.

"No. If Doyle is right, then the vampire Stamford brought back with him has been under lock and key and never been allowed to feed. The creature was being hidden from the Knights, though I think they may have it now."

"So?" Vulk asked.

"So, who killed the people around the estate and created the vampires we have been fighting?"

We all looked at each other like someone smarter than us had just told us something we all should have been able to work for ourselves. Stoker just grinned and held up a newspaper. "I looked for any news about the Stamford estate and found an old story that may help explain what is going on here."

"Well, are you going to tell us or keep us in suspense?" Churchill huffed.

"This paper is five years old and carries an article about the day a waiting horse and buggy broke free and raced through the streets of Chelsea. Here, it tragically ran over the granddaughter of General Wilberforce Stamford."

"The Colonel had three daughters?" Abberline asked.

"No. This granddaughter was named Lucinda."

"Lucinda? What happened to her?" I asked.

"The paper reports she was not killed, but her injuries were terrible. Her back was broken and a head wound all but insured she would never recover any form of sensibility. For the rest of her life she would be little more than a mindless infant."

"Well that certainly does not sound like the girl I met," Vulk pondered.

"Exactly," Stoker agreed, folding the paper up and placing it on the table for anyone to read. "I am thinking perhaps to save his beloved granddaughter the General may have done some sort of deal and had his "pet" vampire bite her. This would explain her miraculous recovery and the numerous disappearances around the estate."

I turned to ask Colonel Stamford what he knew about all this, and exactly where he had hidden his family.

Willkie beat me to it when he asked. "Hey, where did the Colonel go?"

CHAPTER THIRTY-FOUR

In small teams we searched the Stamford house and could find no sign of any of the family. We discovered the upstairs apartments were not only empty, but they were also a mess as though they had been hastily searched.

Batten checked with the men guarding the front and back doors, and both reported the Colonel had not left through either passage. When he returned he brought several squads to ensure we had enough men to search the house safely.

"We need to go back into the greenhouse," Abberline suggested.

"That we do," I agreed, "but there is somewhere we need to check first. Grab your weapons—oh, and we are going to need some rope!"

The roomful of men followed Vulk and I into the house's secret passages. We sent one squad of men up to check on the hidden rooms behind the family quarters and the attic, while the rest of us marched downstairs.

The atmosphere in the passage behind the cellar was cold and damp, and I did not need Vulk's sense of smell to know what had passed through here recently. Checking the old well, the heavy iron lid had been torn away and there were signs that something or someone had climbed through it recently.

Vulk leapt into the hole without any concern, followed by Stoker using rope from one of the work outhouses on the estate. Inside, they discovered a roughly cut second tunnel not ten feet down, and well above the deeper water level. This tunnel travelled in the direction of the greenhouse.

"Well I guess we now know which direction the Colonel went," the reporter called up from the well.

"Are you and Vulk happy to follow the tunnel? If so, we will head over and enter the greenhouse and meet you at the other side," I called down.

"Happy…no!" Stoker yelled back. But when he got a positive sign from Vulk, added, "but we will do it—see you over there."

Leaving a few men to guard the well's entrance and assist as needed, we moved back upstairs and out into the garden. Churchill took command and gathered what men were not needed guarding the doors and gates, and once again those in front created a shield wall, with the rest of us behind. Once we were in position and someone had retrieved some storm lanterns, the entire team entered the dark greenhouse.

Treading through shattered glass and ruined plant boxes, we determined that the entire structure was empty, so we then made our way down through the nest and back into the train tunnel running beneath. By the weak light of our lamps, we searched the entire tunnel and could find nothing until Vulk's head made an appearance out of a dark corner of the wall.

"Good to see you again," he said, wiggling his way free of the tunnel.

"Well, it looks like they were down here," Abberline said, finding fresh footprints on the ground. "Do we know which railway line we are near?"

"This is an old branch running off the Waterloo line," one of the soldiers said from the back of the tunnel. When the men turned and stared at him, the soldier shrugged. "I used to work the trains."

"Waterloo. That was something else I found," Stoker called out as he wiggled himself free from the tunnel to the main house. "The Stamfords are a major shareholder in the LNC, which I found a little strange, considering our previous experience."

"LNC?" Abberline asked.

"The London Necropolis Company. The railway runs out of Waterloo Station."

"Exactly what do you mean by strange?" Willkie asked.

Ignoring the Sergeant, Stoker continued, "As we saw during our trip, the service is only run when there is a first-class funeral to make it worth their while to take the train out to the cemetery. Until that time the LNC stores the second and third class...err...passengers until they are ready for transportation. Luckily, in such a large city this doesn't happen often, but they still need the capability to store these 'passengers' when needed."

"What storage? What passengers?" Willkie asked again, getting frustrated.

"When we went out to the burial of Fortey, did any of you note the emblem for the Necropolis line over the entrance to the station?" I asked, still ignoring the Sergeant, more out fun than anything else. When my previous traveling companions shook their heads, I reached into my shirt and pulled out the silver medallion hanging there. The Order of the Dragon's medallion displayed the ouroboros—a serpent eating its own tail. I could not help but smile at the appropriateness of the symbol.

Willkie looked long and hard at the medallion. "My, that is fascinating," he said rather sarcastically, and then blurted, "What the hell are you talking about? And why would you need to store passengers?"

CHAPTER THIRTY-FIVE

With the Stamfords having fled the estate and with no sign of the General's men, we sent teams, led by Abberline to ensure everything was legal, to search the LNC stations at London and out at Brookwood Cemetery. Again, nothing turned up.

For over a week we searched any location the Stamfords may have had an association with, but they had seemingly disappeared completely. Every night, a platoon of soldiers were stationed in the garden, with at least one of us who knew what was going on to ensure they were not blindsided by some attack, and every night they spent a long, tedious, and thoroughly uneventful evening. It would seem our last attack had destroyed the nest once and for all, and the Order had moved on.

It was our belief Colonel Stamford had escaped to hide his daughters, and they'd likely taken the coffin and the General with them. I believed the Order of the Dragon was in hot pursuit, but others believed they were all in cahoots. Now the fear was that every day we could not find either group was a day they were establishing a new nest...

...and then the murders began anew.

The first occurred on Friday, the thirty-first of August. Abberline ensured he was put on the case after a street prostitute called Mary Anne Nichols was found dead in Buck's Row. Her throat had been torn open, along with her stomach. This last wound we agreed had been done to hide the feeding puncture marks.

Someone knew we were looking for them and was trying to hide their activities, Abberline decided it would be best to have only a small police presence in Whitechapel if we wanted to catch the vampire. If there were an obvious police presence in the area, our prey would just go to ground. The Inspector did clear the murder scene late one night, and Vulk, in partial wolf form, completed a thorough check of the area with that nose of his, hoping to catch the path of the murderer. The street was a busy one, however, and the overpowering scent of the city meant he had no luck at all.

We continued our investigations, but were unable to stop the second murder a week later. Annie Chapman was a flower seller, and her body was found in a back yard with her throat torn out. We hit the streets in force and turned over every brick and rock, yet again found not a sign of the killer. As feared, our search seemed to drive the Stamfords further underground as the next death attributed to a vampire did not occur until Elizabeth Stride was killed nearly a month later. There may have been more murders, but we could find none that indicated exsanguination as the cause. Abberline kept an eye on all murders outside Whitechapel in case the vampire had moved, but none fit the method of death we were looking for.

Evidence that the family had not moved on finally appeared not from the death of Stride, but an hour later when another prostitute called Catherine Eddows was killed mere streets away from the first. The growing hunger the vampire must have been suffering after a month was surely the cause of these deaths; and because Stride had been relatively untouched, we assumed because the murderer had been disturbed before feeding on the body. The killer had been forced to flee, and had found another victim in a less populated area of the city.

The death of a few prostitutes would normally receive little public interest, but the appearance of Abberline on the case certainly had people speculating as to what was going on. Rumours swirled through the streets of London, and Stoker kept us updated of any reports as the story began to grow and more people took an interest.

The gruesome nature of these deaths and the mysterious murderer saw people's imaginations take flight. Suddenly butchers, backyard doctors, and artists came under suspicion; there was even talk that one of the Queen's children was involved in the slayings.

Through it all, I stood back and tried to track the movements of the killer, hoping to find where the family was hiding. I finally had it pinpointed when a fifth victim was found in Whitechapel, meaning the vampire was somewhere near that central borough, but it would be Stoker and Doyle, who had left us early on to pour through city records, who eventually made the break.

The LNC owned warehouse property near the Royal London Hospital, possibly to store bodies coming from the hospital before they could be later moved on to the Necropolis station. The LNC was about to open a new office there as Waterloo Station had asked the Necropolis line to move so Waterloo could start using its valuable and underutilised railway track and station for its own purposes.

This storage space, along with the hospital, was located within Whitechapel. With Scotland Yard leading the way, we gathered a squad of Hussars and marched on the warehouse. The sight of a line of soldiers with rifles, pikes, swords and shields, some even on horseback, marching towards the centre of town, had not been seen on the streets of London in decades, maybe even centuries.

Moving into Whitechapel as quickly as such a large force could through the narrow streets of the London borough, we formed up in front of the warehouse. Shield wall at the ready, we charged inside and found evidence that people had been living in the warehouse, but had recently departed. Abberline figured the Order or the Stamfords likely had a man on the street watching us and, when we marched, had subsequently got word to the family to move on.

Despite missing the Stamfords, for once I felt we were ahead of the game. Having searched through the evidence the cousins had brought us; we had uncovered the suggestion the Necropolis line was moving. The current LNC was looking to move to an unused space at the very edge of Waterloo station on Westminster Bridge Road. Abandoned for years, the spot had access not only to the Waterloo underground tracks, which we knew the Knights and their vampires used to move through the city undetected, but it was only three miles from the LNC office in Westminster.

It took the better part of an hour, for our small force to line up at the front of a large building sitting under a wide railway arch, secured behind two enormous, ornate gates. We later discovered the gates had been built for the Great Exhibition in 1850, and had been transported to Westminster Road in preparation for the upgrade of the Necropolis station.

Though the iron gates proved to be locked, some of our more energetic men clambered over and levered them open. The opening was wide enough to allow the rest of us to start squeezing through the gap, passing our weapons through before we did so. Once everyone was inside we reformed into small teams and began searching the enormous, dark space. Inside, we could see waiting rooms, and even a small chapel had been planned; places where the bereaved could sit, mourn and pray.

It was Abberline who found them. Sitting in a pool of shadow, well away from the rays of sunlight spearing through gaps in the roof and walls, was the Stamford family. Father and daughters huddled together, waiting for nightfall so they could escape the city by a late train from Waterloo. About them were the small pieces of luggage they had managed to carry when they escaped our raid on the warehouse.

Dealing with three vampires in such a space was going to be dangerous, so as a united front we moved forward behind our shield wall, pistols, rifles, swords and pikes at the ready. Catching the movement, Colonel Stamford leapt up and, raising his hands, moved towards us.

"Just stop where you are," he called out.

Abberline stepped forward. "Take another step and we'll fire."

"Wait!" I called out, sensing something was not right. I moved up to the Inspector and whispered in Abberline's ear. "Look where he is standing."

The Colonel, trying to step between his daughters and us, had walked directly into a long ray of sunlight.

"You haven't been bitten?" Stoker asked from behind his raised pistol.

"Me? No, just Lucinda. She was dying, it was the only way," the Colonel admitted.

"Then why did you run?" I asked.

"I knew what you were thinking. I was in the room and heard what you had planned. You think she killed those men and, in turn, you want to kill her."

"If she did not kill the people around the estate, what about Jerome De Gois? What about your wife?"

"She had nothing to do with their deaths either," the Colonel yelled, keeping himself bodily between his family and us.

I stepped in front of the shield wall, looking around the Colonel at the girls hiding in the shadows. "Of course she did. She's your little princess, used to the finest things in life and taking what she wants."

Lucinda returned my stare, stood and walked to the very edge of the sunlight, her flowing white dress reminding me of the vision I had seen running through the house.

"We were going to have dinner. We can still have that dinner if you want."

I could not help but reflect on how such a simple suggestion over a meal had stuck with the girl all this time. It explained how restricted her life must truly have become since becoming bitten and how starved she had become for human contact outside her family.

"Come with us." Lucinda smiled at me. Her voice was like honey, warm and inviting as the ocean of sunlight that separated us. I recognised there was something of the serpent in that voice, dangerous and hypnotic. She had sadly picked the wrong person to try that trick on.

"You have killed at least three people that I know of. You are not going anywhere."

"I was dying," she said flatly, the honey gone.

"Being an inhuman monster does not mean you have to be inhumane."

"Dying means you do whatever it is you need to survive. If you are drowning, you reach up and grab the nearest hand, even if it means dragging them down with you."

"Your argument only goes as far as the first death. After that you were simply feeding, filling your basest desire by devouring the life of another."

"You think I wanted to? I tried to feed from the animals my family brought me, the sheep and pigs. I stole away and fed from cats and even a horse. Nothing felt nourishing, and most just made me ill. Only feeding from a human helped."

"Then you killed people to save yourself. You complained about your sister and her blood-sucking nature, yet you have become a predator of the worse sort."

"I was just trying to survive. Surely you can understand that."

I watched as the girl took a step back into the gloom, but lifted one arm, hand outstretched. "And now we are going to leave. Come with us. Those feelings you were talking about, loneliness, and loss of friendship. Come with us, come with me. We can see the distant future together."

I could not help but laugh, most likely not the reaction she was looking for, judging by how her hand closed and dropped back to her side.

"You are trying to tempt me?" I grinned.

"I am," she said, a hard edge now in her voice.

"May I ask one question of you then?"

"Ask it."

"The vampires we have encountered, they are little more than mindless beasts. How is it you have managed to keep, well, I suppose you could say, your identity. How have you stopped from losing every aspect of your humanity?"

Even in the dark, I saw Lucinda reach and pull out one of the silver medallions from under her bodice. Now we knew the full purpose and likely origin of the medallions. They had likely been originally forged by Vladislaus Draculam to help the monster keep his own identity.

As Lucinda presented her own medallion for inspection, I pulled my pistol and shot the windows directly above her head. Before she could react, lances of sunlight fell about us, catching her in their illumination.

The girl screamed in agony as she burst into flames. It only took seconds, for her entire body to be alight. Batten barked an order and a number of soldiers ran forward and began striking into the flames with their swords and pikes. Even with her unnatural energy, Lucinda soon fell to the ground and her struggles ceased.

Once the fire had died down, one man stepped forward and removed what remained of the vampire's head with a single sword stroke. The decapitated head rolled out of the sunlight and into the dark room beyond.

With his daughter's body still smouldering behind me, I walked over to where the Colonel stood, shielding his remaining daughter from the horror as cowered beside her father. "Where is the General and the Order?"

The man just stood there, eyes unfocused and glassy, clutching Robyn to his chest. I waited, and then repeated the question, but he refused to answer. A man used to the horrors of the world had just seen one horror too many.

From our group Stoker stepped into the sunlight and bared his sword. I watched, a little confused, until his next move. Using the long blade like a mirror, the reporter caught the sun and began reflecting it at the Colonel and his daughter. The light splashed across both with no reaction. He then returned the weapon to its scabbard and said: "Just checking."

With the two Stamfords placed under armed arrest, the rest of us moved into a quiet corner of the room to plan our next move.

"What have we missed?" I asked the group.

The two cousins, Vulk, Abberline and his sergeant, along with Batten and Churchill, all looked blankly at each other and then back to me. No one said a word.

"Come on gentlemen, there must be something? Abraham, Arthur, did you find any other holdings by the General or the LNC?"

"Nothing. There really is very little we could find other than the office and the storage space."

"I thought we were looking for the General?" Batten injected quizzically.

"Your point?" Abberline asked.

"My point is why are you only looking into the General's holdings? Surely you should be looking into what he owned?" With a flick of his head Batten gestured towards the Colonel.

That group of blank looks we had been giving everyone earlier, well they returned.

As though explaining to a group of dim-witted children, Batten went on in what I considered an unnecessarily condescending tone. "It was the General who worked for the railways and helped plan and build the LNC, but it was the Colonel there who was charged with actually running most of the Stamford holdings, including their warehouses and wharfs.

"Maybe we should look around the warehouse on the docks. If the General or the Order are trying to escape, the docks surely would be the best place to find a ship, would they not?"

CHAPTER THIRTY-SIX

Once again we left a murder scene under the care of the Metropolitan Police and, gathering our forces, marched down to the Millwall Docks on the Isle of Dogs. Even in this remote area of the city's long shoreline, this sort of activity could not be kept a secret for long, and our conspicuous column of armed troops was soon joined by Sir Charles Warren.

The Police Commissioner was under increased pressure to end what had been dubbed the Ripper murders and had decided to find out how his chief inspector was using the resources he had been asking for. We would eventually learn that Warren's interest in the affair was far more personal than professional.

Afraid the Order could have spies amongst the crowd watching our parade to tip off the General and the Dragons to our approach, we marched as quickly as we could onto the Isle of Dogs. Batten led the way to the remote storehouse that lay by the edge of a field of overturned small boats resembling turtles lying on their backs. The boats had been dry-docked to have their hulls cleaned and repaired, and were being stored to save them from rot or further damage.

Though one of the General's men, Batten had been nothing but helpful in our efforts to suppress the horror that had befallen the Stamford estate, and I got the feeling he was trying to make amends for being associated with the murders.

At a signal from Batten we slowed and returned to the formations that had proven so useful in battle with the vampires. Above us, the sky began to darken as foreboding clouds boiled over the false-cliff face of the buildings and warehouses.

Batten had given us a layout of the warehouse and the surrounding docks. When we arrived, an old style East-Indiaman called the *Demetrius* was anchored outside the building. Though the *Demetrius's* sails were squared away, the large cargo ship was clearly ready to depart.

Batten ordered two squads onto the ship and the rest of us hunkered down. These men inspected the entire vessel, and signaled that it was abandoned.

With the chances of being attacked from that direction gone,

196

we entered the warehouse. Each squad moved deeper into the building from a different direction, and just as I was starting to think we had either missed the General or simply had the wrong building, the first vampire struck. The monster came up through the floorboards from a hidden platform that sat at water level. It was able to kill three men before being shot between the eyes. Once the vampire was slowed, men with Enfield rifles opened fire, and the large slugs smashed the creature to the floor. Wounded, but still very much alive, the vampire flailed around for prey as our men charged forward to end its struggles.

The Order of the Dragon had learned its lessons well, and instead of coming at us with their traditional handspikes, rushed us with more modern weapons. Many of these Knights had fought the Turks over four centuries earlier and knew how to use their swords and shields. I recalled thinking they must have scoured every pawn shop and antique store in the city to find so many, until I noticed some weapons carried the crest of the Stamfords. The Knights were attacking us with the weapons they had collected from our own dead.

Men were being killed everywhere and it looked like the Knights were going to win the day. And then the old war-dog Batten stepped in. He screamed, and kicked the men around him into some sort of formation, organised the few men with rifles into a line and began firing into the Dragons. Shields were handy for protection against sword and vampires, but there was a reason they were no longer standard issue on the battlefield.

The bullets from our powerful rifles smashed through the shields as though they were not there and cut down the men cowering behind them. Taking his time and waiting for an opportunity—but most importantly not exposing our men to a counterattack by rushing forward—Batten used the long reach of the rifles to move about the room and take the surviving Dragons down.

Out of the chaos, one Knight charged into our men and punched a hole into our defensive line. Rifles and pistols fired, and he was shot half-a-dozen times, but before he dropped dead he had managed to cut down two of our men with his sword. This was no suicidal attack though as another Knight followed up this attack by pushing through the gap the now dead Dragon Knight had made.

I could see what was occurring and could do nothing about it.

Even as I called out a warning and raised my own pistol, the second Knight pivoted through the gap, swinging his own sword around in an arc that sliced through the neck of two men with rifles, before spinning and turning the strike into a thrust and running Batten through.

I fired, and my cartridge smacked into the Knight's head as he was rotating to continue his attack on another group of soldiers, killing him instantly and sending his body pin wheeling to the ground.

Thanks to Batten's work the soldiers kept their formation, allowing us to move up in support. I yelled at Doyle to check on the old soldier, and the rest of us helped overcome the Order's attack. This time we made sure none of them escaped.

Commissioner Warren entered the warehouse once he had been told it was safe, and then immediately started abusing the men who had started their beheading of the dead. I almost laughed at the police commissioner's sudden change in attitude and his joining of the beheading party when two more vampires, possibly held in check and then freed by the death of the last Knight, rushed into the room to feed.

We lost five more men, and nearly twenty more were wounded in the battle, before we finally killed them both; and the Commissioner never queried the possibility of anything we reported from this point on.

Once we were sure there would be no more attacks we placed our wounded under care. Dr Doyle sadly assured us there was no help to be found for John Batten. The old soldier had died, and we all agreed without his valiant defence there'd be many more of us lying next to him.

Vulk appeared and beckoned for us to follow. I had not seen the old wolf since we entered the warehouse, and he explained he had missed the entire fight as he had followed the scent, in wolf form, of the General through the enormous warehouse.

The werewolf led us to the old man, once more the invalid, stretched out on a cot. Stamford was barely breathing, and looked far worse than he had during any of our previous meetings. He looked as though he had been deflated, and it did not take a doctor's skill to note the dozens of puncture marks running up and down both of his arms.

I looked into the face of the General and saw no longer the spark of intelligence that had always animated his face, no matter how poorly his body had been feeling. It was clear that the Order and their now aging bodies had become desperate enough to get an infusion of whatever vitality Stamford contained and had been drawing the General's blood as quickly as they could. They were desperate for whatever remained of the vampire's essence in his blood after being cut off from the true source.

It was my opinion the General and the coffin had become separated. The Order of the Dragon had infiltrated the Stamford estate and kept the old man alive as a backup until they regained control of the true vampire. I doubted they were aware there was a second source, another vein they could have tapped into—Lucinda.

As they were no longer injecting the General with vampire blood to keep him alive, the few Knights at the house had drawn as much blood from Stamford as they could and had injected it into themselves. They did this so they could escape, or perhaps to help recover from wounds from our last battle. This explained why he now resembled nothing as much as a skeleton lying in a bag made from human skin.

Doyle pushed past me to inspect the body, pointing out where the General's original wounds had begun to open again now that he no longer had the vampire's blood holding him together.

"Any hope?" Abberline asked, peering at the General over my shoulder.

"None," I said, running a hand over the man's cold, sweaty head.

"We can't just leave him like this, can we?"

"Not a chance Inspector, unless you want whatever blood he has left being used for someone else's nefarious schemes."

"I do not," the officer from Scotland Yard said in a flat tone.

I asked the man next to me for his sword. With care I moved the General's body, shocked at how light he had become, and positioned him into a more comfortable position. I lifted the weapon high over my head and brought it down and through the man's exposed neck. His body did not even twitch as the spine was severed.

The grizzly work done, I handed the weapon back to its owner. Vulk leaned in and, after a long, quizzical sniff said, "we are not done yet!"

CHAPTER THIRTY-SEVEN

Vulk led me back outside and towards the ship waiting at the dock. We climbed the gangplank and stepped onto the *Demetrius's* deck.

"It's down here," he said, turning himself around and backing down the narrow, steep wooden ladder into the ship's hold.

I turned about and did the same.

Though Vulk's eyesight was far better than mine, my vision was good enough that I didn't need his help this time to navigate safely into the dark vessel's interior. We were both so fast we left those behind that followed us, and who suddenly found the need to head back outside for torches. At the Orlop deck—the lowest level of the ship and with only the ribs and skin of the hull now below us—we had reached our destination.

Sitting amongst old ropes and worn out sails was a large, ornately carved coffin. Made of stone, it had small holes cut into the lid and one larger hole along one side. These had been cut to ensure there was vision into the coffin for those outside, without allowing the creature inside to see or attack. The side hole was situated roughly were the occupant's thigh would be, allowing access to the leg to draw blood.

"Help me," I asked Vulk, indicating the lid. The werewolf looked like he was going to argue, but stopped when I indicated those above us with a tilt of my head. "We do not have a lot of time."

Between us we undid the large latches and simply cut the rope wrapped around the coffin, most likely placed there to help move the heavy object rather than as a means of security. With Vulk standing at the far end and myself positioned at the other, we grasped the enormous lid of the coffin and began inching it up.

For a few heartbeats nothing happened, and then with a creak the lid gave and opened. Dropping the heavy cover to the ground, I stood up and looked inside at a face I had not seen in several centuries.

Inside was a vampire, still very much alive, though it could not move. Its limbs were bound, the straps looking old but still hardy enough to keep the beast in place.

Leaning in, I grabbed the plug that had been driven into the creature's mouth, ensuring it could not scream or bite, and pulled it out. It took some time as the creature had clearly been trying to chew through the wooden wedge and had embedded its teeth in the wood.

I dropped the disgusting plug to the floor and looked back at the vampire as it began to smile. It then worked its jaw, before finally saying, "Father, how did you find me?"

The language was an old one, but the words came back to me easily enough. "I have told you not to call me that, and this is not a conversation. You cannot talk your way out of this Vladislav."

"Me?" it asked indignantly. "What did I do? I have been stuck in this crate for centuries—at least, it certainly feels like centuries."

"Vlad, you have spread your particular disease across Europe and now into England."

"England? That little sheep station of an island? Why would I care about England?"

"Things change, and England has changed. It is now my home and I cannot tell you how unhappy I am to be following the trail of bodies you have once again left behind you. I am no longer going to clean up after you. I am through with this—we are through."

"But father…"

I lashed out, striking the vampire across the face with the back of my hand, an age-old gesture used to shock more than hurt. "Do not call me that. I look back on the day I met your mother as one of the darkest in history."

"You're his actual father?" Vulk gasped. I had forgotten the werewolf had once lived in central Europe and likely knew as many of the older languages as I did.

I refused to be derailed from my mission and as such, ignored Vulk.

"You loved her, and you loved me," the vampire pleaded, and I once more heard the small boy I had indeed known and loved all those years ago. I had believed it impossible for me to father children, so when this true son of a dragon was born, it had been the happiest day of my life.

"I loved the child, the promise of what you brought. You were an impossibility, a true miracle, the chance to have a family of my own."

"That's right father. You sired me, so how can you hate me? How can you despise the very thing you created?"

"Quite easily as it turns out," I said, finally looking at Vulk. We could hear footsteps above us—our time was growing short. "Vulk, please, for me, keep them busy for a few more minutes," I asked of him.

The werewolf looked at me, at my son, then back at me. He then nodded once and loped out of the hold.

"It is my nature, father and you know that. I was born this way. I did not choose it," the vampire whined.

"No, but you chose to continue. You chose to destroy the lives of your victims."

"Cattle for wolves! What's the price, the worth of a life that is over in the blink of an eye? It's like mourning for a season. They come, they go, and each is as beautiful as the other, but they must eventually give way. The seasons are not eternal—we, dear father, are eternal. Why are you trying to stop me, father? You should join me. Together we could rule this world."

"You are making the same mistake so many have made in the past. They all assumed I was on the side of the Morningstar, when nothing could be further from the truth. I was part of the plan; I was always part of the plan. My intervention was as inevitable as the coming of night after a long day...I will not be the cause of..." I turned away, feeling the old anger rising once more. I collected my thoughts and took a deep breath.

Once more in control, I returned to the coffin. "You say 'nature'. I say you have no standing here. If, and I do mean 'if', you had limited yourself to finding minimal victims to survive, well then you may well have grounds for what you have done over the years. You really did what you had to do."

"But...?" the vampire asked.

"But you did not limit yourself to simple survival. You created others in your own image, and you let them loose on the world. What of the lives they took? Your children of the Dragon..."

"Your grandchildren, father."

"I have told you not to call me that."

"Why not? It's true. The joy you admit to feeling when I was born, the knowledge that you would not be alone anymore. No longer a solitary freak watching those in the world live and die and love all about you, while all you could do was eternally watch. Feeling everything, except that you ever truly fit in with the rest of the world. Children mean a family, a community, and a face to recognise after a century. Familiarity!"

The vampire looked me directly in the eye. "You of all people should understand the value of familiarity."

"I thought I did, but no longer. I refuse to have any more…"

"What?" Vlad spat, believing he had finally found an opening. "Any more monsters created in your image?"

You live long enough and you will hear every argument, and this was proving no different. "I have been blamed for unleashing one sin on the world. I refuse to be forever marked by releasing another."

"But what a sin! Knowledge was the first, and it will prove be the ruination of us all. Look at the world about you. Bigger, more powerful and faster, mass killing weapons. The Morningstar will never be able to fill hell as you have helped create it here within paradise."

I looked down long and hard on the creature I had helped bring into the world. "This is not paradise, this was never paradise. Some sins can never be forgotten, nor forgiven. Some mistakes, however, can be amended…and Vlad, you have also made your own mistake?"

"How so, Father?"

"I told you, this was never a conversation."

I plunge my sword into the vampire's chest, aiming for its heart. The blade barely penetrated as the ancient creature's bones were like iron and turned the weapon away.

"Fatherrrrr," the last member of the House of Drăculești screamed, thrashing at the bonds that had held him in place for decades.

I ignored the noise and the approach of my companions. Instead, I raised the sword again and struck at the vampire's neck. This time the weapon bit deep, and Vlad's violent struggles to free himself threatened to snap the bonds holding him in place. I yanked back on the sword and, as the vampire attempted to say something, struck again. This time the sword severed my son's head from his body.

There was no time to waste, as the sounds of approaching footsteps grew louder. I found an old lamp and opened the valve, and poured the stored liquid over the coffin and the ship's timbers. I fished a box of safety matches from my pocket, removed one and struck it. The head ignited, a small flame illuminating the ship's hold. I used the light to take one last look at my son, before dropping the match inside. The tiny flame ignited the lamp oil and began to spread, first throughout the coffin and then across the wooden floorboards.

The heat inside the small hold increased rapidly as the fire grew. I was walking out as Abberline and a few of the others arrived. They looked like they wanted to argue, and Stoker tried to squeeze past me to run towards the flames and see inside the coffin, but I grabbed him by the scruff of the neck and pulled him away like a child.

We got out of the vessel before the flames boiled out of the hold and consumed the wooden ship completely.

I stood on the dock and watched the flames and glowing ashes rising into the sky and realised I was alone once more. I had also completed the long promise of Ouroboros as the serpent, indeed, had devoured its tail.

CHAPTER THIRTY-EIGHT

It took another month, but eventually we were confident enough to consider London free of vampires. Legend suggested that killing the source of vampirism would end all the vampires it had sired, but that was just country folk looking to sleep secure at night. Like a plague of rats, you could only be sure they were gone by killing every last one of them.

There were no more deaths on the streets of Whitechapel after we had flushed out Lucinda, and there were no more incidences with the Order of the Dragon either. With Abberline and Commissioner Warren leading the way, the Met began canvasing the regions where we had encountered the vampires and the Order to collect any bodies we may have missed. These were all destroyed, including a number that we had missed buried around the Stamford estate. All were fed into the large boilers that helped warm the Royal Hospital, destroying any chance of them turning.

It was Commissioner Warren who proposed to hide the truth of the matter. The connection between the Stamfords and the Necropolis Railway meant a lot of political pressure came down from on high to hush it up, despite the connection to the infamous Ripper murders. The city's newspapers and the public remained on edge, believing 'Jack' was still out there, stalking the foggy streets of old London, but there was little we could do about that.

The Colonel and Robyn Stamford returned home to rebuild their shattered lives. I saw them one last time at a secret inquest. Here evidence was presented as to their culpability in the murders.

Though we had strong evidence that they had first-hand knowledge of what was going on, and at the very least had helped cover up the murders on the estate, it was finally decided both Stamfords would be released. The death of the General and Lucinda had removed the stain of past sins and they were free to go home.

I believe any further investigation may have uncovered other secrets, both local and national, and no one wanted that at the time. The link to the failing LNR meant people might stop using the service; and as a number of powerful politicians had been partners with General Stamford in the company. They insisted the business' name be withheld else their own reputations become tarnished.

As the last Stamfords walked past me, Robyn stopped and slapped me across the face. She then left without ever saying a single word. During the inquest the little witch never shed a tear for her dead sister, nor once did she look ashamed when her own part of what occurred was recounted. Instead, in her mind, she seemed to blame me for all that had occurred.

With little interest from the family, and none from the Met, I ensured Batten's body was buried in the soldier's section of the Brompton Cemetery, well away from the Stamfords and the murder victims. We made sure there were at least a few men in uniform during his funeral. Batten deserved that at the very least.

I spent a number of weeks ducking both Doyle and Stoker. I knew both had questions they were desperate to have answered, most of which I did not want known. During his last minutes, there was one thing Vladislav had been correct about; knowledge was indeed a dangerous thing. You live long enough, and you learn there are some apples that should never be eaten.

EPILOGUE

The full moon's reflection glittered along the long, serpentine Snagov River, illuminating a small island, empty but for a large, domed monetary with three spires rising over its roof. The island was a little larger than a sports field; and I stepped off the boat that had carried me across the waterway and started climbing the short, steep rise to the spired building, making as little noise as possible.

Walking across a well-manicured lawn, I reached the building's ornate doors and pushed my way through. Bright moonlight pierced the church's dark interior, and though there was an ornate chandelier hanging from the roof and large candles strategically located about the room inside, none were lit. This did not matter as I could see perfectly well inside, and was astounded that such a small room could be filled with so many decorative panels showing biblical scenes and pictures of saints with golden halos.

Walking along one wall, I ran my hand along the artwork, wryly smiling as I passed an image depicting the Garden of Eden. The wall ended at a large stone tomb, the reported final resting place of Vlad Țepeș, the last of the Drăculea and my only son.

Finding the hidden latch, I flicked the lever and pushed. With a sound of grinding stone, the tomb began to shift, revealing a narrow stone staircase beneath.

I stepped down into a cavernous space that had once held the treasures of the Drăculea. The vault had been built by Vlad himself centuries ago, as part of the island's fortifications against the Ottomans. This space at times had been a prison and a torture chamber, all part of Vlad's personal crusade against the Ottomans after he answered the call of Pope Pius II to help keep the Muslim empire out of Europe.

Sultan Mehmed II, who sent envoys to insist he pay tribute to keep the peace, had claimed Vlad's kingdom of Wallachia. In response, Vlad began his infamous war by killing the envoys, gathering an army and intercepting the first Muslim invasion force into his homeland. The Battle of Târgoviște ended with a Wallachian victory and the impalement of thousands of Muslim survivors.

Vlad next moved along the Danube, massacring every Turk he

could find, including entire populations around Oblucitza and Novoselo. Here he beheaded more than 20,000 people.

The history books later explained that this horrific act was intended to force Mehmed II into withdrawing from Wallachia, but the history books have it wrong. I had attended the massacre, and there was a reason why the Battle of Târgovişte had taken place at night. To match the overwhelming numbers of the Ottoman forces, Vlad had unleashed his own undying army on the invaders.

These vampires fell on the Ottomans with a hunger that could not be sated, and Vlad followed up their attack with his own conventional forces to behead the corpses and stop any of his enemies from turning. What Vlad did not expect was the actions of his nightmare army after the battle.

After interrogating a member of the Order of the Dragon, I uncovered something startling, hidden within the Vatican. The amulets had been created by the 'Societas Draconistarum' and allowed Vlad's men, all of who had accepted the Pope's order to punish the heathens, to move in after the battle and take control of the vampires they found. Vlad ordered the Society to kill all vampires on sight, but they missed a few, which then rampaged throughout the countryside, killing and feeding and creating many more children of the night.

I had heard about the coming war between Vlad and the Sultan, and had arrived looking for the child I once loved. What I found was the man he had grown into, impaling the beheaded bodies of his victims along the Danube. His anger at the world was palpable and I decided to help him, if only to rid this young man of the consuming hatred that fuelled his rage.

When stories of people being butchered in Bulgaria reached us, together Vlad and I organised his army into smaller units, and then moved into the countryside to hunt vampires.

It took months, and by the time we arrived at Oblucitza and Novoselo the infestation had reached a critical mass. So many people had been bitten and so many vampires created that the entire region had to be cleansed to end the infestation. More than 23,000 bodies later, the plague of vampires my son had released on the world had been destroyed.

Of course, the Ottomans knew nothing of this. The Sultan

simply ended his war against Corinth and marshalled an even larger force to hit the Balkans like a sledgehammer. The Ottomans captured most of Wallachia, including the island fortress of Snagov. Here they killed everyone stupid enough to not have run away, and their searches found the very vault I now stood in. They captured the hidden treasure of the House of Drăculeşti.

My time at the Vatican had been worthwhile. Before his unfortunate death by knife, the Knight had laid out what had occurred since my last visit to Wallachia. The Societas Draconistarum had realised the strength of their master's blood when one of the Order was mortally wounded. A favourite soldier, the Voivode had visited the dying man after one nasty battle and blood from the vampire's healing wound dripped into the Knight's injury. The man began to recover, and so the Order of the Dragon started plotting to tap into this well of everlasting life.

As a society formed during the Crusades and backed by the Holy Roman Emperor, this order of Christian Knights had just discovered something so many orders, such as the Knights Templar, had been searching for; the Holy Grail. In a plot worthy of Shakespeare, the Order trapped Vlad in an inescapable coffin and began siphoning off his blood to save themselves. A young member of the order and a future physician to Pope Innocent VIII, Giacomo di San Genesio, had pioneered this technique.

Strong and healthy, the Order grew increasingly paranoid that their secret would be discovered and the coffin confiscated. To protect themselves, the Knights began to withdraw from the world, hiding themselves on the small island where they could control who visited them.

This they did successfully for a number of years, but the world found them again when the ruler of the Austria-Hungry Empire, Francis Joseph I, sought them out. For years the Emperor had heard tales of the rejuvenation powers of the Order on the tiny island of Snagov.

Adding to their woes, the Order had little influence with the Greek Mavrocordatos family, who had been given control of Wallachia by the governing Ottomans and created imperial counts by the Holy Roman Emperor. This family was historically Christian yet found themselves backed by the Sultanate.

The Ottomans recognised great power in the Mavrocordats, and often used them as Dragomans due to their ability not only to speak numerous languages from the East and West, but because of their deep understanding of the cultures of both. The Mavrocordats ruled Wallaschi with an iron grip, arresting anyone who raised a voice of dissent. Nicholas Mavrocordatos arrested Anthim the Iberian, a man pushing for the independence of the nation. Nicholas sent him into exile, where legend tells us he was mysteriously killed and his body destroyed.

It took a few weeks' research, but thanks to the information I gained from the friendly Knight in the Vatican, I discovered Anthim the Iberian had been the father superior of the Snagov monastery. Though this all happened over a century and a half ago, the Knight had admitted not only to knowing Anthim, but also that he was part of the Order of the Dragon and it was also around this time the Mavrocordats started investigating the strange history of the monasteries builder, Vlad the Impaler.

Not twenty years later, war swept through the region as Russia, the Ottomans, and Austria fought for control of Eurasia. Things did not go well for the Austrians who, after some shocking defeats, were forced to sign the Treaty of Belgrade—a treaty devised by yet another Dragoman.

Nothing was really settled however, and when the three nations looked like they would go to war again a century later, it was a Dragoman who stepped in and argued to keep Austria neutral. The mystery as to why the Austrians agreed was explained when the Vatican Knight admitted that the only son of the Austrian Emperor, Crown Prince Rudolf of Austria, was on death's door, and the price of their neutrality was healing the boy. It was the Ottoman Dragoman who organised for the boy to be bitten, as there was no way of keeping up a constant transfusion without giving away the entirety of their secret. The Prince was healed and the order went back into hiding. This all occurred just after the Crimean War and at the time General Stamford's men were desperate to find him a cure for his battle wounds. The Knight admitted the Order had not been as secretive as they had hoped, and word about their ability to miraculously cure the sick and injured had escaped. This explained how Vlad's coffin had eventually ended up in the hands of the

THE ORDER OF THE DRAGON

Stamfords.

Before heading to Snagov, this story brought about the realisation I had an important stop to make first. It took me nearly a year, but I finally caught up with Crown Prince Rudolph at the Imperial hunting lodge buried in the dark woods of Mayerling, near Vienna. Here the Vampire-Prince had been keeping out of the sun, and when I arrived he had just bitten his teenage lover, Baroness Mary Vetsera. As I entered the lodge the two vampires were busy making plans on their long future together.

I managed to stake Rudolph through the heart, and had nearly been killed myself when the girl, driven mad at the death of her lover, attacked me while I was sawing his head off. A pistol shot to the heart slowed the Baroness enough for me to take her head; and with their deaths the last bloodline of my son was scoured from the earth and the existence of vampires became little more than legend and the source of bedtime fairy stories.

I stepped deeper into the torture chamber under the Snagov monastery and surprised the last members of the Order of the Dragon as they gathered what treasure they had managed to accumulate over the years.

I stood quietly at the foot of the stairs, waiting for one of the Knights to notice my presence. As the first gestured to his brothers and said something in the strange language the other Knights we had encountered in the Stamford garden had used, the rest turned to face me. Facing them, I bowed at the waist with my best court flourish.

"Gentlemen, I have been watching the island for a month. It is so nice to finally have you all together at last," I said in the same tongue I had used with the Drăculea.

The fourteen men at the far end of the room turned and pulled what weapons they had. Some were armed with single shot pistols, others knives. Two of the Knights even removed twin spiked gauntlets from their belts and slipped them over their hands.

"I recognise you," one man said, pointing a wary finger my way. "You were with us in Bulgaria."

"Good memory, I was. I am also the one who took the Impaler's head and fed his remains to the flames."

"You killed our Master," another Dragon said, lifting his

weapon.

"I did, though calling him your master after the way you treated him for the last few centuries might be stretching the facts a little."

"Why? If you were with us before the fall of Târgovişte, then you know what we did, what we earned and what he made us do?"

"I fought by your side against the Turks and the undead. I know your bravery, which is the only reason I did not burn this building down around your ears."

"We do not understand. Surely you too have the blood of the Drăculea in your veins to have lived this long. How can you blame us for desiring the same?" the first Knight asked, keeping his pistol aimed at my head.

"You are closer to the truth than you realise, but this conversation is only reminding me of the final chat I had with my only son. I have spent the last centuries cleaning up the bodies he and you have left behind due to your stupidity and desperation. I simply refuse to do so any more."

"Meaning?"

"Meaning, say your final prayers, gentlemen, you will not be leaving this room alive."

The grim eyes of the men narrowed, and I could see many steeling themselves to rush me. One of them even smiled as he stated, "Those are mighty words from a man who, as far as I can see, is alone and without a weapon."

I walked forward a few steps and allowed a cold, reptilian smile to spread across my face, revealing my true nature for the first time in years. "Why, whoever said I was alone?"

From behind me stepped Vulk in full werewolf form. The monster padded forward on all fours. Gone were the human elements of his body except for a large hunch in the shoulders. The werewolf stood by my side, and though his long back was only slightly lower than my chest, I ran a hand warmly through the thick, mane-like fur bordering the enormous head. The werewolf gave me a little snarl, suggesting that was maybe a little too familiar.

"Your particular brand of horror ends tonight," I said, pulling a pistol from my coat pocket and shooting the first Knight between the eyes. Vulk took this as a cue and he sprang forward, catching a

Dragon by the throat in his massive jaws.

Together we brought our own brand of horror to the Order of the Dragon, whose long existence ended forever under tooth and blade.

Until my next adventure…

Author's note

Playing with history is fun, researching parts of history to either inspire or fit a story line you have in your head, well that can be a challenge, and we all like rising to a challenge. I generally write history books about forgotten or overlooked events and people, so have been storing away little interesting titbits that I believed would make a great story ... fitting these events together, however, is an interesting jigsaw and leads us to this section of the book.

I am not sure about you, but I have read a number historical fiction novels and always find myself slightly missing the authors breadcrumb trail because I am either too involved in the story to notice some literary or historical link or my own knowledge on a subject simply isn't broad enough to notice when such a link appears.

Now I am not saying that has happened here, but the following are the true associations for my characters and incidents throughout the book and they are in no specific order.

Elements of this story are based on Raymond Chandler's classic noir story, The Big Sleep. What some of you may not be aware of is there is another, similar story that I adore from my favourite author, Glen Cook. Cook is clearly a student of Noir and his Garrett PI series contains themes and nods at the genres classic authors such as Chandler, MacDonald, and Stout. All the books are great, but Old Tin Sorrows is my favourite and was clearly influenced by The Big Sleep.

General Wilberforce Stamford was not just based on General Sternwood (The Big Sleep) and General Statnor (Old Tin Sorrows), but the very real Field Marshal Sir John Lintorn Arabin Simmons. Stamford's entire career is based on Simmons, who was: "*employed for three years in the disputed territory on the N.E. frontier of the United States in constructing works for its defence and in making military explorations. Happening to be in Turkey in 1853 he was specially employed by Lord Stratford de Redcliffe on several important services: joined Omer Pasha in March 1854; escorted the new Governor into Silistria after the former one had been killed, and was present during part of the siege of that fortress; laid out and threw up the lines of Slobodzie and Georgevo on the Danube, having entire charge of the operation with 20,000 men of all arms under his command, a Russian army of 70,000 men being within seven miles: was present during the occupation of Wallachia and had frequent charge of reconnaissance's upon the enemy's rear. Went to the Crimea in Dec. 1854 to concert with the allied Commanders in-Chief as to the movements of the Turkish army: was present at the battle of Eupatoria, laid out and threw up the entrenched camp round that place; afterwards was before Sebastopol from April 1855 until after its fall, and then went to Mingrelia and was present at the forced passage of the Ingur, where he commanded the division which crossed the river and turned the enemy's position capturing his works and guns: Omer Pasha in his dispatch attributed the success of the day chiefly to Lieut.-Cu!. Simmons. He served as Her Majesty's Commissioner to the Ottoman army throughout the war and was employed in all the negotiations having reference to the movements of Omar Pasha's army. Has received the Crimean Medal and Clasp, the Turkish Gold Medal for the Danubian campaign, the Order of Medjidie, 3rd Class, and a Sword of Honour from the Turkish Government* (THE NEW ARMY LIST, 1857)."

Even the newspaper report from the Hobarton Mercury, dated October 25th, 1854, is word for word the real article, with only a few name changes.

"*It was in leading a charge against the Russians that poor Captain Stamford, of the royal engineers, received his death wound. His loss is very deeply deplored, as he was an officer who was both loved and respected by all the members of his profession. Only about a fortnight ago he had set out to assist in the defence of Silistria.*"

Of course it was not Captain Stamford leading the charge, so in reality the article read: "*It was in leading a charge against the Russians that poor Captain Bourke, of the royal engineers, received his death wound.*"

The *Dunbar* was a real vessel that carried cargo and passengers between London and Sydney during the 1850s. After a number of successful such voyages, one night in1857 the ship was approaching the entrance to Sydney Harbour when her captain,

James Green, mistakenly believed the vessel had already passed through the heads when in reality the *Dunbar* was headed straight for the cliff.

High winds drove the vessel forward, and it wrecked on the large sandstone cliffs, killing all on-board except for a single sailor called James Johnson, who had been working in the rigging. As the vessel hit the rocks, Johnson was flung forward into the cliff, and spent the next two days holding on for dear life until he was rescued.

The Order of the Dragon (or Societas Draconistarum) was a real chivalric order of knights founded by Sigismund, the King of Hungary and the Holy Roman Emperor. With the fear that the increasingly powerful Ottoman Empire would soon invade the West, the order was required to help defend Christianity. Based in central Europe, the Order was mostly located around Hungry and Romania, and the most famous Knight of the order was King Henry V.

Vladislaus Draculam III was the Prince of Wallachia between 1431 and1477, and was the last member of the House of Drăculeşti. His father was Vlad II and is a folk hero in Romania and Bulgaria for his stance against the Ottomans. He was dubbed Vlad the Impaler, as a former captive of the Ottomans Vlad used his knowledge and ability to speak Arabic to infiltrate Ottoman camps and destroy them.

His cruelty is legendary, and he did indeed deserve the name Impaler as his preferred method of torture and execution was by impaling his victims. Estimates run between 40 to 100, 000 people were killed by Vlad's war, and one legend suggests he even impaled 20,000 of his own people and had them hanging as a gruesome message to an oncoming Ottoman army. The message was simple, if I do this to my own people, what do you think I will do to you?

Vlad won battle after battle against the numerically and militarily superior Ottomans, but all came undone when he ran out of money and sought support from neighbouring Hungary, or more specifically Matthias Corvinus. After negotiations with Hungary ended, Vlad returned home, only to be ambushed by his supposed ally and captured, yet he somehow managed to free himself and returned home.

No one is sure exactly how Vlad died after this. Was he killed in battle fighting the Turks, killed by his own men, or perhaps killed during a hunt? The Turks claimed they removed his head, which was preserved in honey and later sent to Constantinople as a prize.

Though later accounts claimed his body was buried at Snagoz monastery, there seems to be little, if any evidence of this having actually taken place.

Snagoz Monastery still stands today within the village of Snagoz on Snagoz Island in Lake Snagoz, Romania. Built in the fourteenth century, then modified by Vlad III into a fortress, it is supposedly the site of his grave. Archaeology digs around the monastery have uncovered human remains, but there is no evidence any of these belong to Dracula, or even if he was ever buried there.

The Kingdom of Wallachia is today located in the nation of Romania. At times it has been part of Hungary, the Ottoman Empire, Russia and a free state. At times Wallachia was ruled by the Voivode, a complex term that sort of means the leader of the military but was more like a duke. Vlad was Wallachia's Voivode on three different occasions.

Arthur Conan Doyle and Stoker were indeed cousins. After school and a stint as a doctor on a whaling ship, Conan Doyle became a partner in a small medical practice in 1882. None of these were very successful ventures, so to fill the time between appointments he began writing short stories.

Abraham 'Bram' Stoker was an Irish author who spent time as a theatre manager and writer for a number of newspapers. This did not include the London Daily Gazette, as this was the newspaper Edward Malone worked for in Arthur Conan Doyle's second most famous story, The Lost World.

The author was most certainly inspired by his environment when he began plotting Dracula, as can be seen by his inclusion of Whitby in the story. Stoker holidayed in the town in 1890 and became inspired by the gothic nature of its architecture and a major part of the story formed when he learned about a Russian schooner called *Dmitri* that shipwrecked there just a few years earlier while carrying a load of dirt (silver sand used in building). Dracula of course would arrive in Whitby on a ship called the *Demeter*, which also shipwrecked and lost its cargo of crates full of earth.

From this wreck leapt a large black dog, which would prove to be the shape-shifting Dracula. While on holiday Stoker likely also came upon the local Whitby legend of a large ferocious black dog, called the Barghest, with fiery eyes that stalked the night.

Squire Richard Cabell was Lord of the Manor of Brook and supposedly murdered his wife in a particularly brutal manner. Upon Cabell's death a pack of spirit hounds appeared and ran throughout nearby Dartmoor Moor, howling and ready to escort the murder's soul to hell. This legend was a major influence in Arthur Conan Doyle's The Hound of the Baskervilles.

The English version of the name, Henry Saint-Martin-de-Boscherville, would be Henry Baskerville.

The Úlfheðinn were the legendary Norse Berserkers, warriors capable of almost inhuman, uncontrollable fighting by falling into a trance-like state before doing battle. These warriors were said to wear the pelt of a wolf as they charged into battle, "and were mad as hounds or wolves, bit their shields...they slew men, but neither fire nor iron had effect upon them."

The London Necropolis Railway first opened in November 1854, with trains taking the dead and their mourners out to the largest cemetery in the world (at the time) in Brookwood, a location specifically chosen to be far enough from the city to be unaffected by future expansion of the city. Once the trains reached Brookwood they would choose one of two stations, one for Anglican funerals and the other for all others. The service ended in 1941 when more practical transportation options began to appear and much of the operation was destroyed by German bombings during the Blitz.

Winston Churchill had to take the entrance exams three times before he was finally accepted into the Royal Military College at Sandhurst. Upon graduation he joined the cavalry, before accepting a position in the 4th Queen's Own Hussars.

The Isle of dogs is not really an island but a stretch of land off the East End of London that is surrounded on three sides by the River Thames. The name goes back at least to the fourteenth-century and the swampy land eventually became a busy dock area.

Richard Lower was a 17th century physician who was the first scientist ever to perform a blood transfusion. Dmitri Ivanovsky was a Russian botanist and the first man to discover a virus in 1892, but had been working on the problem since 1887. Similar experiments had been attempted earlier, including the unsuccessful attempt by the physician, Giacomo di San Genesio, to have Pope Innocent VIII drink the blood he had collected from three 10-year-old boys. Neither the boys nor the Pope survived the experiment.

Frederick Abberline joined the Metropolitan Police on January 5, 1863, and quickly impressed his superiors. He was promoted to Inspector in 1873 and was transferred to Whitechapel, before later receiving a position with Scotland Yard. It was due to his experience in Whitechapel that Abberline was sent back to the borough to investigate the Ripper murders. Later he retired, became a private investigator, before accepting a position as head agent with the European arm of the infamous Pinkerton National Detective Agency of America.

Born in 1969, Phil likes to point out he was one of the last children born before man walked on the moon. Working at Australia's National Dinosaur Museum since 2000 and as an educator at the Australian War Memorial since 2006, he has previously worked at Questacon Science centre and could be seen haunting the halls and specimen rooms of London's Natural History Museum and The Smithsonian's National Museum of Natural History. Here he even played famed palaeontologist O. C. Marsh during the Smithsonian's centenary celebrations, and when asked why the 19th century palaeontologist was speaking with an Australian accent, happily pointed out that everyone on the 19th century spoke with an Australian accent.

Published in newspapers and magazines across the globe, since 2007 Phil has been the paleo-author for the world's longest running dinosaur magazine, The Prehistoric Times. He has also been a comic shop manager, a cinema projectionist, a theatre technician and gutted chickens for a deli. All of these influences seem to make an appearance in his writing, especially the chicken guts bit.

Raven's Head Press

Brings you some cool gothic horror

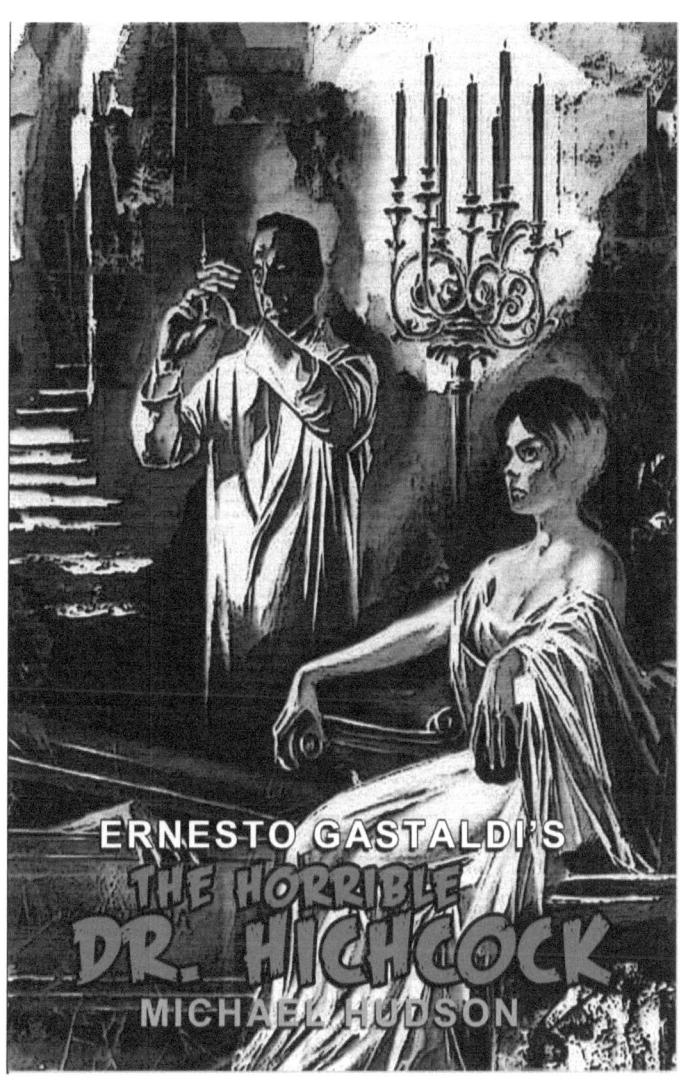

www.ingramcontent.com/pod-product-compliance
Lightning Source LLC
Chambersburg PA
CBHW050524260626

47157CB00004B/1456

* 9 7 8 0 6 9 2 6 2 0 4 4 1 *